The Case Files of
Case File 2
Honor Raconteur

Charms
and
DEATH
and
EXPLOSIONS
(oh my!)

That...was not what I called the report

Yeah, your naming scheme is boring.

Raconteur House

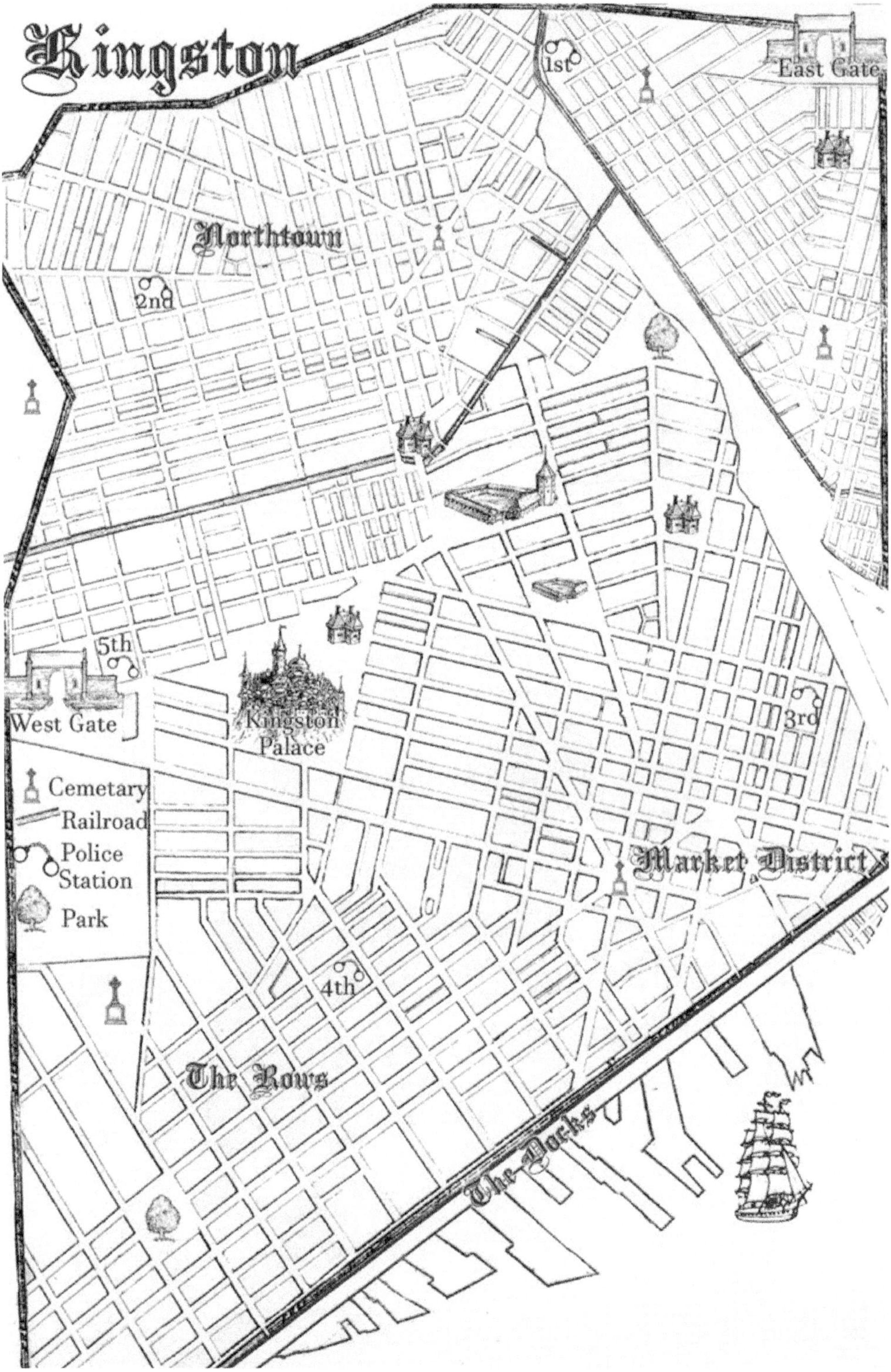
Kingston
1st
East Gate
Northtown
2nd
5th
West Gate
Kingston Palace
3rd
Cemetary
Railroad
Police Station
Park
Market District
4th
The Rows
The Docks

Published by Raconteur House
Murfreesboro, TN

THE CASE FILES OF HENRI DAVENFORTH: Charms and Death and Explosions (oh my!)
Case File 2

A Raconteur House book/ published by arrangement with the author

Copyright © 2019 by Honor Raconteur
Cover by Katie Griffin

This book is a work of fiction, so please treat it like a work of fiction. Seriously. References to real people, dead people, good guys, bad guys, stupid politicians, companies, restaurants, cats with attitudes, events, products, dragons, locations, pop culture references, or wacky historical events are intended to provide a sense of authenticity and are used fictitiously. Or because I wanted it in the story. Characters, names, story, location, dialogue, weird humor and strange incidents all come from the author's very fertile imagination and are not to be construed as real. No, I don't believe in killing off main characters. Villains are a totally different story.

All rights reserved.
No part of this book may be reproduced, scanned, or distributed in any printed or electronic form without permission. Please do not participate in or encourage electronic piracy of copyrighted materials in violation of the author's rights.
Purchase only authorized editions.

For information address: www.raconteurhouse.com

Report 00: The Beginning

I had unfortunately reached that state in which I'd utterly stopped paying attention, so I tried to focus. Then found myself focusing so hard on focusing that I still wasn't paying attention to Seaton's musings.

"—should work, don't you think?" Seaton finished thoughtfully, his finger tracing some spell design in the book on his lap. Unfortunately, he had the book tilted just so, and it blocked me from being able to glance down and actually discern what he might be discussing.

Fortunately, I had a catch phrase to use for situations like this. "Seaton. I'm not sure if I can agree."

Sighing, he pushed the book off his lap, letting it thump to his desk. "Yes, well, I must admit the math didn't total out as it should have done. I just hoped you'd see something I hadn't."

"Afraid I didn't, old chap," I responded noncommittally. There, see? It hadn't been necessary for me to pay attention anyway. Even he didn't think it was a good idea, whatever the idea had been.

Normally I'd feel bad about wool gathering, but Seaton and I had been closeted away in this office for nearly six hours, and that was after my shift had ended. I was tired, famished, and wanted nothing more than a hearty snack and the softness of my bed. We'd normally not meet like this on a work day, but both of our schedules had been so heinous in the past month that we'd not met up as promised, and we'd forcefully made time for it today.

Not that it had done much good in the end. We still had no answer on how to incorporate any healing spells, revival spells, or anything of that ilk into Jamie's system. And despite the fact that two registered geniuses had bent their considerable intellect unto the problem, we still hadn't found a permanent way to sort out Jamie's fluctuating magical core either. Belladonna's madness was not just that—it had been ingenious and crafty as well. I had faith we'd find some means around it, but the solution would not come quickly or easily.

The mantel clock chimed the eleventh hour and I grimaced. Just as well I had the weekend stretching ahead of me. I'd dearly like to have a sleep-in tomorrow. "Seaton. Our eyes are crossing and our minds fatigued. We'll make no more progress tonight."

"We barely made any progress," Seaton growled, vexed. Then he wearily lifted a hand in either acknowledgement or apology. Perhaps both. "I do like your thought of mixing potion ingredients without magic influence. If nothing else, putting the correct healing mixture of herbs into her system will help—even if her own magical defenses don't use them as a healing potion."

"We'll need to test the theory, of course, but I strongly believe that Belladonna was not stupid. Mad as a hatter, perhaps, but not without cunning. If she'd so safeguarded Jamie against every possible attack, but left her open to nature? There had to be a reason for it. I can only theorize that she has a signal lying dormant in Jamie's system that can turn potion ingredients into an active potion when properly introduced." I shrugged, as I had hypothesized the theory but didn't have complete faith in it.

"We'll ask Jamie to do something harmless, perhaps some peppermint leaves, to see how her body reacts." Seaton shifted forward, as if to rise, then paused. "Davenforth. There is one more thing I want you to be aware of."

Wearily, I asked, "Now what?"

"The anniversary is coming up."

Anniversary? What in the devil could he—oh. Struck with sudden understanding, I glanced to the hanging wall calendar behind his desk, checking the date. I didn't know the exact day that Jamie had fought her way out of Belladonna's cave, only the date the newspapers reported it, the day we all celebrated the mad witch's demise. I was not sure if I'd ever heard the exact date.

That point was not important at this moment. What Seaton meant was something else entirely—how this anniversary would affect Jamie. People track and acknowledge anniversaries for a reason. They have an emotional impact on us, for good or ill. We celebrate or mourn them, depending on their significance. In this case, I didn't know which way my friend's emotions would fall. Would she mourn her lost world? Would she celebrate her survival?

"I don't anticipate she'll take this well," Seaton continued, his words delivered in a weary and sad rasp. "The events of those months still haunt her dreams. I'm afraid that with the reminder of it—because you know well the paper will run an anniversary article at the least—she'll suffer for it."

Grimly, I nodded, as I agreed with him. I feared something else, too. Jamie's likeness would also be printed in the paper, the savior that killed the witch. People would celebrate, would likely thank her, but no matter how good their intentions, they would draw attention to her. Jamie already noticeably stood out from the rest of us—she didn't look like anyone else on this planet. Her skin was noticeably a different shade, a duskier golden tone that didn't exist in this world, her stature and bone structure noticeably slimmer and more angled, just different enough to set her apart. People already looked at her askance, wondering where she came from. With this visible reminder, they wouldn't just wonder—they'd know.

"Jamie hates spectacles," I groaned.

"That she does. And while most of it, I think, will be positive, some of it won't. There will always be those who will fear her, and what people fear, they scorn. Just…keep an eye on her, Henri. Kingston will not be a comfortable place for her in the next month or so."

Whether I could be of any assistance, I did not know. But I'd certainly try to be a support to her. "I'll do my best."

"And keep me updated, won't you?" Seaton requested—well, it was more of a demand really.

"Same to you."

Boys.

May I remind you that I'm a highly trained federal agent?

We're of course just looking out for your magical welfare.

And that's your story, and you're sticking to it.

Report 01: Death and Explosions

I love how you see an explosion and think of me.

Are you making fun, Henri?

Perish the thought.

Sweat dotted along my forehead as I stood outside on the sidewalk. The oppressiveness could have been due to the early summer weather but I blamed the crime scene as the source. Heat radiated from the area, clinging along the pavement and brick walls. Quite the crowd had gathered around us on all sides, most of them fairly alarmed by the wreckage, and they murmured about it to their neighbors.

I must admit, I well understood their morbid fascination.

Gerring stood nearby with a hand covering his mouth and a green cast to his skin, which was no mean feat for the dark-skinned Svartalfár. His elongated ears lay flat against his head in silent dismay. Or perhaps it was the smell that bothered him. I certainly found it offensive. No human should smell as if they had been turned into crispy bacon. The churning of my stomach made me suddenly grateful I had not had anything pork for breakfast.

As a Magical Examiner, I often found myself called to disturbing scenes, and after so many years on the police force, I had thought myself largely immune to things of this ilk. Humanity, however, seemed quite enthralled with discovering ever more creative methods of killing each other off. This method, specifically, I had never seen before.

I hoped not to ever see it again, for that matter. I'd paused on top of the wagon, using the superior vantage point for an overall bird's eye view. The grimness of the scene was stomach-turning, and I wished for a peppermint or candied ginger to settle my stomach before wading into that black patch of scorched earth and death. Alas, I had nothing of that sort on me. Resigned, I gathered up my black bag and descended lightly to the ground. Clutching it with a white-knuckled grip, I strode grimly toward the epicenter of the blast, my eyes searching for my colleague. With a body on scene (what was left of the poor sod) there had to be a coroner. Ah, as expected. "Weber!"

Weber poked his head up above the ruined top of the car, blinking behind his thick glasses. Smoot already smudged his milk chocolate skin, turning his coloring into something that resembled a char boy's. "Davenforth, excellent. Do come and help me make sense of this. I've never seen anything like it."

I stepped very gingerly around the charred remains of the car—what seemed to be the latest model with its red paint job—taking it in as I moved around the rear bumper. It looked as if someone had put an explosive element inside the interior and then blown it up, killing, of course, the poor driver. If I hadn't known the model of the car, I wouldn't have been able to put a name to it, the frame of it twisted past all recognition. The hood remained intact, somehow, but warped, as if a giant had driven a fist upwards into it. The doors were both twisted open, barely hanging on their hinges, and scarcely anything was left of the engine block. All the windows had been blown out, the tires half-melted against the cement. I found it amazing that nothing large had come away from the frame, but although debris lay scattered about, nothing was larger than my forearm. It was incredibly tidy, all things considered.

This close, the scent of well-done bacon and scorched metal turned even more overpowering, and I started breathing through my mouth to ward off nausea. There was a very good reason why I had not sought any degree in the medical line. "Morning, Weber. What do we have?"

Making a face, Weber responded, "An utter mess, that's what. I'd say it in stronger terms if there wasn't a reporter dead behind me."

The reporter in question snorted amusement and got off another shot with his camera. He'd stayed behind the police line, but the distance was a bare ten feet, so he could both clearly hear us and get a good shot for his article without strain.

I shot the man a quelling look, not that it did much good, and focused on Weber again. "The…that is a man, correct?"

"Correct," Weber confirmed, rattling off, "Human male, possibly thirty or forty, and according to the little paperwork that survived the blast, I believe he was the owner of the business right in this building."

I glanced up at the sign, now marred with flames and smoke, but readable despite that: Charm-A-Way. "A charm company? Is that why I was called out here?"

"He's at least some sort of magician," Weber answered with a blasé shrug. "That, and this exploding car beats me. It's not my line."

Weber was young for his profession, only two years out of school, and the newest coroner to join us at Fourth Precinct. In the two weeks he'd been with us, however, I'd found him to be intelligent and competent. I didn't question his findings like I did with some of my other colleagues. "Indeed not. Anything else you can tell me?"

"Explosion point was likely the engine," he reported, pointing a pencil illustratively in the right direction. "I say that because of the way it impacted the body. The steering wheel, some of the engine parts, and the glass all shot out at an angle and upwards. The man didn't die instantly; it took him a few minutes, and it was internal damage that did him in. That, more than blood loss, as the heat and fire of the explosion seared all of the wounds."

A ghastly way to go. The remains of the body in the front seat looked like a prop from one of those third-rate haunted houses—nothing but a burned-up husk with trace amounts of blood and oozing wounds. I shuddered in sympathy for the poor victim. "A horrendous way to kill someone."

"I quite agree." Weber sighed, taking a step back, allowing me more room to observe with. "Not much else I can tell you until I cut him open. I might not find anything else to contribute, actually. The explosion would do a good job at destroying evidence."

"Unfortunately true. This I can say, however: It wasn't magically done." I let my eyes rove over the car from front to back. Magic has its own aura, a presence of light and shades of color, like a visible spectrum. The intensity of the light and saturation of the colors could tell any magician worth their salt a great deal about the potency of the charm, hex, or spell itself. I saw no trace of magic anywhere about the engine but a faint residue of white light swirled up visibly from the back seat. Charms, no doubt—the cheap versions people liked to buy and paste onto their walls to ward off sickness, fire, and things of that ilk. From the nature of the aura, I judged this to be an anti-sickness charm. "The only magic I see is from the mangled briefcase in the back seat."

Weber blinked at me, brown eyes wide behind his glasses. "You don't say. Well, I didn't expect that. What else could cause an explosion like this?"

Lips pursed, I didn't answer him, as I had no answer to give. Even though this was not in my line of expertise either, I had the notion it would fall on me to solve the mystery regardless. Especially since the victim was a magician. A niggling memory teased the back of my mind, and I focused for a moment on it rather than the sight in front of me. This type of explosion wasn't familiar to me, but I'd heard about it somewhat recently. Where…?

The memory came back to me all at once. Jamie and I had been lingering over an excellent meal of something she called lasagna, trading stories about the craziest cases we'd investigated. She'd mentioned something about a car bomb. I stared at the car in front of me with new eyes, matching up her description with what I observed. There were too many similarities to dismiss it.

Taking out my 'texting pad' as Jamie called it, I scribbled a note: Jamie. Are you free?

Almost a month ago, Ellie Warner, the inventor of the texting pad, had come up with a breakthrough of sorts. She'd devised a magical battery to attach to the back of the pad, serving as a source of energy. Unfortunately, the battery only lasted a week at a time, but still, it allowed normal citizens to use the device, and Jamie adored it. She always had it on hand, usually in a pocket, and it had proven the best means to reach her. I kept it charged religiously for that reason.

I am, why? she scrawled back.

For her sake, I used simple words, as she was still learning Velars. Although, all of the texting was improving her vocabulary by leaps and bounds. I need you. Corner of Maple and King Street.

Coming.

Weber leaned his head over my shoulder to peer owlishly at the texting pad. "I say, isn't that the instant communication device that Ellie Warner designed?"

"Indeed. Detective Edwards and I are two of the field testers." I tilted the screen so he could get a better look at it. "Guildmaster Warner is still tweaking the design so that normal citizens can use it, but currently a non-magical person can operate it for a week before it must be magically charged again."

"That is brilliant. And convenient. If she needs another person to field test, let me know," Weber volunteered eagerly.

Almost everyone who saw it said the same thing, so I gave him an indulgent smile. "Of course."

"But, if you don't mind my asking, why call for Detective Edwards? I know that she's your partner, but this isn't exactly your case, is it? Detective Berghetta is over this area."

It was a valid question, so I lowered my voice to explain, as I didn't want the reporters gathered behind the crime scene rope to overhear. "I believe she's seen something like this before."

Weber blinked at me. "Has she? Well, if you don't mind, I'll stick around a little longer and see what she has to say. Might help me figure things out later during my own examination."

I saw no issue with that and learning on the job was something a smart man did. "Not at all. Help me keep everyone back while I take a recording of the scene, will you? That way she can move things as she likes when she arrives."

Ducking under the police line, I retreated briefly to the wagon. Pulling a black box from the carriage, I set about recording the area. In slow sweeps, I took in the scene as a whole, then maneuvered toward the front of the car so that my back was to the building. For all intents and purposes, I was simply gaining a different view point for our records, but if the last case had taught me anything, it was that the odds of the criminal watching our investigation were quite probable. I scanned the crowd of faces as well, just in case.

"Detective," Gerring greeted, a happy note in his voice. The dark elf half-turned in his position, and for a man who had been nervous around Jamie when she'd first arrived, he'd certainly done an about-face in attitude now, as his grin winked out in his dark skin like a welcoming sign, pointed ears perked up under the black brim of his hat.

Glancing up, I found Jamie had arrived on scene. She caught my eye, winked, then stopped long enough to murmur something in Gerring's ear, which delighted him to no end judging from his expression. They'd become rather fond of each other since Gerring had joined the ladies in the auxiliary training Jamie held for the policewomen. The young policeman was of the firm opinion that Jamie Edwards could do no wrong.

Well. He was not entirely wrong about that. I raised my voice a notch so she could hear me. "Three seconds."

Jamie halted, waiting that count of three, already pulling on gloves. I studied her from the corner of my eye as I did so, looking for any signs of fatigue or strain. We were not yet to the anniversary, although it loomed closer by the day, and I feared how she would respond when the momentous day arrived. So far, she had not shown anything like irritation, sleep deprivation, or other ill symptoms. Although, she could be keeping a strong front, considering the reporters who seemed intent on capturing her every public moment.

Almost as if my thoughts had triggered it, the five reporters gathered on scene scented their prey and jostled people, quickly coming around to capture several photographs of her, their lenses flashing obnoxiously. I knew precisely why the reporters risked it.

The Shinigami Detective had arrived.

With her penchant of wearing male clothing, and the exotic look of her features, Jamie couldn't be mistaken as just another policewoman. Still, I knew that such fame grated on her nerves. Eventually, her fame of killing the most famous rogue witch in the country would die down. At least, for her sake, I wished for that to happen.

"Detective Edwards, why are you called here at this scene—"

"Detective Edwards, is a rogue witch responsible for this incident—"

"Detective—"

She gave them a flat, unamused look. "With all due respect," she said, her tone indicating a very miniscule amount of respect due, possibly none, "I am here to investigate a crime. You will remain behind the police line, quietly, as we investigate. If you do otherwise, I will forcefully remove your arses from this scene."

They gulped, put the cameras down, and went back to meekly standing at the cordoned rope. All except one. A middle-aged woman wearing a flashy dress of lavender pulled a notebook from her purse, pencil poised. "Detective Edwards, just one question: How do you feel about the upcoming anniversary of Belladonna's death?"

"Banzai," Jamie deadpanned.

I choked on a snorted laugh. Perhaps no one else in this world knew that word, but I certainly did. I could read the reporter's frustration, practically coming off in waves, but she didn't dare try again. Not with the visible glee in Jamie's expression, daring her to cross the line so Jamie could officially get rid of her.

I finished the recording, closing up the box, before approaching the two of them. "Jamie, thanks for coming. I think this will fall more in your area of expertise than mine."

Her brown eyes moved from the reporter to take in

the scene without flinching, her only sign of discomfort a downturn of the mouth. "Yes, it unfortunately does."

That answer made me wonder—had it been more than the one case she'd related to me? No doubt she'd tell me later. "Gerring, if you could replace this on the wagon. Thank you." I handed it over before turning on a heel, falling into step with Jamie as I retraced my steps towards the left side of the vehicle. "Weber has already done a preliminary examination of the body and he believes that the epicenter of the blast is, in fact, the front engine block."

"He's quite likely right." Several bulbs flashed as the reporters took pictures of Jamie striding through. She paused, shooting them an unamused look.

After that one-second glare, which cowed the reporters into retreating a step and lowering their cameras again, she continued forward. I found it vaguely impressive that they would step down for her, when no matter of words or frowning on my part would have had the same effect. Then again, Jamie had more presence than I did.

"Weber," she greeted with a cordial nod. "Wow. Poor guy. Did he die instantly?"

"No, unfortunately not," Weber answered, returning the greeting. "Took about fifteen minutes, or so I estimate. He was gasping his last when I arrived, and I was pretty quick to get here."

"Poor guy," she repeated with more sympathy. Stepping around Weber, she knelt, taking a careful look without touching anything. "I can see why you think the blast point is in the engine. It all blew up at him. Anyone try to lift the hood yet?"

Shaking my head, I answered, "No. We thought to wait on you. You've prior experience with this."

Her eyes came up sharply to mine. "Not magical, then?"

"Not at all."

"Ah." Jamie grimaced. "I'd hoped that this world wouldn't figure out how to do car bombs yet, but I suppose it was inevitable." Blowing out a breath, she stood straight again and motioned for me to get on the other side. "We'll likely have to muscle this off."

I did not doubt that if Jamie wished for the hood to come up, it would, as she possessed far more strength than the normal human. But I humored her request. She would no doubt have a good reason for my assistance, and it could be as simple as not displaying her full strength in front of a crowd. I pulled on gloves myself before getting a good grip on the edge of the hood.

With the force and heat the metal had experienced, lifting the hood was not an easy exercise. Its clasps had been warped past any redemption and they squealed in protest as Jamie and I forced them up. If not for her strength, I suspect I would've had to use a few judicious cutting spells to get it off. After fifteen seconds of wrestling with it, the hood finally gave, then torqued so badly to the side that Weber had to step in and hold it up so it wouldn't come crashing down again on our heads.

Jamie took in the mess of the engine compartment with a low whistle. "Definitely has seen better days. I don't see an incendiary device, but it was likely blown to bits."

I didn't doubt that. Nothing about her expression clued us in to her thoughts, so I prompted her. "What do you think it was?"

"Not a bomb expert," she denied thoughtfully, leaning down to crane her head this way and that, poking at one thing carefully with a single finger. "We'll definitely need to take this apart and give it a good combing. But my guess? Someone figured out how to tie a stick of dynamite to the spark plugs. As soon as the man turned the engine over, it would have lit the fuse and—" her hands spread out in an expansive gesture as she made an exploding noise.

That basic step-by-step process alarmed me. "It's that simple?"

Jamie grimaced like she'd just stepped in something questionable. "Unfortunately. If you know what you're doing with explosives, at least. All it takes is the right spark to light the fuse."

I felt grateful beyond measure that she'd lowered her voice, as that wasn't information the masses needed to know.

"Weber, I think you can take your body," Jamie continued before looking up and giving Detective Berghetta a sharp look. The detective had been working the crowd, searching for witnesses when Jamie had arrived, but the man must have had a sixth sense. As soon as her eyes latched onto him, Berghetta turned about sharply, uneasy. It amused Jamie, in a dark way, that the man feared her so much. "Henri."

"You want us to take this case," I guessed dryly.

Stripping off her gloves, Jamie grinned at me, fully delighted. "You do know me so well."

I certainly tried to. "I don't mind. I think this case demands your expertise, and it might tie into the man's business as a charm maker at some point, which means it might need a little of mine as well. But just asking Berghetta to hand the reins over isn't sufficient in this case, you do know that."

She flapped a hand at me. "I know, I know, but let's not step on toes."

I felt absolutely certain that if Jamie spoke to the man directly, Berghetta might keel over on the spot from cardiac arrest. I had a morbid enough sense of humor that I found the notion entertaining. That, and Berghetta's attitude toward Jamie irritated me. With a sort of evil anticipation, I accompanied her over to where Berghetta stood. He did have the sense to move away from the crowd, meeting us more in the middle of the cordoned off area, although from the way his feet dragged, he'd rather be in the drink.

"Detective," Jamie greeted civilly, a professional smile on her face. "I understand this one's yours?"

Berghetta nodded, his wide face looking a touch pale, dark eyes shadowed as if trying to brace himself for the upcoming conversation.

"Do you mind if I take it?"

For some reason the man looked alarmed by this request. He pulled his suit coat sharper around his paunch, almost hunched in defensively. "W-why?"

Oh for deities' sakes— "Detective Edwards has experience with this sort of thing. And the victim was a charm maker—his business might tie into the motive of his death. We believe this case might hit more in our wheelhouse than yours. We'll speak with Captain Gregson, of course, if you're amiable."

Berghetta would not have dreamed to cross Jamie, not for all the money in the world. He focused on me as he responded, the easier of the two for him to face. "Y-yes, of course, I don't mind."

Remember, Henri, you can't go about belting people in the mouth for stupidity. For one thing, you'd be hitting people from dawn to dusk without any end in sight. For another, you need your hands for other things.

"Excellent, thank you," Jamie chirped, slotted her arm through mine, and hauled me physically away. As we moved, she lowered her head just a touch to murmur in my ear, "Don't punch the man."

Had that desire been visible on my face? "I dislike his attitude towards you. Immensely. There's no cause to act so terrified of you, and reacting as he does sets a bad precedent with civilians and others at the precinct."

"I know," she responded, the words vibrating in amusement, "but still, don't punch him. You don't want to do the paperwork that involves punching a fellow officer, trust me."

"You would know." Jamie had struck three of her previous partners before partnering with me because they'd solicited her for intercourse, which still appalled me on some level. It was part of the reason I had been so relieved Captain Gregson declared us permanent partners. That, and working with Jamie always proved intellectually stimulating.

Well. I might just enjoy her company too.

"Shall I run to the precinct real quick and get permission to work the case?" Jamie asked. "You can collect evidence while I'm gone. It shouldn't take more than thirty minutes."

That seemed the sensible approach, as technically, she was not allowed to investigate a case that was not hers, and couldn't even take witness statements on her own accord. "Yes, go. I'll get Berghetta to hand over any statements he's already taken in the meantime. In fact, I'll ask Gerring to help us. This crowd is a bit much to handle on our own."

Jamie took in the onlookers, possibly fifty or more people gathered around as if this was some spectator sport, and nodded in agreement. "For that matter, I'll see if I can borrow Penny. We might need the manpower."

I knew Penny McSparrin would appreciate the chance to do real investigative work in any case. As the only other female officer at the station, she had been regulated to handling the domestic troubles until Jamie had joined us two and half months ago. Jamie had pulled her into the first case we'd worked on together, and McSparrin proved to have a good head on her shoulders. Jamie had unofficially taken the young woman under her wing, and this would be another good opportunity to get some field experience. "Please do." I turned to the wagon, retrieving the coverall suit I used to preserve my clothes, then paused as a thought occurred. "Jamie? How much dynamite would it take to do this sort of damage?"

"That," she acknowledged with a wry expression, "is a very excellent question."

Awwwwwwwww, Henri! Just for that, I'm making you macaroons

Well it's true. Macaroons!

sweets

Excellent.

Report 02: Volatile Elements

Hauling the ruined remains of the car into my lab was not possible, of course. There were no viable means to cart it inside of the building, for one thing. Fortunately, we had an outdoor warehouse for evidence of a larger nature, and I made plans with the collection officers to take it there.

As I arranged for all of this to be done, I had a thought on who might possibly be of use in determining the amount of explosives necessary to do the deed with. I sent Gerring off to inquire if Herbert Drake would be available to come and examine the car.

I'd just finished seeing the car loaded onto an evidence wagon when Jamie returned, her face set in grim lines of satisfaction. She swung out of the cab and made a beeline for me, Penny McSparrin in tow. "Henri. We have permission to work the case."

"I rather thought so, considering you brought Officer McSparrin with you." I gave the young woman a quick smile and nod of the head. "Happy that you can join us."

"Thank you, Dr. Davenforth," she returned with a quick bob of the head, but her cornflower blue eyes darted to the ruined car and lingered. Tipping the policeman cap to expose more of her forehead and wisps of blond hair, she whistled. "Cor, look at that. How in blazes did that happen?"

"That is entirely the question," I agreed ruefully. "Jamie, I'm having this hauled over to the evidence warehouse. It's the only place with sufficient size."

She nodded, not surprised. "Penny and I will work

the crowd and meet you there. Where's Gerring?"

"I sent him off to make a request of a colleague. Have you by any chance met Herbert Drake?"

Frowning, she looked steadfastly at the sky as she thought. "I don't believe I have. Name isn't ringing any bells."

"Ah, well, I thought the chance remote. Drake is one of the few demolition experts in Kingston. He is routinely called in as an expert and material witness in such matters."

Her eyes flared in relief. "So you do have one? I wondered if you did. Good, that should move things along quickly. Gerring can fetch him, I hope."

"I would think so, although he might not have the time today. It's entirely up to his schedule." I had only met the man once previously and possessed very little knowledge of him. I did have experience with his work, however, which was quite excellent. "At any rate, we'll hope he can come in quickly. I'll meet you back at the station."

Nodding, she moved off, already splitting the work load with McSparrin as she did. I left the ladies to it, as they were far better at taking witness statements than I, and left to follow the evidence wagon in my own wagon. I had to be sure that nothing untoward happened in the offloading of the car, as I didn't want the evidence skewed or damaged because of some mishap in transit.

To my relief, nothing happened, and the car was lowered carefully to the cement floor of the evidence warehouse without issue. I thanked the technicians who had worked so diligently, took the time to settle the wagon and cart, brought my black boxes and equipment back to the lab, and then returned to the car with a different tool kit. I might have known very little about explosives, but the charms in the back seat nagged at me. They might or might not have anything to do with, well, anything. They might tie into the motive of why the man had been so brutally killed in such a fashion, or they might be completely innocuous, but I wanted to at least determine what they were and have them on record.

The backseat of the car, while charred and smoky, was strangely untouched in comparison to the front of the vehicle. It was as if the blast force had gone up and over, the heat and force of the explosion twisting the metal of the frame. Perchance the fabric roof overhead had something to do it, not being an adequate barrier to that sort of heat and force, and it lay in tatters, a mute testament of this. The fabric of the backseat, more amiable to movement, had torn but otherwise maintained its general shape. Strange and morbidly fascinating how some of the fabric escaped any significant damage. With gloves on, I carefully retrieved the briefcase, charred thing that it was, and retreated to the table nearby. It took a little judicious prying to pull the contents of it free.

The top two papers were invoices, detailing an amount of charms ordered by businesses along Market Row. I unfortunately recognized both stores. They were popular—they sat on the respectable side of town, offered cheap charms, but maintained an air of propriety. Most of the charms were either perfectly useless, or so anemic as to be useless.

I more or less knew the quality of the charms even before I lifted the top invoices off. The paper was discolored and warped, of course, but the charms themselves still perfectly readable. I considered that to be (un)fortunate. It took no more than a casual gander to discern that the charms were very shoddy work indeed. In fact, I think a printing press had been involved at some point, which made the professional in me shrivel up in protest. A printing press could not relay even the smallest amount of magic into a charm. To use one during the process of charm construction completely nullified all efforts and rendered the charm either dangerously unstable or entirely powerless.

My sympathy for the dead imbecile dropped by half.

"Dr. Davenforth?"

Lifting my head, I turned toward the hail and found Gerring with Herbert Drake. It had been a good year since I'd seen Drake, and aside from the new beard he sported, I detected no change in his appearance. Still broad as a keg, dark eyes sharp in his lined face, salt and pepper hair flying about in every direction.

Stripping off my right glove, I approached. "Thank you, Gerring. Mr. Drake, I'm not sure if you recall our meeting last year."

"You're a hard man to forget, Dr. Davenforth," Drake denied, accepting my hand in a firm clasp. He smelled faintly of black powder, which inclined me to think that my summons had interrupted something. His eyes darted to the car beyond me and hardened visibly. "Gerring here explained what happened, and I'm happy to come and look it over, as this isn't the sort of nonsense I want to see in my city."

"Indeed not," I agreed wholeheartedly. "Please, come take a look. Ah, do wear gloves. It avoids contamination of the scene."

He accepted the gloves I handed him without a qualm, pulling them on while carefully maneuvering around the car to view it from all angles. "When did this happen?"

"Roughly two hours ago."

"Gerring said there was a victim?"

"A man. The driver."

"Did the hood come off in the explosion?"

I enjoyed the rapid-fire questioning, as I could see his mind taking in facts, absorbing what knowledge I imparted and what his eyes alone told him. "It did not. The hood was warped but stayed more or less on. My partner and I removed it to see if we could find any trace of an incendiary element."

He stopped abruptly at the boot and looked up sharply. "Was there?"

"Not that we could determine in a cursory examination," I denied with a shake of the head. "However, neither of us are experts in demolitions, which was why I thought it wise to ask your opinion."

"Hmmm." He went back to walking around the car. "Anything taken from the car, aside from that briefcase? I assume it was in there."

"Yes, backseat. And no, we've not touched the vehicle otherwise, aside from the removal of the corpse, of course—just transported it here."

"How much damage was there to the car's surroundings?"

"Scorch marks for the most part, superficial damage. The explosion seemed very localized to the vehicle itself." I observed that Gerring hovered nearby, still and quiet, as if unsure he should be here but unwilling to leave. It was to his betterment that he learned about things like this, as such knowledge might help him in the future, and I knew he was another of Jamie's ducklings she'd taken under her wing. I caught his eye and gave him a nod to indicate he was fine where he was. Only then did he relax.

Because of my momentary preoccupation, I nearly didn't pick up on Drake's discomfort at this information. Straightening, I asked tautly, "That says something to you?"

"Easiest thing in the world is to pile on too much powder," Drake answered slowly. He came to stand at the hood of the car again, staring intently down into what remained of the engine compartment. "It's much, much harder to use exactly the right amount for the job. That's either the luckiest fluke in the world, or it means you have someone with a lot of skill and knowledge behind this. I'm leaning towards the latter."

I was not at all inclined to argue. I doubted anyone not in the demolitions business would think to hot wire a car to explode to begin with. Human beings tended to stick to their comfort zones. "Who would have the necessary expertise?"

"I don't know enough at this point to answer that question," Drake responded semi-apologetically. "Let me get a good look of the inside, see if I can backwards engineer what they did."

That was entirely reasonable and I waved him to it. "Yes, of course." As I detested having people hovering over my shoulder while I worked, I did him the courtesy of turning my back to him and focusing once again on the charms at the table. In fact, since I still had Gerring, I decided to make use of him. "Gerring."

He obeyed my summons and came to stand next to me. "Yes, Doctor?"

"There's a bit of unpleasantness here," I explained to him, gesturing towards the charms. "I'm not sure if it will provide motive or not, but we should definitely investigate it. These charms are some of those fake off-the-press sorts that cause all ends of trouble. I'll message Jamie now, informing her of this finding, but can you go to Legal and inform them that I need a warrant issued to have these things pulled from the shelves? I shudder to think there's a batch lot available to the masses."

"Yes, of course," Gerring assured me with a distasteful glare at the charms in question. "What are the charms for?"

"They're anti-sickness charms, so hopefully they

haven't done too much damage." I crossed my fingers when I said it, then nearly laughed at myself. That was very much a Jamie maneuver. Strange how quickly I picked up her mannerisms. "Here, take these top invoices and this charm. Don't worry, this one is powerless, but they'll need the information from all of them in order to issue the warrant."

Gerring still picked it up as gingerly as he would have a moldy, dead kitchen rag. "Yes, Doctor. I'll be right back."

Shooing him on, I retrieved my texting pad and scrawled a quick message: Jamie, charms are bad.

It took a minute for her to respond: Possible motive?

Possibly. Do not enter business building without me.

Dangerous?

Could be. I honestly didn't know. But if the man was careless enough to mess with printing presses and charms then he most likely hadn't been the sort to take proper work precautions. Magical booby-traps could be set up, just waiting to be sprung. I did know that I didn't want my magically unstable partner anywhere near that potential landmine. Not until I had done a proper sweep through first and made it safe for her.

Roger that, she responded promptly.

Bless her for being so sensible. Relieved I wouldn't have to worry about her, I tacked on, Demolitions expert here. Then I frowned. Did she know the word demolitions? Well, she knew the word 'expert' so surely she could infer what I'd meant.

On our way back.

Good. That way I didn't need to repeat myself later. Repetition of any sort made my skin crawl.

"What is that thing?" Drake inquired, coming to stand at my elbow.

"Ah. It's a new invention of Guildmaster Warner's. It allows instantaneous communication with a similar device."

Drake's thick eyebrows shot straight into his hairline. "Like a telegraph?"

"Similar principal, yes."

He eyed the device in my hand with considerable respect. "Brilliant, that. You're testing it, I assume? I haven't heard of something like this on the market."

"Yes, I'm one of the testers," I confirmed, setting it back down on the table. "It's still in the experimental stage. There are a few kinks to work out yet. My partner tells me that she's on her way back. Do you have findings to report as of yet?"

"Not quite. I think I see something, but I need a magnifying glass and a pair of tweezers to get to it. Can I borrow a few tools?"

"Yes, of course." He'd come with nothing on hand, but then, I didn't know what he'd been doing prior. It could well be he'd hadn't the opportunity to pack up his own tools.

I opened up my bag, then went to my lab to fetch a few other things, including a journal so we could record his findings and preserve the chain of evidence. My nose kept itching from the acrid smell of gunpowder prevalent in the air. It took willpower to not rub at the appendage every five seconds.

Gerring returned with the warrant, which I quickly perused, making sure that all of the pertinent details were correct. They were, fortunately, and I folded the warrant to rest inside my pocket. Thanking him, I let him linger again to watch as Drake half crawled inside of the engine compartment. The man would be perfectly filthy after digging about. I'd offer him a cleaning charm before he left as a professional courtesy, I decided. Only fair. He'd done me a very good turn by showing up as quickly as he had, and I'd not wish him to ruin a good set of clothes in the endeavor.

Drake made several satisfied grunting noises, pulling out scraps of various sizes and makes, everything from shreds of paper to something that looked suspiciously like wire. Charred, twisted wire. He laid it out on the table next to the charms, in a precise little row, then went back for another look.

I heard her footsteps before I saw her—the quick and ground-eating stride—and turned to greet my partner. "Jamie, Officer McSparrin. What did you ladies discover?"

"Nothing good, but informative," Jamie reported, coming to stand next to the table. "Did we miss anything here?"

"He has yet to report his findings to me," I confided with a glance at Drake, "but he's making happy noises at what he's found, which is indicative enough, I believe."

Drake paused in his rummaging enough to pop his head up and correct, "Not happy, satisfied. I think I know what the powder monkey did. This who we were waiting on?"

"Indeed, sir," I confirmed.

"I know enough to give you the general picture, at least." Drake picked himself off the car and came closer, pulling off a glove so he could offer a hand.

Since I knew all parties, I made the introductions. "Demolitions expert Herbert Drake. This is Detective Jamie Edwards and Officer Penny McSparrin."

"Pleasure," Jamie said as she shook the man's hand. "And thank you for coming quickly."

"Downright disturbing, this is," he responded, then shook Penny's hand with the same professional courtesy. "I wanted to know what happened, once Officer Gerring got across the problem. I certainly want to catch the devil who did it before the mechanics of how-to gets about. Now, near as I can tell, you've got an experienced powder monkey behind this. He knew precisely how much powder to cause damage and kill the poor bloke, but to not hurt innocent bystanders. He wired up precisely one stick of dynamite to the engine, the wire keeping it in place with the fuse attached to the spark plug. Common materials, but he knew what to do with them."

"So we're looking for a demo expert." Jamie looked somewhat pleased by this, and I understood why, as it narrowed the suspect field.

Drake hesitated, mouth visibly mulling the words over before releasing them. "I think more than one person. I think he'd need a mechanic of some sort, too. This new model of car, the spark plugs are hard to get to. You'd have to know where they are, where to attach the wire to get the most voltage."

My brows rose. "You believe two people were behind this?"

"Yes. Powder monkeys make good money; it's not often they change professions. Same for mechanics. Doubt you'll find the same skillset in the same man." Drake shrugged, allowing us to come to our own conclusions.

I rocked back on my heels and thought about it. The man made an excellent point.

"Murder," McSparrin murmured with a disturbed look at the car. "But how can we be sure he was the right victim? I mean, it was a business car."

"That was something we discovered today," Jamie filled me in, almost as an aside. "The car was a registered vehicle to the charms business. He had a painted logo on the side and everything, which you can barely see now. The man—Trevor Garner is his name—had one employee, whereabouts currently unknown. It's entirely possible that the wrong person got into the car at the wrong time."

"Just when I think we are approaching clarity, something appears to muddy the waters," I bemoaned with a sigh.

Jamie gave me a commiserating look. "Tell me about it. The reviews we got on the victim were just as mixed. He was either a wonderful man or a snake charmer. Take your pick. You said the charms were bad, and we certainly heard a lot of war stories about that, but what's bad about them?"

It didn't surprise me others had cottoned onto the charms' less than stellar qualities. Or that Jamie had already heard about it. "The earmarks of the charms indicate that he was using a printing press to make them, then would add a line or two on his own so that they would register a magical signature." I grimaced, nearly shuddering at the shoddiness of it. "If he wasn't careful—and all indication from this stack of charms indicates that caution was not in this man's nature—then any charms misprinted could potentially cause harm."

"Like making people sick instead of preventing it?" McSparrin inquired, her tone and expression indicating it was more a rhetorical question.

Eyes narrowing, I asked her, "How many people claimed to be victims of his?"

"About a dozen," she answered in a flat, unhappy manner.

I took this information to its logical conclusion and winced. "In other words, his potential victims could incorporate half of this city."

"It's why I'm so happy that it takes expertise to pull this job off," Jamie said, leaning over to look at the charms more closely, "as we need all the help we can get in limiting the suspect pool. I'm sorry, Mr. Drake, are we boring you?"

"Not at all, very curious how this case will turn out," Drake assured her. "I want time to look over the car one more time, get up underneath it, you know. I'm pretty sure it went down as I said, but I want to be able to prove it to a court of law."

Jamie nodded in understanding. "As do we, sir. First order of business, though, I want those charms of his pulled from the marketplace. Let's do the city a favor and limit his victims."

I tapped my breast pocket. "I had Gerring get us a warrant while we worked out here. Legal was very quick to give us one. Care to step back out with me?"

Jamie flashed me a smile. "You bet. Gerring, Penny, we could use your help on this."

Holding up a hand, I intervened. "Actually, Gerring, perhaps you can assist Mr. Drake? Take notes on his findings so he's not constantly climbing out from under the car."

Drake, I think, also picked up on Gerring's interest and he was quick to back me up. "Yes, that will be very helpful. And I can explain to you as I go, just in case you see something like this again."

Gerring looked to Jamie for approval, for all the world like a child begging a favor from his mother. I think Jamie saw the similarity, as she bit the inside of her check before giving him a serious nod. "That's fine. Penny?"

"I'm with you," McSparrin stated promptly.

"Then let's be off," I encouraged, already doffing both gloves and striding for the open door. "The sooner we remove those charms, the better."

Report 03: The Missing Employee

Unfortunately, Jamie chose to take one of the cars from the motor pool. Equally unfortunate, I was unable to dissuade her from driving. Something on my face must have clued my partner in, as Jamie rolled her big brown eyes in an expressive manner before promising me, "I won't go over twenty."

Breathing out a sigh of relief, I gave McSparrin a hand up into the vehicle, then climbed in myself. If Jamie kept to her promise, I'd at least be assured that all of my limbs would still be intact upon our arrival.

Once everyone was seated, Jamie drove off, merging with her usual recklessness into oncoming traffic, but she did maintain her speed at a sane twenty instead of the insane thirty she normally favored. With the top down, a wash of warm air scented with petrol rushed around us, the noise of the street more hectic than usual. I noticed signs in the windows of several businesses as we passed them, all offering deals or specials in honor of the anniversary of Belladonna's demise. I shot a look at my companion but Jamie seemed either blind to it or determined to be blind to it. I could not determine which.

As we drove, she inquired of me, "You said the charms were bad. Does that mean you think the charms tie into the motive?"

"I believe it too soon to make any such assumptions," I responded, pitching my voice so that McSparrin, in the back seat, could also hear me. "However, at this juncture I would not be surprised. I hesitate to make any assumptions simply because a man was careless in his work place. It could well be that we're dealing with a jealous husband, a scorned lover, or something of that ilk."

Jamie pursed her lips in a manner that I'd come to learn meant she didn't entirely agree. "And yet he was killed at his business and not his house."

Opening my mouth, I thought about that, then slowly closed it again. That was quite an excellent point.

Leaning over the back bench, McSparrin put her head between us to ask, "Does that mean you think it's professional? That the charms are definitely the motive?"

"Not necessarily, but it does lean more toward that side," Jamie explained to her, not taking her eyes off the road. I felt quite relieved she maintained at least that modicum of safe driving practices, as the traffic was more helter-skelter than normal—pedestrians apparently of a suicidal bent kept darting between the lanes of traffic and getting blown at by drivers for their trouble. The horns sounded so frequently they resembled a discordant orchestra. "It also says something to me, that they hit him at his business. It means they possibly didn't know where he lived, that the business was a guaranteed location. Why else would you choose to hit someone on an open, busy street? Anyone could have seen them set the bomb."

Another point I had not considered, but she was quite correct. Some business areas closed at night, making them easier to rob or sneak through, but the street of this business was a main one, used by everyone to pass quickly from the docks to the downtown area. Even we policemen used it frequently at all hours. It must have been deucedly difficult to get in, get the job done, and not be spotted in the process. "A residential house would have been easier to access. Safer."

Jamie cast me a glance and a nod. "Yup. Exactly. Now, we could be wrong. Could be he doesn't take the car home, or he lives on a very busy street too. I haven't gotten the personal information about him yet. We're still trying to find his business partner."

Yes, she'd mentioned this before. "He has a business partner? Or an employee?"

"None of the neighboring business owners were sure about it," McSparrin explained to me. "They just knew the man handled the finances and they saw him coming in and out of the building at interesting hours. In fact, the business ran interesting hours. They were only open in the afternoons from two until five, three days a week."

I blinked at that, turning my head to give her a baffled look. "And they stayed in business?"

"Did better than that," McSparrin denied with an expression that suggested it was only the tip of the iceberg. "The car? Was paid for in cash three months ago. They said the victim was always bringing by a new girlfriend, eating out at the best restaurants, and wearing the latest fashions."

That did not add up to a good overall picture. "I'm afraid I see. He was churning out charms by quantity instead of quality, cutting corners and costs, and living off the profits."

"You see why I really want to find the business partner," Jamie intoned dryly. "Right now it's a very ugly picture. I give it fifty-fifty odds that it was a jealous girlfriend who got to him. Or paid someone to get to him, I should say. How many female powder monkeys are there?"

"About as many policewomen, perhaps less," I answered dryly. "It's not a profession most women choose to pursue."

"Hmm." She digested this with a noncommittal hum and made the necessary turn onto the main road. We were perhaps five minutes away from the crime scene now. "Alright, you said that the business was too dangerous for us to go into. What are you expecting it to be like?"

Something of this nature was not easy to explain, but for her sake and McSparrin's, I tried to put it into layman's terms. "In order for charms to be accepted into a store, they go through a cursory inspection. Usually a lens of some sort is used to see if the charms radiate magic. They unfortunately cannot tell the average person if a charm is of good quality or not, hence the deplorable state of the market, but they can at least tell if the charms are nothing more than ink and paper. To that end, fraudulent people like our victim have the habit of using bespelled ink, or spelled paper, in order to manufacture enough of a magical signature to pass these inspections. But they're often careless with the storage and use of the items. Spilled ink on the floor is ignored, torn paper not disposed of properly, etc. It leaves a mess of magical energy strewn about."

Jamie's eyes cut sharply to mine and I knew she heard what I did not say. Her magical core was in a constant state of flux, and while coming into contact with other magic was not harmful, per se, being around agitated magical energy would do her no good. Such knowledge of her state was confined to a handful of people—I being one of them—and I protected her as much as possible by keeping that information close to my chest.

"I see," she finally said. "That does sound nasty."

"I'd rather not step through that kind of mess," McSparrin seconded firmly. "Doctor, I assume you can tell at a glance how bad it is?"

"I can, yes, which was why I requested that you not enter the building without me. If I deem it safe enough, you can of course come inside and investigate. Otherwise I'll have to cleanse the place first. It won't be safe for a non-practitioner to enter otherwise."

Jamie pulled to a stop in front of the building, clear

from the crime scene rope still cordoning off the small area of the parking lot and sidewalk outside of the two-story brick building, and turned off the engine. "Then we'll wait here while you take a gander."

"Very well." I climbed out and headed for the business's front door, a truly ugly shade of chartreuse with a bell hanging over the top of it to announce visitors. The red brick front of the building, at least, had not been impacted by the blast unduly. The windows were cracked, the painted gold letters on the panes now less than pristine as it read: Charm-A-Way: Your source for good health. I couldn't stop a snort at the slogan, as I found it ironic in the extreme. Testing the brass handle, I found the door unlocked—interesting—and pushed it open without trying to step across the threshold. Best to get a good look at the situation first.

Even with my bare eyes, I could see that the front room, at least, was kept in an orderly fashion. The tile was clean, the front counter dividing the foyer from the back room polished to a dull gleam, and nothing about the narrow space hinted at trouble. Stepping through, I maneuvered around the long counter and toward the back of the space, finding two offices and a file room. Nothing in any of them indicated magic at all. Conversely, that made me frown. If he hadn't been using this back area to manufacture his charms, then where? He must have a printing press in the building somewhere.

Opening doors at random, I found one leading to a staircase downwards and took it. As I descended, a vile odor assaulted my nose and I stopped dead halfway down. There was a light on somewhere, enough to dimly illuminate the space, but the angle of the wall prevented me from seeing anything more than a sliver of grey floor at the base of the stairs. What was that horrendous odor? It smelled of something dead and decaying, mixed in with the oil of a machine, the metal tang of spilled blood—oh, stonking deities.

I think I knew where that missing partner/employee might be.

Hastily, I reversed directions and ascended the stairs, as I had no means of protection on myself except my wand, and Jamie would have my head if I walked into a potentially dangerous situation by myself. I doubted the murderer was still here if the body was already in such a state of decay that I could smell it, but still. No need to be stupid.

I stumbled to a stop at the edge of the door, meeting both women's eyes, and they looked tense and alarmed at my abrupt reappearance. Either that, or my wild expression told them that something was dreadfully awry. "I think the missing employee is in the basement, and I do not believe he's still living."

Jamie was out of the car before I could complete the sentence, already removing her gun from its holster. "You see him?"

"No, smelled him halfway down the stairs. The odor is...distinctive. I thought better of investigating it by myself."

"Good. I'd hate to have to beat sense into you." She patted my arm as she went through, her own way of saying she was glad for my common sense, then paused as McSparrin scrambled to join us.

I led the way toward the back of the building, explaining quickly as I moved, "There is a set of stairs in the back. There's no sign of anything magical on this floor. I assume the printing press and other materials are in the basement. Do allow me to go first, as I still have not verified the basement area safe for exploration."

"We will," McSparrin promised faithfully, her gun also in hand.

Certain individuals in this city would find it emasculating to have two women armed and ready to defend their unprotected backs. I found it vastly reassuring. Both of these women were better marksmen than I, and it was their task more than mine to take down armed criminals. My focus was to protect them from the elements of magic they could not see. I left the rest up to them.

Descending the stairs again, I breathed through my mouth, and gave McSparrin a sympathetic glance as she gagged. "Vile, isn't it? You'll never mistake this smell for anything other than a rotting corpse. Breathe through your mouth and try not to think of food. It helps."

"Sorta, at least," Jamie muttered, eyes peeled as we descended. She kept her gun trained down, ready to lift and aim at a moment's notice.

We reached the bottom and I carefully put my head around the corner. There was no hint of anything living moving about. The basement was well lit, suggesting that the men actually spent most of their working hours down here. Narrow windows lined the walls on all sides, spaced out evenly, providing something in the way of lighting. The main illumination came from the bare bulbs dangling from the ceiling. There were six printing presses, huge creations of iron staged along the area, with reams and reams of paper, bottles of ink, and two tables of printed charms along the front area. They'd been hard at work before the disaster, apparently.

"Henri," Jamie stepped around me to stand at my side, in full view of the room. "Any magic?"

"Quite a bit, but contained, fortunately. Don't approach the shelves or the table, and it should be fine. They weren't stupid enough to ignore spills, at least." Although I didn't have any higher praise to offer than that. Which was a sad state of affairs.

"Penny, you take right," Jamie instructed with a jerk of her chin. "Let's locate the source of that smell."

"That's about as exciting as chasing down the smell of a dead rat," McSparrin muttered to herself but obeyed immediately.

"I'd rather it be a rat," Jamie retorted, then sighed. I noted she carefully breathed through her mouth and I felt a certain sympathy for her. As vile as the stench was, Jamie's heightened senses would be doubly assaulted. "I hate dead people. They hold no answers."

"Unfortunately true." Since no one could approach the printing presses but myself, I went that direction, wand ready with a stasis spell. It was the best defense I had, as it would keep my attacker down if attacked. I didn't expect trouble down here, however. The area was too open, with too few hiding places. We would have seen him already if there was someone still here.

"Ah. Found him."

I hurried through the rest of my sweep of the back area, following Jamie's voice toward the front. She stood near the charm tables—although keeping her distance and a hand over her nose—staring downwards with the oddest look upon her face. McSparrin, standing at her side, looked just as baffled.

Coming around the other direction, I immediately saw why. The man was in his forties, perhaps older, hair thinning on top, his clothes shabby and on the edge of ruin with all of the ink staining his cuffs and splattering his white shirt. I couldn't see anything of his expression, as the body was on its knees and slumped in on itself. Someone had tied his hands behind his back, then his wrists to his ankles, keeping the body taut and strangely upright.

"Bullet to the back of the head, looks like," Jamie informed me, words muffled, "although we'll wait for the coroner's report to make sure. Penny, take the car and go fetch Doctor Weber, please."

With a nod, McSparrin scrambled up the stairs, gratefully, I think. At least, I would be grateful for any reason to escape the stench.

I studied the man, my perplexity growing. "Why go through the very elaborate prep work necessary to turn the car into a bomb, killing one of them, then execute the other like this?"

"Does seem strange, doesn't it? If they had a gun, why not use it on both men? It would have been far simpler." Jamie holstered her gun and scratched her chin, staring at our second victim thoughtfully. "Assuming that's what happened. We might be looking at this wrong. Garner could have killed the assistant, and then his accomplice, whoever that was, killed Garner later."

"I grant you the possibility, although at this moment I don't see the motive."

"I don't see the motive behind any of this yet. Either way, we're not looking at a single murderer. Drake said before it would take two men, two specialties, in order to pull the car bomb off. I think he's right. We're not dealing with a single murderer. This smacks of being a group of people. Just how many people did these two idiots piss off?"

"That is indeed the question. My second is more practical. Must we stay down here while waiting for Weber to arrive? I'd like to find my appetite again before dinner."

Laughing, Jamie winked at me. "Come on, then. Let's wait topside."

I followed at her heels, each step offering cleaner air to inhale, which my nose appreciated. We gained the main floor and didn't stop until reaching the offices. Inclining my head toward one, I suggested, "We could put the time to use. I, for one, would like to know what other stores carried their wares."

"And finances are usually very telling," Jamie agreed with a thoughtful look toward the filing room. "Let's divide and conquer. My reading skills are up to this, I think."

Numbers were easiest for her to read, after all. We divided to either side, me toward the main office and the massive desk that conquered most of the room. The mahogany surface didn't contain much paperwork, but I had the feeling that the desk was mostly for show. This was a place to impress women, not to actually run a business. Jamie might well have better luck in the file room than I did here.

I went through several drawers, but other than finding a stash of liquor, a half-devoured box of hard candy, and a few potentially useful love letters stashed in the back of one drawer, I found nothing of interest. I did keep the letters, then wandered into the file room to search there.

Jamie already had two drawers out, and three piles on the sole table in the room. As I entered, she glanced up from the ledger in her hands and informed me, "I think our dead man downstairs is named Peter Timms. He's listed as an employee in the books."

"Well, that clarifies that, at least." I pointed to the piles. "What are these?"

Pointing to each, Jamie rattled off, "Invoices, tax forms, bills."

I picked up the first folder on the invoice pile, noted the date was this month, and rifled through them. To my utter lack of surprise, he had more than one vendor for his wares, which meant the warrant in my pocket would need to be revised. Still, it seemed he only dealt with roughly thirty stores, a modest amount in a city of this size. Unless…now that was odd.

"What's the funny look for?" Jamie inquired.

"All of the stores he uses are on this side of the city,"

I answered slowly, conferring with the mental map in my head.

She put the ledger down for a moment, cocking her hips to half-sit on the table's surface. "Really? You're sure."

"Yes, I'm quite familiar with all of them. Some of them are modestly reputable, others not known for their quality."

Shaking her head, she marveled, "You're better than a Wikipedia page when it comes to Kingston."

"I'm sorry, what?" When she waved this off, I put her statement under its usual heading of, Earthling, Strange Statement of, and continued. "I find this odd. There are multiple market places in Kingston, and the east end would be the perfect place to cater to, considering the state of his charms. And yet he doesn't have a single store over there that he distributes to?"

Narrowing her eyes, she stared down at the open ledger in her hands. "You know, when you put it that way...."

"Odd, is it not? What are you seeing in the ledger?"

"The same thirty stores, over and over again. He apparently delivered charms to them once a week, usually an order of fifty at a time. There's a lot of abbreviations and short hand going on—I assume because they had more than one type of charm they offered, and their own way of referring to it."

"Yes, quite. I saw three different types just from the briefcase. More than a dozen types were on the tables downstairs." This did not make sense to me. Why only thirty stores? Why only on this semi-respectable side of the city when the east side would be a better way to offload his merchandise?

"I've got a bad hunch," Jamie murmured. Standing, she put the ledger aside and went to the far right filing cabinet, the one nearly hidden in the corner, then sank onto her haunches. Pulling out the bottom drawer, she drew a leather-bound ledger out and flipped through it. It took her precisely one page before she grunted in satisfaction. "Knew it."

"Do enlighten me," I drawled in invitation, leaning my back against the table's edge.

Standing, she waved the ledger in illustration. "This has a different business name on it. Different stores. I will bet you dollars to donuts that these idiots are charlatans. Con-artists. They go into an area, saturate it with bad charms, and when it gets too hot for them, they pull out. Declare bankruptcy, change their names, change their distributors, and go right back at it."

I let out a soundless whistle. That was entirely possible. I'd seen multiple businesses pull the same strategy, especially bad construction businesses. Unfortunately, the law could not prosecute an individual for certain crimes, per se. Not if the business as a whole was deemed responsible. It was a loophole that the more clever criminals used often to their advantage. I kept waiting for the law to change, to wise up to this tactic and plug the hole. It had not happened yet.

"If you're correct—and I'll lay odds you are—then it should be easy enough to prove the matter. Especially since they were stupid enough to keep their files from the last business."

Jamie nodded in dark amusement. "I think they did it just to keep track of who they'd already burned. Either way, it was stupid. Cocky. Well, Henri, this is a bit of a pickle. It looks more and more like the bad charms are tied into the motive. But if they've done this multiple times, it leaves us with a rather wide suspect pool. There's got to be several hundred mechanics and powder monkeys in this city alone."

"Yes," I agreed, the thought already exhausting me. "This won't be easy, to narrow the field. I think I already know the answer, but do fingerprints survive explosions?"

"Actually, they do," she surprised me by saying.

I blinked at her. "I'm astonished. Do they really?"

"I should qualify that," Jamie cautioned. "Fingerprints made with blood, dirt, or grease can survive fires. A contained explosion like the car bomb wouldn't necessarily wipe away fingerprints."

It truly fascinated me, the knowledge contained in her head. I never tired of asking her questions because of it. "Interesting. I'm doubly glad that I and Drake wore gloves, then."

"Yes, so am I. I'll get on fingerprint recovery when we get back to the car. For now, though…" she regarded all the files with a sort of resigned good humor, "I suppose we'll have to arrange this being carted back to the office. Do you think we can requisition Penny and Gerring?"

"I believe so." At least, I hoped so. Captain Gregson was of the opinion that Jamie's techniques produced good results. He encouraged her to train the newer members of the force, those who were still amiable to learning, and I'd seen him rearrange schedules to allow our junior members the time to study under her. Phrased correctly, we'd no doubt be able to keep McSparrin and Gerring with us for at least a week. "We'll ask upon our return."

Jamie arched a slender eyebrow at me, part amusement, part challenge. "When you volunteered us for this case, you thought it would be more my end than yours, didn't you?"

Shrugging, I allowed, "I did, yes. I'm doubly glad that we have it now, though. I'm always far happier to take shoddy charm work off the market."

"I know you are. I'm almost disappointed we have to catch the murderers. I'm beginning to think they had a very good motive for doing what they did."

Sadly, she was likely not wrong. If the two victims had pulled this stunt multiple times, that meant the law had failed to catch them multiple times, and no doubt left a string of bodies in their wake. The thought saddened me. As much as I loved the law, I was not blind to its shortcomings.

"Buck up, Henri," Jamie advised, not unsympathetically. "Maybe we can make this case the precedent, get the law changed so that conmen can't pull stunts like this."

"From your lips to the gods' ears."

Jamie's Additional Report 0.2

Poor Henri. I could tell this bothered him. We have the same loopholes in the legal system on Earth, too. It bothers every lawman that sometimes we just can't help. The law hasn't caught up to some crimes, the criminals too quick to create new distinctions so they can skate by. I have faith, though, that Kingston will stomp this out quickly. This is the sort of case that we can really use to get public attention. Sometimes that's all you need for precedent.

> *Jamie, why are you scribbling in my report again?*
>> Now, Henri, it's such a lovely tradition. Of course I must continue it.
>
> *How in the world did you even find it, anyway?*
>> *I hid it rather well.*
>>
>> You hid it exactly where you hide your third stash of chocolates. I don't consider that "well hidden."
>
> *You're worse than a bloodhound, I swear.*
>> I accept the compliment. ☺

Report 04: Bad Charms

I think this should be called

SHERARD'S GRAND ENTRANCE!

Kindly don't encourage him.

The dead man executed in the basement was confirmed to be one Peter Timms by the ID in his wallet. Weber estimated that he'd died the day before, late in the evening, sometime after normal business hours. With the car bomb occurring early morning the next day, I found this gap between murders rather interesting, as did McSparrin and Jamie.

As we boxed up the file room to cart back to the precinct, Jamie ruminated out loud, "The timeline makes me scratch my head a little. So, let's say that Timms was down in the basement working, caught by the murderers, and tied up. They demanded information from him—whether they got it or not is anyone's guess at this point—and then, what? Killed him immediately and rigged the car to explode?"

"Fits with the coroner's finding," McSparrin admitted, pausing with two folders in her hands. She looked speculatively through a window. "So Trevor Garner comes into work, perhaps does something in the office, pops down to confer with his colleague, finds him dead, then tries to run for it?"

"Hence why he died in the car," I finished. "It all rather does fit, doesn't it? Why the briefcase of charms, though? They were practically worthless."

"That's the odd thing," Jamie admitted, hefting a full box onto the table. "But I think it's equally possible he came into work, had the briefcase in hand, and when he saw the dead Timms just ran for it. He never set it down."

Also entirely possible. Although, truly, the matter of the briefcase was idle speculation. It didn't factor into the grand scheme of things whatsoever. "While the timeline helps a little, it gives us no clearer picture regarding suspects or motive."

"I'll take either at this point," Jamie sighed. "Alright, is that all of them?"

I glanced about, double checking the file cabinets, but we'd emptied them quickly between the three of us. "I believe that it is. Officer McSparrin, can I entrust these to you? I truly wish to get the charms this business made off the market before the end of the day. Their shoddy craftsmanship alarms me."

"Yes, of course," McSparrin assured me, shooing us on.

"Excellent. Put them in the evidence locker for now. We'll sort out an appropriate place to cull through them tomorrow." It edged into mid-afternoon now and I fully anticipated that going to the two stores on the warrant would eat up the rest of the work day.

Somehow, Jamie beat me to the car, grinning as she went. I do believe that she enjoyed driving just to tweak my nose. I was not at all sure why she found it so amusing to terrify me, and yet the fact stood that I'd yet to drive when in her company. I found this suspicious. Resigned to my inevitable heart attack, I climbed into the passenger seat next to her, gripping the door for dear life.

My partner had the gall to pat my arm like I was a cranky child. "There, there, Henri. We'll be there before you know it."

I glared at her. "We can get there at a slower pace and

it will make no difference to our agenda."

"Yes, but that would be less fun," she informed me, eyes dancing with laughter.

Why did I even try? After several weeks of being acquainted with this woman, I surely knew better.

Jamie took off in her usual squeal of tires, although she once again managed to avoid every other vehicle and pedestrian on the road. I began to suspect occult powers at play, because with her driving methods, an accident should have been inevitable by now. And yet she had never even come close to any sort of collision. It boggled the statistical mind.

"I learned something very important yesterday," Jamie said in a matter-of-fact tone that suggested she actually laughed internally. "Clint informed me that he kept a log of all cuddle time. I've apparently failed to meet his quota. I was ordered—ordered, mind you—to stay in this evening, as he needed more lap time."

Knowing the feline creature well, I rolled my eyes. "I had no notion when I acquired him for you that he would be so demanding upon your affections."

"Really? I did. Cats on Earth are very similar to Clint. They like long cuddles, laps, scratches, and to be adored. The saying goes that thousands of years ago, cats were worshipped as gods. Cats have not forgotten this."

Bemused, I stared at her. "They were worshipped as gods?"

"In a country called Egypt, long in the past," she answered forthrightly. "One of their goddesses was half cat, half woman. Bastet…I think was her name. Anyway, in Egypt, it was a severe crime to kill or injure a cat."

"But this didn't remain true in modern times?"

"Nope. Hence the joke. The general attitude of cats is that they should still be worshipped and adored. Clint's attitude fits the feline mentality to a T."

I'd been half-afraid Clint would prove to be a nuisance, but Jamie not only seemed to take his attitude in stride, but found his antics entertaining. If she wasn't regretting my somewhat impulsive gift, it was fine. "As long as he's being good company."

"He is. Better than TV, I think." She cast me a glance, speculatively. "Since I've been ordered to stay in, that means I'm cooking dinner tonight."

My ears perked up hopefully. "If I contribute dessert, may I have an invitation to join you?"

"I fully expected that question," she acknowledged dryly. "I thought perhaps I'd make enchiladas tonight."

I'd had these before, and they were mouthwatering and fattening in the best sense. "Sounds delightful. Six?"

"Assuming that we can get done with this in the next three hours." Jamie pulled off the main street and into the parking lot next to a main shopping center. Garden Square brimmed with people even at this hour of the day, many with packages in their hands. The Square used to be a shoe factory, many decades ago, but had been converted over to multiple shops on two levels. The age of the place reflected in the red brick, the slightly crooked sidewalks. However, despite it not being the epicenter of shopping in Kingston, some care had been taken to keep the appearance of it clean. The middle-class citizen chose to shop here, as the wares were plentiful and cheap.

The store we wished to visit was fortunately on the ground floor and not far from the parking lot. It had a charming red brick and white trim exterior, the front window pane boasted the store's name in painted cursive script. The white front door stood open, a concession to the heat, perhaps. As we walked towards it, I noticed that several people had stopped and started whispering behind their hands, their eyes obviously trained upon the woman at my side.

What was this about? Surely they couldn't identify her at a—well, no. Perhaps they could identify Jamie at a glance now. The morning edition of the Kingston Gazette had featured the car bombing front and center, with both my likeness and Jamie's as a side caption. To my resigned frustration, they had recapped Jamie's history with Belladonna as well in the article, illuminating my partner's identity for the masses ahead of the dreaded anniversary article we all anticipated.

People didn't seem to know what to make of her. Some of them edged away, others stared at her in open awe. More than one whisper grew just loud enough that I could make out the sentiment, if not every word, and I glared at the perpetrator until the man flinched and hastily looked away. Idiot. I wouldn't be surprised if he was related to Sanderson in some form or fashion.

Jamie caught this reaction, naturally, and a dark frown grew on her face. She disliked fame and notoriety but, in this case, one could hardly escape it. For her benefit, I murmured in a low tone, "It'll pass. Some new amusement or shocking news will rise to supplant this story."

"I know," she sighed. "It's just slower without social media. It's alright, Henri."

Not the reaction I'd hoped for, but at least she did not seem outraged, simply resigned. I followed Jamie in through the open door, then instinctively put myself in between her and the majority of the shelves. The shelves themselves were neatly organized, each type of charm stacked in tidy piles of paper with clear labels and prices below each stack. These places tried to keep tabs on their stock, but their efforts didn't always produce good results. I could tell that a few of the charms on the shelves sparked sporadically with magic. It would not be safe for her to come into contact with them.

Looking at me sharply, she leaned in to murmur near my ear, "Is it bad in here?"

"Certain areas of the store, yes. Please stay away from the shelves," I returned in a low tone.

With a wary eye on the right side, she gave me a nod.

Fortunately, the cashier's counter was where we needed to go, and precious little product cluttered up the wide expanse of the wood. I headed there, pulling out my badge as I went and flashing it at the female teller wearing a smart black uniform. "I'm Dr. Henri Davenforth with Fourth Precinct. This is my partner, Detective Jamie Edwards. May I speak with your manager or boss, please?"

The girl's eyes went wide. "Ah, y-yes, just a minute." She disappeared through a door marked 'Employees only' behind the counter, and I could hear her whisper something urgently before another woman appeared, a matron with her greying hair held up in a loose bun, dressed in the same black uniform. Their skirts and lacey shirts with flowing sleeves stood in sharp contrast to the woman at my side, who wore formfitting trousers and coat. I could see both of them do a bit of a doubletake to see Jamie in obviously male clothing.

"I'm Heather Lee, the owner of this store," she introduced herself with an uneasy glance between us. "What's wrong?"

"You're not in trouble," Jamie assured her with a charming smile, and the woman's tension dropped by half. "It's just that some crook has snuck dangerous charms into your inventory. You know Trevor Garner?"

Eyes narrowing, Mrs. Lee answered slowly, "I do. Mr. Garner has five different charms on our shelves, all anti-sickness charms of different types. You say that the charms are dangerous?"

"They're unstable," I explained patiently. "He made

them using a printing press."

Both Mrs. Lee and her clerk gasped in outrage, which pleased me, as it meant they knew enough about charm making to realize how dangerous that was.

"The nerve!" Mrs. Lee spluttered, already flipping open the counter's door so she could come through to stand with us. "I'll have those removed at once. If you know they're here, have you arrested him?"

"He's past that, I'm afraid," Jamie drawled with a wry shake of the head. "He was murdered this morning."

Mrs. Lee stopped dead, brown eyes flaring wide. "No! You don't say. Was it because of the bad charms?"

"We're still investigating," Jamie said with an apologetic splay of hands. "But in the course of investigating, we learned about his charms. We'd like to take everything he had out of your inventory."

"Yes, please. They're all over here."

Jamie stayed planted near the counter, drawing the clerk into a conversation to pump her for information. I drew out a containment pouch from my pocket, which I'd taken from my black bag for this purpose, and carefully sorted everything that Mrs. Lee pointed to inside. I was relieved she had the good sense to not handle anything herself. The stacks were not to be casually approached, as each paper charm sparked against the ones it pressed to, arcs of power and light like static electricity rebounding visibly in the air. With such obvious instability of the charms, I was very careful to not rub them against one another as I put them into the bag. Since I was there, and she seemed receptive, I inquired, "I do, in fact, see three other stacks of charms that are also dangerously unstable."

She stopped, eyeing me carefully. "Are you a magician, Dr. Davenforth?"

"Magical Examiner."

Her mouth dropped in a silent 'oh' of understanding. "In that case, sir, please do take them as well. I've no intention of keeping bad charms in my store; I just don't have the means to always tell good from bad. Some of these fakes are quite well done."

"Yes, I'm quite aware of the problem. If you'll give me the names and contact information of the individuals who created them, I'd be delighted to report them."

This satisfied her and she nodded firmly. "I'll be happy to."

I took out a separate bag from my pocket to contain the other charms, carefully labeling each one to preserve the chain of evidence. As I worked behind the shelves, I heard someone enter with a heavy tread, and a voice I knew very well sang out, "Jamie! Imagine finding you here."

"Sherard," Jamie greeted, equally surprised. "This is a coincidence. I'm here working. You?"

"The same, as it happens. Where's Davenforth?"

I moved quickly, rounding the corner of the aisle so that Royal Mage Sherard Seaton came into view. He wore his usual theatrical red jacket, dark hair combed back in a rakish manner, and his eyes were lined with kohl, but for once, he appeared to be not in a jovial mood. In fact, he sported lines around his eyes that aged him five years at least. "I'm here. What's happened?"

"Bit of bad business, I'm afraid. I'm investigating and hoping I'm in the right shop. Jamie, don't touch this." He pulled out a charm from his pocket and displayed it for Mrs. Lee. "Madam, I'm RM Sherard Seaton. Please tell me, does your shop sell this charm?"

She looked at the charm in hand and we both blanched. It was one of Garner's charms and that boded quite ill indeed. She cast me an anxious look, and I answered for her. "She did, until about five minutes ago. We're here

Charms and Death and Explosions (oh my!)

to take all of those charms into evidence. The man who created them was murdered not eight hours ago."

Seaton's dark eyebrows arched as he let out a low whistle. "Was he, now."

"Sherard," Jamie pressed anxiously, "Why are you here looking for this?"

"As it happens, one of these was in the Kingsmen's barracks," he answered with a long face. "It's made the entire barracks ill. I'm investigating on their behalf. Monkey balls, he really was murdered eight hours ago?"

"Car bomb," Jamie informed him succinctly. When he winced, she gave him a grim smile. "That was my reaction. Sherard, I think it just became a dual investigation."

That, finally, put a smile on his face. "You think? What am I saying? When they discover you and Davenforth are already on the case, they'll insist I work with you. Oh, excellent, I've so looked forward to our next case together."

I thought about protesting—next case? What the devil was that about?—but I sensed a certain inevitability about it all. Besides, in cases like this where volatile charms were involved, another magician to safeguard Jamie would be invaluable. "In that case, follow us to the next shop. We've one other that we have a warrant for, and then we can sit down and compare notes."

"Splendid," Seaton agreed heartily. "Although, if you know some of the other shops that he sold such charms to, you can just give me the list. I'll have the Kingsmen gather them up for us. No need to extend the warrant."

"There's definite perks to working with you," Jamie observed gratefully. "Yes, we have a list of several other distributors. Or I should say, Penny's working on the list now."

"Penny? We get her officially this time around, then? Good show," Seaton approved. "I quite like that young woman. She shows intelligence. Here, give me the list. I'll message it over."

Because of his friendship with Jamie, Seaton had horned in on field testing the texting pad. He in fact had ten in total, half of them scattered among the upper ranks of the Kingsmen, the others being played with by the royal family. Ellie Warner, I understood, had almost daily updates from people asking for tweaks or offering suggestions. She might regret having given Seaton any of them by this point.

As he messaged the appropriate parties, I jotted down the information for the other bad charm makers. I also wrote Mrs. Lee a receipt so that she could report the inventory as claimed for evidence and get a tax deductible for it, which she appreciated.

As we left the store, I kept a weather eye out for trouble, or for stupid people who might try and crowd us. It might have happened if not for Seaton's presence. He gave them all one scathing look and that was sufficient to make people suddenly remember their own business. I do wish I had the same ability. Apparently I'd not a sufficient reputation in order to manage it. We walked unencumbered toward our own vehicle. Seaton had somehow parked next to us, so we stopped to catch each other up on the particulars.

In a low tone, Seaton leaned toward us, standing close to avoid being overheard. "One of the Kingsmen—Georg, actually—has a sweetheart, and it was she who bought the charm. There's been flu going about and she didn't want him catching it. A sweet sentiment, of course, but she bought the wrong charm. Georg, not knowing, pasted the charm up in the hallway near the front door. Everyone in the barracks, which is twenty-four men, are now very ill because of it. I had to quarantine the entire Kingsmen compound on the palace grounds to keep it from spreading."

Charms and Death and Explosions (oh my!) 59

Jamie startled. "Wait, this charm caused them to be sick?"

"Yes, that's what I feared." Meeting her eyes, I managed a one shoulder shrug. "Part of the problem with using a printing press—"

Seaton slapped a hand on the car, his mouth loosing several foul curses strong enough to shame a sailor. "The devil you say! They couldn't be that stupid!"

"Six printing presses in the basement," Jamie stated sourly. "He's quite serious."

Spluttering with incoherent rage, Seaton stared at her. "Six?!"

"All of them in recent use," I tacked on sourly. "You now understand my and Jamie's concern. We've no notion if every charm they printed was of the same terrible quality, or if only some of them cause sickness like the one in the Kingsmen's Barracks. I suppose I will spend tomorrow examining multiple charms in the effort to figure out if this is a result of poor training or negligence."

"I'll help you," Seaton promised darkly.

"At any rate, I meant to say that it's because of their usage of a printing press that caused issues; while the design might go on the paper quickly enough, you sometimes get splotches. Blemishes. Parts of the ink might be fainter than it should be. All of these discrepancies hinder the spell, and if you have enough imperfections, it will actually turn the charm into an antithesis of itself. None of the charms I examined today are to that point, but I saw enough in their methods to fear that at least a few would have this effect."

Jamie's golden-brown eyes shone as she put the pieces rapidly together. "You think they made a charm bad enough that it got someone sick. Mortally ill, even?"

"Healthy people do not typically think to buy anti-sickness charms. Such things are bought by those who are ill, or have a tendency to become ill easily. If you put a bad charm, such as the one in the Kingsmen barracks, next to a person already struggling with a serious condition…" I trailed off suggestively, not liking my own dark theory.

"They could very well have killed someone indirectly," Jamie finished lowly. "Yeah, okay, that's a good motive for murder right there. And it would explain why Timms got offed too."

"'Offed?'" Seaton repeated in amusement. "Is that really the term you use?"

She flapped a hand at him. "You know what I mean. I don't think we can firmly call it just yet, as jealous people are not rational, and we could still be dealing with a scorned lover, but I'm ninety percent certain this was about the charms. Although how we're going to narrow down the suspects is beyond me at the moment. Sherard, you don't know this yet, but this is actually their second business. They had to shut the first one down and change to a totally opposite end of the city."

Seaton's dark eyes went black with anger. "I cannot state that I am surprised to hear that. Not with the charms I saw. But you're correct in that it will leave us with a very wide suspect pool."

"First step," I encouraged them to load into the vehicles, "let's do what we can to prevent more victims."

I must say, I do feel that Davenforth's observation about me looking older than my years was unkind. I am always precisely put together.

Oh, for deities' sakes. Seaton, not you too!

My dear fellow, who do you think helped Jamie read the first one?

But you refrained from scribbling in the first one.

Yes, I do wonder what I was thinking. It's much better to add to the fun.

Clearly, I need to find a more secure location to hide this. *Challenge accepted, dear fellow.*

Report 05: A Dinner with Colleagues

We finished the day by gathering in Jamie's kitchen. Even Gerring was invited, and the dark elf happily accepted. I had the notion that he'd overheard talk of his mentor's cooking before and was ecstatic to finally be able to taste it himself. It made for an interesting crowd with myself, McSparrin, Seaton, and Gerring all gathered around the bar. Jamie didn't seem to mind; in fact, a wide smile split her face as she pulled the ingredients from the refrigerator and started mixing things together.

Clint introduced himself to the group—I had to explain what he was to both Gerring and McSparrin—and then chose Seaton to perch upon. Seaton lavished both praise and affection upon the egotistical creature and soon enough Clint sprawled across the mage's lap, purring loudly.

"I sent a note to my superiors and the other Kingsmen," Seaton informed us as Jamie browned the beef on the stove. "I've no doubt that we'll be issued orders for a dual investigation. Officer McSparrin, Officer Gerring, I included a formal request that you work with us. We need all hands on deck for this case, I think."

Gerring perked up hopefully. "Truly, sir? I'm very happy to hear it. Detective Edwards has methods I've never seen taught in the Academy and I'd like to learn from her as much as I can."

That wasn't surprising. Jamie's methods weren't even from this world, after all. I decided to hold my peace, focusing on chopping an onion for Jamie instead, our elbows brushing together as I worked. The glance Jamie shot me said she knew very well I'd bitten my tongue and found it amusing.

"I'm inclined to think you'll make a good detective," Jamie informed the young man, and Gerring's ears swiveled in a happy movement. "Penny as well. It's why I'm glad I can pull you in on a case like this. It gives you both good experience and introduces you to colleagues you might otherwise not meet. Although, I'll be honest, I'm not quite sure what's the best tactic from here. I know what I'd do in my own country, but not all methods can be translated over. Unfortunately. We have a huge suspect pool."

Gerring blinked at her. "We do?"

Leaning forward, McSparrin shifted so that she could see around Seaton and explain to her colleague, "We found today that Timms and Garner actually had a charms business before this one on east end. They had to shut it down and start up a new one. There's a lot of files that we still need to wade through, so we're not sure why, but it doesn't look like bankruptcy. I took a quick look at the ledgers on the way to the station and the first business was making good money."

"Which means that it's more likely they had a lot of complaints about quality, or something went seriously wrong," Seaton inferred, hand still rhythmically stroking behind Clint's purple ears. "I'm inclined to think both, considering the state of their charms."

Clint reared up in his lap, tapping Seaton gently on the cheek with a paw.

"Yes, my feline one?" Seaton inquired in amusement, pausing in the petting.

"Sing to me," Clint requested in a slight whine.

I stabbed the knife in Seaton's direction. "Don't you dare. That creature is incorrigible and has a terribly accurate mimicry ability. Whatever you sing to him, he will use it against you."

Jamie snorted but notably did not disagree.

Foiled, Clint shot me a dark look before slinking back down in Seaton's lap. He nudged the hand nearest to him to resume the petting. Visibly biting back a laugh, Seaton indulged the Felix with circular rubbing behind his ears.

"Speaking of," I stayed paused in my chopping, not willing to lose a finger in pursuit of my question. "Seaton, you examined at least one of the charms. How thoroughly?"

"Not very, I'm afraid. I was more inclined to dash off and find the dastard who'd made it. I checked only for the maker's mark and the store stamp to give myself a location. I barely paused long enough to put it under strong warding to prevent any other mischief." Cocking his head in question, he queried, "Why?"

"I've a question that needs answering," I admitted frankly, one eye on my partner. "I'm certain you've wondered this as well, Jamie. Are the charms intentionally terrible, or a product of negligence? Or perhaps they are a result of someone who is simply not skilled about their craft. I gave it a cursory inspection, but aside from it being printed on a press—"

"Don't remind me of that," Seaton moaned, the sound coming from his gut like a mortal wound. "The stupidity of that brings horror to my soul."

"Some people just need a sympathetic pat," Jamie soothed him mockingly. When he gave her a dark look, she grinned and finished, "On the head. With a hammer."

"Anyway, aside from it being printed on a press, any number of errors could be involved, and it will take study to determine what exactly made it the antithesis of what it was designed to do."

Jamie poked me in the side and I belatedly realized I had a half-chopped onion in front of me. With an apologetic glance at her, I went back to dicing it into small cubes.

Charms and Death and Explosions (oh my!)

"Before we got sidetracked by that, I meant to say that because they had a business over at the east end of Kingston, we have a very wide pool of suspects," Jamie stated. She picked up a wheel of cheese and started grating in a smooth motion, the scent of fresh cheese mixing pleasantly with the grilling meat in front of us. Enough so my mouth started to water. "From everything you two have told me, it's very likely that these bad charms have either made people deathly sick or possibly even killed someone. On the other hand, we know that we had at least a powder monkey and a mechanic involved in the murder. Possibly a third person with a gun. I'm not sure which is the best approach to start narrowing our suspect pool from. Do we try to eliminate by profession first? Do we search for deaths in the past six months that are related to charms?"

I did take her meaning. We could approach it either way and find both searches equally time consuming.

Gerring leaned a little closer to her across the wooden surface of the bar. "You don't think it will be any faster to search for the powder monkey and then work our way out?"

"I think the powder monkey might be tricky to find," she explained patiently. "You heard Drake as well as I did—a single stick of dynamite was responsible for the explosion. Odds are he's not going to find any trace of it left to identify. We don't have the technology for that. Now, think about this. How easy is it for a citizen to purchase dynamite in any quantity?"

McSparrin and Gerring shared a speaking look before Gerring offered slowly, "I would imagine difficult. He'd need a very good reason for it and it'll surely be recorded somewhere that he purchased it."

"Yes, exactly. So odds are this man didn't purchase it. He's a powder monkey, he has open access to his company's supply of dynamite. It would surely be easy for him to fudge the numbers, especially if it's only one or two. I imagine that they tested this at least once, to make sure it would work, so say he took at least two sticks. All he would have to report was that there was a weak charge with a detonation, it took two sticks more than he expected, and bam. Perfect cover."

Seaton's face screwed up in glower. "You're making too much sense. But that's likely what happened. Even a close audit won't reveal this person if they did it that way."

"I'm personally hoping for a stupid criminal," Jamie admitted to him, stirring the meat to prevent it from scorching, "but frankly? I don't give it good odds. We'll still investigate every company that does demolition in the city to cover our bases. Who knows? Maybe we'll get lucky."

"Maybe if we cross reference?" McSparrin glanced between all of us. "Isn't that what we did on the last case? We got a list of all the possibilities and started cross referencing. We narrowed it down that way to people who needed actual investigation."

I had to admit, the notion was a good one. It would not be a quick method of investigation, but it might be the only viable option. "I am inclined to think that's a good idea. But it would mean some of us are regulated to searching the morgues for histories on recent deaths, and there's hundreds of those in the city."

"Not to mention interviewing hundreds of powder monkeys to see who they've lost lately to compare names with," Jamie sighed. "Good heavens, but that's giving me a headache just thinking about it. You're right, though, Penny. It's the only way to do this. I'd kill for a computer right about now."

I'd heard, of course, about this 'computer' contraption

before. If we'd possessed the technology capable of making one, I had no doubt that Jamie would own a machine. As it was, I gave her a sympathetic pat on the back. "We'll make do. Seaton, because this is now a Kingsmen's case, does that mean we can call upon the Kingsmen to help investigate it?"

"My dear fellow, you think that you can keep them out of this?" Seaton retorted, rolling his eyes expressively. "They're hot under the collar right now, make no mistake. They'll leap at the chance to help investigate this. But with so many out of commission, I'm afraid we'll be shorthanded. I can probably only spare three or four of them."

"Even three or four would help," Jamie mused. "Who all do you think can come?"

"Lewis, Evans, and Bennett," Seaton rattled off immediately. "They made sure I understood that they would do everything in their power to help."

The names meant nothing to me, but they did to Jamie. She perked up immediately. It was only then that I remembered Jamie had spent six months with the Kingsmen, in an unofficial capacity, recouping and learning all about this world from them. She had close ties to several of them, and regarded them as close friends. I'd heard her tell stories but I'd never actually made their acquaintance.

"Gibson?" she inquired hopefully.

"I'm sure if you ask, he'll come," Seaton answered wryly. "That man denies you nothing."

Gibson...Gibson...the name rang a bell with me. "Wasn't he the first Kingsman to respond after you escaped Belladonna?"

Jamie gave me a quick nod, pleased. "You've a mind like a steel trap. Yup, that's him. Cool guy, Gibs. He's the biggest teddy bear I've ever met in my life, right up until you cross him. Then he's like an enraged grizzly bear on steroids. He spent the first four months after I met him kicking out reporters and making sure I could breathe. He's the big brother I never had."

"He's also one of the people with a texting pad," Seaton hinted strongly with a wink at her.

"Oooh, is he really? Wait, how come I didn't know this?" Jamie demanded.

"Likely because he only acquired it this morning." Tapping a thoughtful finger to his mouth, Seaton glanced to the policemen on either side of him. "Really, I think we should see if Warner has anymore to spare. If we're going to be divided up all over the city, it will aid us if we can stay in constant communication with each other."

I thought that a splendid notion and said so. "If she has any on hand, we should acquisition them. I'm sure in this case she won't mind, even if it's temporary to this case."

"No, likely not," Jamie agreed. Taking the onions from me, she started mixing cheese, spices, and meat together in a blur of efficient movements.

Wisely, I stepped out of her way and joined Gerring on his side of the bar. At this stage, I would be more hindrance than help. Previous experience had taught me that quite well. "Seaton and I will start tomorrow by examining the charms, then. Who wants morgue duty, and who wants to interview the powder monkeys?"

Gerring and McSparrin stared doubtfully at each other.

"Rock, paper, scissors," Jamie instructed.

We all stared at her in confusion. She'd said it in such a manner that it seemed obvious to her what it meant, but I couldn't begin to fathom her meaning. Sometimes I could infer, but this was not one of those instances.

"Right," she groaned, head tilting back to stare crossly

at the ceiling. "You don't have that game here."

"Explain," I requested of her. It always intrigued me when she taught me something of her world. It inevitably made my own perceptions of this culture broader, more enriched.

"It's a simple game, really. Your hand conforms to different shapes," her free hand rose in demonstration, changing shape as she said each word, "rock, paper, scissors. You play opposite someone else and choose a shape on the count of three. Each one trumps another. So, rock beats scissors, paper beats rock, scissors beat paper. Whoever wins chooses what to do."

I believed I followed the rules of the game, if not the logic. Why would paper beat rock? I would think it quite the opposite. "And this is a method you use to divvy up duties and so forth?"

"Right," she confirmed easily. "Is there a Kingston equivalent?"

"There is." I paused as she slid the prepared enchiladas into the oven to bake. "Sails. A challenger starts, they do a brief chant of 'Choose, oh choose which way the wind blows,' and both players turn their hands as they chant. The players both flip their hands horizontally or vertically. If they match, the opponent wins. If they don't, the challenger wins."

"Huh." Jamie pointed at her two underlings and instructed, "Okay, then, you two plays Sails. The winner gets to choose."

Gerring faced McSparrin forthright and said, "I challenge you to Sails. I choose powder monkey."

Nodding, she twisted on her barstool to face him, raising both hands in front of her. Seaton leaned back so they could properly see each other without straining, and they performed the chant in perfect unison, ending with their hands in the horizontal position. Gerring groaned, slumping forward.

"Sorry, I can take morgue if you rather," McSparrin said kindly. "I know the smells make your eyes water."

"No, fair's fair," he responded, resigned. "I think it more suitable you take the demolition companies. They'll likely tell you more. Strangely enough, people say more to a female police officer than they would a male."

I'd noticed the same strange phenomena. People were always more amiable about sharing details, gossip, and other bits of information to Jamie than to myself. With me, they were strictly business. But with my partner, they were more inclined to shoot the breeze. It was fascinating psychology to say the least, although tiresome at times, as it left Jamie the onerous of interview duty.

"I've a notion there's more morgues than demolition companies in Kingston. Am I right, Kingstonpedia?" Jamie asked me with mock authority.

Staring at the ceiling briefly, I answered deadpan, "You are correct. There are sixteen demolition companies, three government owned, that I am aware of."

"Sixteen places won't take us long to get through," Jamie mused as she set a timer and set it aside. "Penny, how about you and I tackle the demolition companies first? Aside from Drake, I have a better idea than anyone here how the car was detonated. I know what questions to ask. Gerring, I'll have you meet up with the Kingsmen and coordinate the search through the morgues on the east end. Start there. We'll divvy up the other section of Kingston in two days, assuming Penny and I are done by then."

"I'll send in a formal request for any charm-related deaths in the past six months from all of the relevant stations as well," I volunteered. "If we submit it now, we might get an answer from at least some of them by the end of the week."

Jamie regarded me doubtfully. "That sounds like wishful thinking."

"I'll sign it too," Seaton threw in cheerfully, the smile on his face edging toward evil.

Nodding, she agreed blandly, "That will encourage them to speed things along, alright. Does that sound like a plan to everyone? Good. Then let's eat."

Report 05.5: 🎵 I'll Be There For You~ 🎵

Should I just start leaving several blank pages between every chapter for your use? This haphazard method you have of pasting pages in is unsightly.

Why thank you, Henri, that would be helpful. Given up on my "scribbles?"

More to say, resigned.

Somehow it ended up being just Sherard and I after dinner. He cradled a cup of coffee in his hand, looking tired but not as vexed as earlier. With me finally sitting down, Clint abandoned him utterly to curl up in my lap. Or I should say sprawl. He lay belly up, demanding rubs, and purring loud enough to start an earthquake.

Staring at us, Sherard commented over the rim of his cup, "He's a truly remarkable creature. Although I'm not sure if he actually performs the function that Davenforth intended."

"He does, actually," I disagreed. "I know it might seem a strange idea to you, but the use of therapy animals is quite common on Earth. People started out using mainly dogs, but cats, horses, even chickens are used. Clint especially is excellent at it. It was very easy to train him on what I needed him to do. He's an expert on waking me out of a nightmare, aren't you, fuzzball?"

Clint flicked an ear at me, not deigning to reply when I had fingers massaging his belly.

"You still have the dreams, then?"

"Not as often," I admitted freely. I knew that Sherard worried, as did Henri, so I didn't mind being frank with them that I was getting better. "It used to be nightly, remember? Now it's more like once or twice a month. When I do have them, Clint pulls me out pretty quickly."

Sherard softened into an almost smile, visibly relaxing. "I'm glad to hear it. Gibs, Marshall, Evans, and some of the others were asking about you the other day. They haven't seen you in the past two weeks, what with our duties pulling us all different directions. Gibs says he's craving curry."

I shook my head in amusement. "Of course he is. He and Henri are addicted to it, I swear. Well, maybe this weekend we can all get together for a curry night. I miss those rascals."

"That sounds grand. They're a mite worried, what with all the brouhaha coming up," Sherard admitted with a general wave toward the outside world.

Meaning the anniversary of Belladonna's death, the looks I kept getting from people, and all of that nonsense? I snorted in dark amusement. Yes, I could see why my Kingsmen friends would be worried about that. They knew how I felt about the attention. It didn't compare to what I'd lived through those first few days out of the cave—I don't think anything could compare to that—but at the same time, I didn't appreciate the atmosphere now either. I get that people were stupidly relieved that Belladonna was gone. Truly, I understood that. I'd lived through her circle of hell after all. But the unwanted attention grated, to say the least.

To him, I only said, "It's not as bad as last time. Usually people leave me alone if I glare at them. I think I have it more or less under control. I just have to put up with their enthusiasm for the next couple weeks, and that's doable."

Shrugging, he allowed, "As you say," and went back to sipping his coffee. "But let us know if you need help, won't you?"

"Of course," I answered, and meant every word. I was not the type who thought I had to climb every mountain without help. I stood here today thanks to all of the help and support of the people in this world. I would not discount that, ever.

I greeted Penny at the evidence warehouse the next morning with a cup of hot coffee. She took it with a groan of thanks. Every strand of her dirty blonde hair was tucked into a demure bun, her uniform crisp, but it was clear she had not slept well the night before. "Bad night?"

"My walls are thin," she explained to me, holding the cup

under her nose and inhaling deeply, as if the fumes alone would revive her. "And my next-door neighbor had a bit of a domestic with his wife. I went over to tell him to knock it off, and he took a swing at me. Idiot apparently didn't realize I'm a policewoman. I had to slap cuffs on him, haul him down to the station, and do the paperwork to throw him in jail. All the while, his wife wailing about how he is a good man, just drunk. Her with a bruise on her cheek, no less. I told her flat out, no good man gets drunk enough to hit his wife. Makes me mad, every time I hear a battered woman say that to me."

Sympathetic, I patted her on the back. "Me too, Penny. Me too. I'm glad I picked up the extra coffee now."

"Me too," she whimpered in relief, then took another swallow. "So, what first?"

"Fingerprints. I've mentioned these before, right?" At her nod, I continued. "Believe it or not, even with an explosion like this, sometimes fingerprints can survive. If there was a heavy enough coating of blood, grease, or dirt on the hands, the print is strong enough to survive the blast. What we're looking for, mostly around the motor area, is any signs of fingerprints. If we're lucky, someone left one behind and we can match it up to our perp later."

With a game shrug, she accepted the white gloves I handed to her, juggling the coffee cup to put them on, then we bent over either side of the car to take a close look. I let her have the magnifying glass, as I didn't really need it. The fine charcoal brush in my hand worked better for obscure prints. The metal around the engine compartment was rough, jagged along the edges, and not comfortable to lean against. I borrowed a thick mat to soften the area and help keep my clothes from becoming a sooty streak.

A few times, she pointed out something hopefully, but when dusted, it didn't turn out to be anything. We went all around the engine, the steering wheel, the lever on the inside that lifted the hood, all of it. No dice. Whoever had touched the car had either worn gloves (unlikely) or had had clean hands. Regular skin oil wasn't sufficient to leave a trace in this situation.

"Well," I sighed, slightly disappointed, "That's that. No luck on this. Let's put everything back up."

Charms and Death and Explosions (oh my!) 75

"Sure," Penny agreed, straightening with a groan. I mirrored it exactly. Leaning at the forty-five degree angle for an hour really did make the lower back protest. Removing her white gloves, she inquired of me, "What next?"

"Demolition companies," I said decisively, locking the place down. I ran an eye over the area, then grunted in satisfaction when I saw nothing else that needed tidying. Signing on the clipboard, I continued, "Kingston Removal Company is literally down the street. I say we work our way outwards." Henri had been a sweetheart the night before and marked every company he knew of on a map for me so that I could navigate to them easily today. There were days I could just kiss that man. Of all the things that I missed about Earth—and there was a megaton that I missed—GPS placed right up there at the top of the list. Fortunately, more times than not, my Kingstonpedia came through for me.

Pulling out into morning traffic took a certain amount of skill and timing, which I managed, although I came within inches of hitting another car that swerved into my side of the lane. The installation of traffic lights in the city was slow going. I couldn't wait until all of the streets had at least one. It would cut down on the madness some.

Kingston reminded me sometimes of New York in the 1900's. I'd only seen photographs, of course, but still the resemblance stuck in my mind. It had the same cluttered feeling to it, with brownstones clustered wall-to-wall, streets just wide enough for cars to pass each other and sidewalks to exist. Metal balconies jutted out almost at every level, giving people the outdoor space to hang laundry, have cold boxes on their windows, or lean outside and have a smoke. It was a strange mix of cars, technology, and horses and buggies. Despite the clutter, people made an effort to keep the place clean. I could breathe without inhaling raw sewage.

The chatter of other people's conversations and the honking of horns distracted me so that I didn't realize at first that my companion sat very still at my side. Penny's silence held weight, as if there was something she wanted to say or ask, but she couldn't find the words. Or perhaps she wasn't sure what my reaction would be. The traffic was heavy enough, the pedestrians bold in their crossing, that I didn't dare take my eyes off the road long. Still, I dared a glance. "Just ask, Penny. I won't take your head off."

"No, I know that," she responded, then paused as two idiots got into a honking war.

I paused in the middle of the intersection, flashed a badge, and pointed them sternly back to driving. Sullenly, they both did. Idiots. The ego of people just drove me straight up the wall some days.

Waiting until we were in motion again, Penny offered, "I'm just not sure how to ask. You mention sometimes that you're from a different country. And what you cook, the things you say…all of that says clearly you're not from here. But I don't know of anyone else like you either. Where are you really from, Jamie?"

I'd expected this question sooner or later. Perhaps it was the anniversary, and all of the articles that talked about me that drove her curiosity higher. I assumed my seniority had kept Penny from asking it sooner. I took it as a sign of comfortableness from her that she could ask the question now. Still, I hesitated. What I said next could completely change her view of me, and while I didn't mind if people knew, I was selective in who I told for that reason. Feeling a knot of nerves clench in my chest, I dared to glance at her from the corner of my eye, evaluating. I thought Penny the type to ride the surprise. At least, she had enough common sense and an even keeled personality that I didn't think she'd be weird about it. "I'm not from this world at all."

Startled, she jerked in her seat, head whipping toward me. "What?!"

Her reaction amused me. People's shocked reactions never failed to tickle my funny bone. It helped combat the nerves. "Belladonna grabbed multiple people from all over the universe. It was completely haphazard on her part. I'm from a planet called Earth."

She went stiff as a statue, staring at me blankly. If I'd announced that I was a wererabbit in disguise, she could not have been more astounded. It took several seconds before her mouth moved, and even then, she struggled to form actual words instead of sounds. "B-but you look like us…"

"On a cell level, I'm a little different, but very similar to everyone on this planet, yeah. Fortunately. Otherwise I wouldn't be able to exist here—breathe, Penny. Deep breaths. I'm an alien, but a nice alien."

Startled laughter poured out of her mouth and she croaked, "You are that."

She needed a minute. For that matter, I needed a minute. She was taking it rather well, actually. People had responded worse. If she could laugh about it, I gave it good odds that she wouldn't have a freak out later. I gave us both that minute, just driving, which was a challenge enough in and of itself. Were early drivers on Earth like this? No wonder they kept crashing Model T's, if that was the case. I swear half of these drivers could fit right into the set of Keystone Cops.

"Dr. Davenforth knows," Penny blurted out. "And RM Seaton."

"Yes to both." I found it interesting that was the first thing she said. "Sherard because he's constantly re-aligning my magical core. Belladonna did a number on it. Henri I actually told when we first partnered up together. I don't really make a secret of it, where I'm from. I'm just selective of who I tell. Henri's more cautious about it than I am."

Her blue eyes regarded me thoughtfully. "He is highly protective of you. I've noticed that before."

"He is," I agreed. I didn't mind it, as I understood the cause, and Henri really did have cause to worry about magical mishaps. But I knew that he trusted me to protect him too. That balanced the scales, kept our friendship even. There'd been many a time that I blessed Captain Gregson for partnering me with Henri. If I had to live out the rest of my life on another planet, at least I had excellent friends around me to pass the days with.

"I'll keep it quiet too." Penny gave a firm nod, pleased with her own decision. "I think it will just cause you trouble if everyone knew."

"Likely so." Penny McSparrin really was a good friend. I was glad to have another girlfriend I could pal around with, too.

"What do you miss? What's different?" she asked, half-turning in the seat to face me comfortably.

"Oh wow, how to answer that? I miss cats. Clint's the closest version you have here, but cats on Earth are many shades, and purple isn't one of them. I miss strawberries like you wouldn't believe—small, juicy red fruit. Very sweet. I miss a lot of my world's inventions, things that entertained or made life easier. My friend Ellie is literally making them as fast as she can, and I give her ideas often, but there's still such a technological gap between our cultures. She's struggling to invent even the basics to build upon." All of that was practical. My voice softened as I admitted, "I miss home. Family, friends, colleagues. There's no way for me to even get a message out to them, to assure them that I'm alright. That, I think, is the hardest part."

Penny leaned in for a moment and gave me a hug around the shoulders, which I appreciated. Reminders of home left me feeling emotionally raw even on the best of days. I hated that I couldn't call home, couldn't reassure my family that I was alive and well. They had to be worried. I certainly would be, in their shoes. I was an FBI agent, for heaven's sake, I knew they'd been braced for me getting hurt or killed in the line of duty, but straight disappearance? That wasn't something anyone would have expected.

"The anniversary of you killing Belladonna is coming up," Penny said thoughtfully, "and I bet that doesn't help, that reminder."

"It doesn't, but I have a plan of sorts. Ignore it as much as possible and eat mass quantities of chocolate."

Snorting, she relaxed back into her seat. "That sounds like a grand plan to me. Will it be Dr. Davenforth's chocolate stash you raid?"

"Among other places." I winked at her, pleased when she snickered. "He just makes it so easy. If he wanted to keep me out of his stash, he should change his hiding places."

"Perhaps he's resigned," she suggested archly. "It's not like changing his hiding spots will do him any good."

I shrugged because that was basically the truth of it.

We arrived at that point and I pulled up in front of the building, hugging the curb and throwing the car into park. Kingston roads were thankfully wide enough to allow this maneuver. At least, in most of the city. Some places, not so much. The building looked like a standard office, no more than one story, red brick in good condition and a white washed door standing open in the summer heat. We climbed out and headed inside, the interior barely any cooler than the outside. Air conditioning. Why can't air conditioning spread faster? I gave Ellie the rundown on it, dangit.

The inside was barely more than a foyer with a desk. I saw signs of a hallway stretching out toward the back, and I could smell the gunpowder clearly, so I assumed they actually made their own explosives and such. A very young man that might be eighteen popped up from behind the desk and greeted, "Hello, Officers. Can I help you?"

"I hope so," I answered, stopping right in front of the desk. I could tell from the expression on his face he thought I looked familiar, but couldn't place me. I do bless people's poor facial recognition sometimes. "I'm Detective Edwards, this is Officer McSparrin. Is your boss around?"

"He is, Detective. One moment." He scurried toward the hallway and disappeared for a few moments.

Penny leaned in to whisper, "What's our tack here?"

"We're friendly and concerned," I whispered back. "They're not in trouble. Good cop, good cop routine."

"Got it."

A werebadger with gunpowder streaks on his hands and a rounded belly stepped quickly into view. His whiskers quivered with alarm, but he kept a smile on his face as he offered a paw. "I'm Reynolds, owner of Kingston Removal Company."

"Detective Edwards, and this is Officer McSparrin," I introduced again patiently. His eyes flared wide, alarmed, and I knew that he at least recognized me. I followed up with something I hoped would settle him. "Master Reynolds, first let me assure you that you and your company are not in trouble. We're just trying to track down a lead and hope you can help us."

As I'd expected, he calmed right down hearing that. People always did. "Yes, of course. What can I do to help?"

"You heard of the car that exploded yesterday morning?"

"I did," he confirmed with a short bob of the head. "Terrible business."

"That was actually caused by a stick of dynamite," I informed him. You had to give a little info in cases like this to get anything.

His dark round eyes flared wide. "No! I was just saying to my powder monkeys yesterday that I wondered if it had been dynamite. The epicenter of the explosion, you understand, it made me think of it."

"You weren't wrong," Penny pitched in. "Our demolitions expert confirmed it was dynamite."

"Which is why we're here," I picked it up smoothly. "We suspect that the powder monkey who set the charge didn't buy the dynamite. It would leave too obvious of a record. Odds are he snuck in somewhere and stole a stick or two. Can you confirm your inventory hasn't been touched?"

Now he truly looked alarmed. "We haven't done an audit in a good month. I'm afraid I can't."

"Do you mind if we go back with you, do a quick audit? I'd like to know if he broke into your shop to get the goods."

"I'd like to know that very thing," Reynolds declared, hot and bothered now. "You come straight back with me, please. Dreadful, dreadful business."

Following him back through the narrow white hallway, I dropped casually, "We think the motive was because the victim was making bad health charms. They were actually causing people to get sick."

Reynolds cast me a startled look over his shoulder. "Truly? Dreadful. I hear from time to time that people get sick from those shoddy anti-sickness charms."

"Know anyone specifically?" Penny asked, matching my stride. "We're trying to track down the charm maker's victims. We want to make sure all of those bad charms are scooped up and disposed of."

"Well, now, that's a splendid idea. I'm glad you're on top of that too. I can't say off hand I can think of anyone—" he paused just outside the back door, his paw on the brass knob and a wrinkle in his forehead. "No. Wait, I did hear of someone, a daughter of a friend at church. Allison, Allison Watts. But I'm not sure if that was really charm-related; just that they'd bought a dozen charms to keep her healthy and they'd all failed."

I hid a smile. Gossiping people were the best at information.

"Really? I'll drop in and visit the family, make sure they weren't one of the charm maker's victims. Anyone else you can think of?"

"Well, now that I think on it...."

Penny pulled out a small notebook, jotting down names as he said them, me egging him on. The dynamite was likely a lost cause, but just maybe I could find a powder monkey who'd lost someone recently. And that was information I'd dearly like to lay my hands on.

Report 06: Intention of the Act

"I remember your lab being more cluttered than this," Seaton mused, taking in the scarred work table, the multiple bookshelves, the equipment tucked away along the shelves. He'd shed his outer coat as he'd come in and hung it up, a necessary precaution when working with any sort of chemicals or magical elements in a lab.

"The addition of another colleague has taken a considerable amount of work off my shoulders," I informed him factually, retrieving the charms from the protective pouches I'd collected them in the day before. We had more than Garner's work, of course, but I thought it best to deal with all of the charms I'd collected at once. Especially if I could apply Seaton's signature to the warrants, it would ensure a quick response in rounding up the shoddy charm makers. "I'm no longer doing the work of three people, so naturally the area is tidier. Garner's charms first?"

With a decisive nod, Seaton agreed, "Yes. Hand me two or three."

I obligingly did so before taking the chair next to him. We spread the charms out side by side on the table, Seaton borrowing a magnifying glass from me, and we both bent over them to peer carefully at every line and word written. Charms of this nature served three purposes: to cleanse the exposed air of communicable diseases, prevent the cross-contamination of any shared items, and to bolster a person's vitality to fight off any contracted illness. I could tell in a glance that the power of this charm wasn't sufficient to do anything of that nature. But I would still need to perform a more in-depth analysis to truly understand how the 'charm' had been crafted.

I started with the paper, as any decent charm

maker understood that the weight of the paper was very important. Thin paper easily stained, wrinkled, and so forth. Any alteration of the paper directly impacted the charm, usually in an alarming manner. The best charms used a heavy weight paper, something that could be embossed on.

This was not that sort of paper.

"Cheap, isn't it?" Seaton observed, distaste curling his upper lip. He flicked a finger against the edge of the charm.

"Indeed it is," I agreed sourly. "I do believe my utility bills come in on heavier paper than this."

"Shoddy, shoddy, shoddy," Seaton grumbled. "The ink isn't appropriate for this sort of use either, not that I'm surprised. Not with a printing press being involved."

"I find dye ink in the use of charms alarming, no matter the fashion it was applied." I held the charm up at an angle, closer to the lamp on the table, and felt the strongest urge to curse. There were two different types of ink in the world: pigment ink and dye ink. Pigment ink was essentially a waterproof ink made to stick permanently to paper without any runs. Artists, charm makers, magicians, and tattoo artists all used some solution of pigment ink because of its solid permanency. There were downsides to it, of course. They were more difficult to write with, as they didn't dissolve completely in water, and they didn't offer the same brightness and vibrancy in color as other inks.

Dye inks were quite the opposite—not permanent, easily smeared with water, and tended to fade with time. However, because they mixed well with water, they were the ink of choice for fountain pens, printing presses, and some artists. They were also considerably cheaper than pigment ink.

In this particular case, I believed that Garner had used dye ink for two simple reasons: it would work with the printing press and it was cheaper than pigment ink. Which, in my humble opinion, was a truly disgusting reason to use the wrong ink for a charm that another human being depended upon for safety.

I scraped a sample of the ink into a small glass dish and ran it through several chemical analyses, frowning at the results. "Destroying Angels is mixed in with this."

Seaton went taut, warding himself instantly. "How active? Sproutling?"

"The trace of it is small enough that I believe so, yes. However, I want to take a sample from the other charms to determine that before staking my reputation on it."

"With their printing process, they actually used Destroying Angel ink," Seaton muttered in disgust. "I realize it's a powerful ingredient, but the wrongful use of it could not only have killed them, but every person within range of their charms!"

"Have you ever noticed," I inquired of my companion acidly, "that greed directly leads to stupidity?"

"They certainly share the same bed," Seaton agreed, dropping his charm in disgust. "Cheap paper, cheap ink, and the charm has been compromised to the point that it does the opposite of what it's designed to do; however, I'm not finding a fault on the charm design itself. What do we know about Trevor Garner?"

"Precious little," I admitted frankly. "The coroner is still working on the autopsy. He submitted a request for information with the government, but that hasn't come in yet. However, I think the earmarks of the design tell us something about our victim. The design structure itself is sound. I see no fault with it. It's also unique—I haven't encountered any other charm with this design before. See the element here?"

Seaton nodded, staring at the small wind and light symbol incorporated into the corner of the design. "I noticed that earlier. He called upon air and sunlight to keep the charm powered. It's rather ingenious in theory, although I'm not sure how well that would have worked in practice. Even if he'd used the proper paper and ink."

"I agree, it bears testing, but my point is that he wasn't copying someone else's design. The man wasn't a thief, or a plagiarist. He knew what he was about in designing the charm. I wonder if we're perhaps looking at someone who actually attended school for charm making."

Seaton's gaze sharpened and he regarded the charm in my hand with new eyes. "A drop-out, perhaps?"

"Or simply a poor student—one who didn't pay attention as he should have. There are those who believe that marginally passing grades still nets a diploma and suffices." My tone made it very clear what I thought of that mentality. "This man might be of that school of thought."

"Perish the thought," Seaton grumbled with a shudder. "But I take your meaning. Then, you believe this isn't a case of criminal negligence, but stupidity?"

I phrased my response carefully, as truly, I didn't have enough evidence to support my instincts at this time. "I'm inclined to believe that he didn't properly understand charm making. He was going off half-cocked, as it were. If I could find an example of a charm that he made on the east side of town, from his first business, it would clarify matters. If he used the same design in the first business, the same methods, then he's obviously a crook. But if he changed anything, it would make it clear that he was trying to learn from his mistakes."

"Hmmm." Seaton sat back and regarded me thoughtfully. "The difference between mensa and actusa?"

I twitched my mouth up in a quick smile. The intention of the act versus the action itself. Sometimes it was a very fine line where the law was concerned; it wasn't always necessary to know if there had been criminal intent or not to prosecute someone with. "In this case, I'm not certain how it will aid us. Even if we can prove that he had no ill intentions while creating the charms, it won't change his state. But with such little information to go off of, I think anything we add to the evidence pile can only be helpful."

Shrugging, Seaton allowed, "I certainly can't argue that. For what it's worth, I think you're correct. But I'd like to have that confirmed with his schooling history before I say that definitively."

"Understandable," I assured him. "I'll note it down as just an opinion."

"Very good. Well, if you'll write up the findings, I'll turn my attention to the other charms you confiscated."

Agreeable to this, I fetched the appropriate form and set about writing out an analysis on the charms and our own findings. Naturally, I stated things more in-depth on the report than Seaton and I had discussed. Such reports were often quoted verbatim in a court of law, and I'd learned early in my career to make them as simply stated as possible, with explanations as appropriate, so that both judge and jury could understand the facts explicitly. Nothing irked me more than having evidence thrown out by a judge because he couldn't comprehend it.

My mind suddenly sparked with a remembrance. My first case with Jamie, we had by necessity gathered a list of all the students who had graduated from a magical university in the past few decades. I still had the list here in the lab, a reference that I hadn't gotten around to submitting to Archives yet. Heading for the shelf on which it sat, I mentioned to Seaton, "I do actually have a list of graduated students here in the lab. Remember how we needed that for the Nightfox Thieves case?"

Alert, he snapped a finger and straightened on his stool. "That I do. That should tell us at least if he properly graduated or not."

"Indeed." Pulling it out, I thumped it on the table, dividing the list so that he could look through one set of university graduates while I took the other. With them in alphabetical order, it didn't take long to page through. When I failed to find Garner's name, I went back through more carefully. Still to no avail. "He didn't graduate that I can find in my list. Yours?"

"No, he's not listed. Nor is Timms."

Timms. Now there was a good idea. We actually had no proof that Garner had been the one designing the charms, after all. I went back through looking for Peter Timms' name but came up equally blank. "No, nor him. I know for a fact they had a business license. Bit tricky to do that when you can't produce a magical license, unless—"

"Your magical license is a forgery," Seaton completed the sentence with a wry expression. "I'll bet you anything you care to name that it is. Where is the magical license?"

"If memory serves, it's framed and hanging nicely upon Garner's wall. I'll have to swing by and fetch it today or tomorrow. That bares a more proper examination as well." I sat back, thinking. "It might behoove us to look more into Timms and Garner. Jamie's lead of the dynamite might or might not pan out, but the possibility of a jealous lover being behind all of this still bears investigation. If nothing else, I would like to cross out the possibility."

"Yes, and if nothing else, an investigation of their homes—"

The door to my lab abruptly burst open. Only one man possessed the gall to stomp about in my lab like a wounded elephant, so I didn't bother to look up.

"Davenforth! This is the outside of enough!" Sanderson snarled, slamming a hand down on the table, dangerously close to the more unstable of the confiscated charms.

"You bloody fool, are you senile?" Seaton demanded of him sharply, yanking the charms away before Sanderson could actually land a digit on the charms themselves. Sanderson was sparking enough errant magic that he shouldn't come in direct contact with anything remotely magical, much less unstable charms like these. I actually quite fancied the idea of him losing a hand through his own stupidity, but it would likely set my table on fire in the process, which I didn't fancy. Seaton's quick reaction was likely the better avenue.

Sanderson looked at Seaton without any recognition. Then again, members of the Endangered Species list had better survival instincts than Sanderson when he's lost his temper. I relaxed back into my seat, fully anticipating a show that would rival anything I'd purchased a ticket for. At my most genial, I inquired helpfully, "Why, my dear Sanderson, whatever could be the matter?"

"It's not enough that you shuffle your work off to the

rest of us, no," he thumped his hand against the table again, hard enough to make everything on the surface jump, his temper adding strength to his small stature, "now you're stealing cases! That car bombing should have gone directly to me! How dare you call in that woman and force Berghetta's hand. You know he's terrified of her!"

Seaton's face set in an interesting manner. It reminded me rather of Clint's expression when a bug had deigned to crawl into his line of vision. "Davenforth, who is this blustering fellow?"

"Dr. Sanderson, one of the Magical Examiners here," I introduced briefly, purposefully failing to introduce Seaton in return. "And Sanderson, Jamie was given permission by Captain—"

"Oh, it's Jamie now," he snapped, mobile features morphing into an expression both suggestive and ugly in its contortion. Pugnacious monkeys had a more pleasant demeanor about them.

I knew very well what he insinuated. But my relationship with my partner had little to do with romance and more to do with mutual respect and genuine liking. I refused to be baited. "Sanderson, you are only here stomping about because the car bombing has enough splash to it that it made the morning paper. Being the Magical Examiner on the case would have boosted both your career and ego, assuming that you managed to solve it."

Sanderson made to step around the table, hands flexing in clear threat of a physical altercation. He barely shifted a foot before abruptly halting, Seaton's hand on his chest stopping him in his tracks.

"Jamie Edwards is the expert on car bombings," Seaton informed him flatly. "It was she the case was given to, not us. And don't think I haven't noticed that it's him you take your complaint to and not her. Jamie would flatten you before folding you like a sheet if you dared to throw this tantrum in front of her."

For the first time, Sanderson blinked the rage out of his eyes, at least a notch. He looked at Seaton in acrimonious regard, tense with residual anger. "Who by magic are you to call her that way?"

An evil smile on his face, Seaton practically purred, "Royal Mage Sherard Seaton."

Sanderson blanched. I'd never seen blood drain so quickly from a human being's face. I doubted even a vampire could manage a drain that swift. He backed up two steps, hastily, the motion jerky. Then he stared up at Seaton, jaw flapping about, making croaking noises like a beached fish.

"I am here on Queen's business," Seaton added, practically jovial in his menace, "which ties into the very case that you're blustering about. Let's be clear on this, Dr. Sanderson. Detective Jamie Edwards is the crown's preferred expert, and our beloved queen is both delighted and relieved that she is already working this case. Queen Regina is equally delighted that Dr. Davenforth is lending his considerable expertise to the magical side of this case, as am I. By coming in here and throwing such a fit, you are putting a noose about your neck and attempting political suicide. A wise man would apologize, remove the noose, and hastily beat an exit."

Miserable and with the grey coloring of a corpse, Sanderson stared at me mutely. He couldn't bring himself to apologize—or at least, his mouth failed to deliver anything that I could interpret as such. He stumbled out the door and out of sight.

"What in all deities was that about?" Seaton demanded of me, throwing his arms out in an expansive gesture of incredulity. "Does he routinely pull such nonsense? You didn't even look up when he barged in."

"Unfortunately so," I admitted with a long sigh. "Sanderson is not the most sensible man when it comes to social graces, and he regularly runs roughshod over his colleagues. I've been picking up the man's slack for years. I've jested that he only maintains his position because he's courting the police commissioner's daughter, but I'm afraid there's more truth in that than anyone cares to admit."

Seaton listened intently, the wheels visibly turning in his mind. "And why is he so belligerent where Jamie is concerned?"

"She's gotten the best of him, publicly. He's also one of those chauvinist pigs who believes a woman shouldn't be in the workforce. At least, not in this line of work." I shrugged, as Sanderson's idiocy was a known evil in my life. "I generally ignore him. Reporting him has yielded no results."

Dark eyes narrowing, Seaton repeated, "'Reporting him has yielded no results.'"

Seaton and I might only be into our third month of acquaintance, but it hadn't taken a significant amount of time to be able to read the man properly. He possessed a very emotive face, after all. Even if he had not, I knew that there were certain things in his life he held no tolerance regarding, and insulting Jamie Edwards featured very prominently at the top of that list. To see her so casually disregarded by a colleague, and accused of glory-hoarding, would irritate Seaton.

The expression on his face went past 'irritated.' I do believe dragons readying themselves to raid a town sported similar facial twitches.

A lesser man might have suggested to Seaton that a Royal Mage's report of unbecoming conduct might have more weight to it. That perhaps he would do the favor of pushing the issue. I smiled genially at Seaton, rocked back on my stool, and waited.

The mage did not disappoint. "Davenforth. It's a curious thing, but I'm not a fan of nepotism."

"Truly? Indeed, I must say, neither am I."

"You've reported this multiple times, you say. An organized man like yourself likely kept copies of those previous reports."

"I daresay I have a few lying about," I agreed, my benign smile not slipping.

"Why don't you lend those to me? I'd like to include them in my own report."

My smile finally morphed into one that matched his,

our evil machinations clear.
    Sanderson had poked the sleeping dragon. Oh my.

> Is that why Sanderson got formally written up?
>> It might have been.
>>> good job
>> You won't say that we're being immature?
>>> why? he started it

Report 07: Unpleasant Business

Hear, hear. I did not enjoy any of that.

Hadn't either of these men heard of a broom?

After three days, Jamie and Penny had visited every known demolition company in Kingston. I know because I'd either made them a daily list or gave them directions to the companies in question. After all of that legwork, I'd set up the black box recording of the scene and let them go through it. Sometimes a perpetrator lingered at the crime scene and could be caught that way. Both women carefully combed through the circle of onlookers, but no one stood out.

I entered the station this morning knowing that we'd be doing something of a different ilk and went hunting for my partner. She'd lured me to her desk this morning with the promise of another breakfast burrito, which I'd happily taken her up on.

"There you are," Jamie's voice greeted from behind me. I turned with a smile, perhaps a touch more eager than usual. She could see it, and let out a short bark of laughter before extending a rolled, steaming bundle wrapped in aluminum foil in my direction. "You are such a foodie."

"Guilty as charged," I admitted happily, unwrapping the top right where I stood and biting into it. Ahh, bliss. The cheese, meat, egg, all wrapped up in in a lovely layer of spices. If she marketed this, I predict she would make a minor fortune and be able to retire. In fact, I was quite sure of this.

"Do you have anything you need to do this morning before we go?" she double-checked. "No? Then let's go. Weber found keys and addresses for both men in their personal effects, so I want to get a good look at Timms' and Garner's apartments."

"Apartments?" I queried, then swallowed to free up my mouth. If my mother could see me like this, not only standing while eating, but talking with my mouth half full, she would be utterly appalled at my lack of manners. But every policeman knows to eat while you can, where you can, and to not be fussy about the details. "Not a house?"

"I'm rather surprised by that as well, as Garner at least certainly made enough to afford a house, but I believe it was a matter of convenience." Jamie filled me in as we walked toward the back, and inevitably, toward the car park. If she had any pity, she would drive slow in order to avoid upsetting my system. "They already had a short stint with the first business, barely lasting half a year. I think they were afraid they'd have to quickly pull up stakes here, too. Better an apartment, something you can quickly get out of. Houses are like a boat anchor. They moor you in place."

I nodded, as that seemed quite reasonable to me. Although really, it didn't matter if they were in house or apartment, as long as we knew their addresses. "Have we any word on family at this point?"

"That's what I'm hoping to get from their apartments," Jamie admitted. "I put in a notice of death through the Gazette and asked for anyone related to the victims to come meet us, as no one around the business seemed to know of any relations. So far I've had three girlfriends show up for Garner, no one for Timms."

That seemed strange as well. "No one's missing these men?"

"Or at least, no one who knows them by that name." Jamie's eyebrows arched, insinuating several things as she slid into the driver's seat. "I mean, you told me that Garner's magic license had to be forged, as he didn't graduate from anywhere. We know the first business failed because of shoddy products. How much trouble were they in to close up shop and move to the other side of the city? Enough to change their names while they were at it?"

"Could be," I allowed slowly. "I'm not sure if that would surprise me at this point. I suppose we'll have to see." I focused once more on my breakfast and tried to subtly study my partner as I did so. Jamie looked... tired. Not exhausted, but clearly her energy levels sank below their norms today. I had not heard any night time disturbances, which I normally did hear with her apartment being directly above mine, so I could not be certain if bad memories kept her awake or if she had chosen to avoid going to bed altogether.

The city became more alive with specials, mementos, and things of that ilk to celebrate Belladonna's demise. I saw more than one person do a double-take as we passed them, no doubt recognizing Jamie. This was not the worst of it, and indeed we'd have to pass through the anniversary before we regained normalcy. Or what passed for normalcy in our world of thefts, murders, and magical mayhem.

"I'm fine, Henri."

I must work on my subtlety. "You just look tired, is all."

"Well, I am, but that's because I was up half the night talking to Ellie. She's working out some bugs with the texting pad. I mentioned perhaps getting more texting pads out to the others. Our Kingsmen comrades are all over the lower half of the city, combing through the stores and pulling out bad merch, but there's no easy way to keep track of them or their progress. The texting pads would make it easier."

A gesture of my free hand showed that I agreed with her. It would be deucedly convenient.

"That, and I had a notion for another invention I'd like to see here." Jamie slowed at an intersection, stopping at one of the new traffic lights in town. It was a prototype, one of four, and I could already see the difference in how traffic flowed. This corner typically saw three accidents a week, but since its installation, we hadn't nary a one.

Since I was always curious about her inventions, I queried, "Something else mechanical? Or something like the texting pad?"

"Neither, actually. This one is more basic to health care. While I was running around with you pulling all of those anti-sickness charms out of the stores, I had a thought. On Earth we had two different primary cleaning solutions that we used to keep things sterile—alcohol and hydrogen peroxide. Now, I don't know how to make hydrogen peroxide, but I do happen to remember how to distill rubbing alcohol." She put the car into gear as it became our turn, changing streets smoothly. "I do love the traffic lights. People picked up on that quickly."

"May they spread across the city," I seconded wholeheartedly. Finished with the burrito, I crumbled the foil and put it into the waste basket tucked in the side of the door. "This alcohol, what can you sterilize with it?"

"That's the beauty of it. Practically anything. Hard surfaces, fabrics, operating equipment, even skin. It's routinely used on wounds to disinfect them. But a diluted version can be used to scrub a floor, for instance."

My mind carried through the possible implications of this in a blink. "That could potentially cut infections in half."

"Probably more than, if we can get it widespread on the market. Which I'm pretty sure we can. It's a cheap solution on Earth that everyone uses. I can't imagine Kingstonians feeling any different about it, especially since bad charms are so prevalent here." She slowed and took another right, this time entering an area with nearly wall-to-wall apartment buildings. "I think this is right. Cherrywood Lane?"

"Yes, further up this street," I directed, pointing ahead. Still, I wouldn't be distracted from this. "This is something Guildmaster Warner believes she can do?"

"Sure. Simple chemical solution, only takes about two weeks to make. Once I explained the process and how to apply it, she was completely on board. Swears she can get some bottled and on shelves in a few weeks. I think she's got an idea of how to speed the process up with magic," Jamie shrugged, as if not bothered by this.

"Can I field test this one too?" I inquired, very curious about the product.

Amused, Jamie flicked me a glance. "I'm sure Ellie would be delighted to have someone with your reputation stamp endorsement on the product."

Excellent. I normally didn't lean much upon my family's standing in society. We were not aristocrats or anything of that nature, but with my grandfather and father's service in the military, they'd gained powerful friends and connections in the government. With their excellent businesses, we enjoyed a comfortable amount of wealth as well. The Davenforths were well-known in Kingston, and while that sometimes impeded my path, it did leave doors open to me as well. Using that reputation to further promote something good brought me significant satisfaction, and I knew that my family would approve as well.

"I think this is it." Jamie pulled snugly up to the curb

and shielded her eyes with one hand to look up at the sign on the grey brick exterior. "Cherrywood Apartments. Huh, interesting. Timms lived in Ashwood Apartments, directly across the street. Coincidence?"

"Likely not." I pointed to both of them illustratively. "These aren't very old, perhaps eight months. If Garner and Timms moved across town at the right time, these apartments would likely be one of the few with space for tenants. I assume they were trying to stay near their business, as Charm-A-Way sits only six blocks down from here."

Jamie nodded and allowed, "Makes sense. Garner only had the company car, and Timms would have to walk to work. I'd stay close too. Alright, Garner's apartment first? I have keys to both places, so we don't need to bother the landlady."

"After you." I followed her up the stone steps and through the very small front lobby. It barely possessed the room for a body to turn about in and find the stairs, much less anything for visitors. Clearly, the design of this building focused on giving as much space to tenants as possible, sacrificing the other areas. Jamie led the way confidently up to the second story, then stopped at the first door, wrangling a set of keys from her pocket. Only three on the key ring, which made sense—business, apartment's front door, the building's door. He wouldn't need anything more than that.

The plain white door opened on noiseless hinges and we stepped through.

My apartment had a certain functionality to it. Kitchen and living room combined into a great room, bathroom and bedrooms closed off with doors. This apartment barely had any privacy to offer. The kitchen, living room, and bedroom all stood open to each other. Only the bathroom had a door and walls, and even the door stood open. The furnishings looked new and barely used, the kitchen sporting not a single dish. With the exception of the iron-wrought bed, which had not been made, the apartment appeared unlived in.

"He didn't cook, but ate out. The area's not messy, but not clean. Clean enough to bring female company over, but not as tidy as it should be. Huh. His laundry's in a pile on the other side of the bed, most of it just missing the hamper," Jamie noted as she swept through the area. Turning, she stared hard at the bed before approaching, scenting with a deep breath. "Bedsheets probably haven't been changed in three months at least. They're a little ripe. He has all the earmarks of a man who isn't used to picking up after himself."

Sensing her thoughts, I took a closer look about as well, bringing my wand into play. "You think Garner's divorced?"

"Or separated from a wife, perhaps. A man who's not interested in staying clean will have piles of dishes and clothes and trash stacked everywhere. He's sort of making an effort, but it's half-hearted, as if he's in the habit of doing specific things but not others. Well, I could be wrong. Maybe he's still sticking to habits from home when mommy did everything."

We'd find out, either way. Moving through the room, I swept the wand from side to side, seeking trouble before Jamie stumbled across it. If Garner had been careless—and he'd certainly not proven to be careful—then he might have things here that he shouldn't. "He's not brought any of his work home with him, at least. I sense nothing magical—no, wait. That's not correct. There's a strangely condensed residue of magic lingering on his clothes."

"Brushed up against his ink while working, perhaps?"

"Some of it is that. Some of it is something else. I'll have to take it back to the lab to properly examine it."

Charms and Death and Explosions (oh my!)

Pulling a containment box from my black bag, I snipped off a few samples of clothing and placed them inside.

Jamie rifled through a rolling top desk, searching the papers, then whistled low. "Ho, I'm right. He's divorced. Recently, too. Aimee Williams Garner. I do love divorce papers, they insist on putting everyone's addresses down under signatures." Freeing the sheet entirely, she slid it into an evidence folder. "Let's see what other goodies we can pull up."

Aside from some cards from various lady friends, most of which we could use to track them down, there was nothing else in Garner's apartment worth our time. We switched to Timms' where Jamie found the 'typical bachelor' apartment. I doubted a single surface had anything less than three layers of clothing, decaying dishes, or paperwork on it. We followed paths from room to room, weaving our way around piles of…things I didn't actually care to examine closely.

"Worse than a college dorm," Jamie muttered to herself, wading through. "I suddenly feel like my shots aren't up to date enough for this place. How do people live like this? Henri, anything magical?"

"Nothing of the sort. Not even residual." I blessed the fact my wand could tell me such information from a distance. The foul odor of the apartment offended not only my nose but my sensibilities. "Either Timms was more careful about wearing protective gear while working, or he had nothing to do with the magical spectrum of the charms. I'm inclined toward the latter. The only magical license we found was Garner's."

"Yeah, I'm thinking Timms was the printer, Garner

the charm maker." Jamie bent to lift a crate full of cards and letters, shuffling through the first inch of the stack. We fell to searching for several minutes in mutual silence until Jamie broke it, singing a strange song under her breath: "Clean up, clean up, everybody everywhere. Clean up, clean up, everybody do your share."

This song sounded odd, rather simplistic, which didn't match her normal repertoire. I stopped shifting through a pile of papers on the desk and regarded her in bemusement. "What's that?"

Distracted, she glanced up. "The Clean Up song? Ah, it's a children's song. Timms obviously should have learned it."

"I cannot disagree."

Straightening, she went through a stack of cards in her hands. "Hmm. Timms had family, at least. He's got letters from a mother, brother, sister, and what looks to be a very young niece. No romance letters yet but maybe some are buried in here. Let's haul this back."

I didn't see anything else worth taking or further examining, and after thirty minutes of poking about, Jamie seemed to share this opinion. We thankfully left the apartment behind, and I absently sent a sympathetic prayer to whoever was forced to clean out that place later.

As we returned to the car, I saw more than one person turn, tracking Jamie's movements. One woman audibly gasped, hand over her mouth, alarmed to see the Shinigami Detective stride out of what was obviously her own apartment building. I shook my head, refusing to stop and reassure her. She'd realize on her own there was nothing untoward about the building.

If Jamie saw their reactions, she gave no sign of it. I knew her to be too sharp to have failed to miss them, however. In this situation, the best thing to do was to ignore it. I could not fault her tactic.

Sliding into the car, I inquired, "Which would you rather do first? Verify that Garner's magical license was a forgery? Or track down the relatives for both Garner and Timms for questioning?"

Lips pursed, she considered the options. "We're fairly certain it's forged, even without you looking at it. I mean, it had to be if he didn't graduate. Still, I think it would go over better if you officially confirmed that. And I don't know about you, but I want to know how Garner got a business license with a fake magical license."

I shared her shark-like smile. "Yes, that question does indeed weigh on me. Shall we go to City Hall and make some inquiries?"

Report 07.5: No Love Lost

I woke up in a cold sweat, a rough tongue bathing my temple. The annoyance of it, that tactile impression slashing through the dream, had brought me out of it. I flailed a little until I realized Clint was wrapped around my head, then I stopped, breathing hard.

"Jamie?" he asked softly, in that gentle, high voice of his.

"Yeah, bud, I'm awake." Gently disentangling myself from his paws, I sat up, then stayed there with my feet off the side of the bed, shoulders hunched as I tried to orient myself again to the present world. I went through the routine—grounding my senses by touch, scent, smell, sight, until I felt like I was present once more. Only then did I turn and scoop him up, cuddling him against me. Clint came with a purr, pressing his chin to my collarbone, a warm and vibrating bundle in my arms.

Bless Henri for giving me this cat. He was exactly what I needed—a touch of home in a world that looked just different enough to offset my sense of normality. Clint's purple fur still threw me sometimes if I caught a glimpse from the corner of my eye, but he was so like a cat in every other aspect I felt like I'd brought him with me most of the time.

I knew Henri worried about me. I knew Sherard did too. With the anniversary coming up, of course they would worry. I'd even gotten a call from Gibs earlier, expressing concern from all of my Kingsmen friends, and saying in his own way that I had their support and protection. That I could hide out with them until the world went back to normal, if I wanted to.

The idea held some appeal, I wouldn't lie. But it didn't really tempt me. I felt better out here, working, rather than focusing on the one event that had changed my life. Nightmares aside, unwanted fame definitely aside, I was okay. I'd decidedly been worse.

Not wanting to fall back to sleep, I got up instead, feeling the coolness of the apartment brush against my sweaty skin. "Hey, Clint. How about I wash up a little, then we have a midnight snack. I'll read to you some."

Clint adored books. It frustrated him that he didn't know the words, but he could learn them, as I could. In fact, we were almost on the same reading level now, as he had more time to study than I did. He perked up immediately. "Books! And snuggie."

"You gotta explain this to me, Clint. I mean, you're covered in fur. You can't possibly feel a blanket through all of that. So why do you always go for the softest one in the house?"

He pulled back to give me a superior look that adequately expressed how stupid that question was. "Snuggie."

"Yeah, okay." Heaven forbid Lord Furball not have his blanket. Notice how he dodged that question? Far be it for a cat to explain anything to us pitiful humans.

I'd only gotten three hours of sleep, and I might be able to go back to bed at some point tonight, but for now I was going to do nothing more complicated than curl up with my cat, a blanket, and a book.

Because Henri had a stack of other cases that needed his magical assistance, I took Penny with me the next morning and let him catch up on his workload. I'd hoped that with an additional Magical Examiner now at the precinct it would lighten his workload, and it did seem to. Slightly. Sanderson was throwing more fits than usual, though, and that showed. I do wish someone would fire that man. We'd work more efficiently as a whole without him stumbling around causing trouble.

Penny had the file in hand, perusing it as I drove to Garner's ex-wife's house. Yes, house. She'd gotten that as alimony in the divorce proceedings.

"Says here they were married for barely more than a year," Penny noted. "Filed for divorce for 'irreconcilable differences.' Catch phrase for they're not being abusive or cheating, but I don't want to be married anyway."

"Basically," I agreed with a shrug. Morning traffic was dying down, now that most people were already at work. It made fighting my way through the four-way a little easier. I hoped they'd put in a traffic light at this corner next. "Henri and I did go and talk to Timms' family yesterday. I didn't report, it as there wasn't much to report on. They were horrified to learn their son is dead—apparently Peter Timms is a popular name in Kingston, they thought it was someone else—and there was so much crying I couldn't get a sensible word out of anyone. Not that I blame them. As far as they knew, though, Timms worked as a printer and made a good living from it. He didn't have anyone in his life romantically, and he showed up every other weekend for family dinner with his parents."

Penny shook her head, sighing. "Poor people. Did you tell them how he died?"

"No. Just that he'd been shot, and we were investigating who'd done it and why." That was the strange thing about this whole case. Why shoot poor Timms? If it was a jealous lover, or what have you, then why Timms too? I'd followed up on the connections of the people around these two men because only a stupid investigator wouldn't, but the continual lack of evidence chipped away at that ten percent chance of the motive being non-charms related.

"I'm not sure if the ex-wife had anything to do with Garner's death." Penny drew a finger down the page as she read. "She's the one who filed for it. They've been divorced nearly eight months. She's already changed back to her maiden name, too."

"Sometimes, Penny, people divorce someone and then belatedly realize they don't want to be divorced. They get back together."

"Why? I mean, the relationship failed enough that you went through months and a lot of money to get divorced in the first place. If it didn't work the first time, why would it work the second?"

"You know, I ask that question a lot. I never have gotten a good answer." It seemed to be a universal truth no matter what planet I was on. I wasn't sure what that said of our species as a whole.

The house of Ms. Aimee Williamson was a cute little cottage on the eastern section of the city, right at the outskirts and along the channel. She had an excellent view of the water, although paid for it by having a miniscule yard. I pulled up in front of the white picket fence, parked, and we crossed through the colorful flower beds to the sunny yellow front door.

A woman opened it after the third knock, her auburn hair done up in a twist, dressed in a delicate ensemble of linen and white lace that made her the ultimate soft beauty so popular in Kingston. She looked quite taken aback to see me and Penny, both of us in pants, Penny in the black uniform of a policeman. I pulled out a badge and introduced us both. "You're Ms. Aimee Williamson?"

"Why, yes," she answered, her free hand fluttering at the base of her throat, blue eyes wide with alarm. "Officers, whatever is the matter?"

"I'd like to talk to you about Trevor Garner."

Her expression and demeanor instantly changed. She went from being a delicate flower in distress to a scornful woman with the potential rage of a dragon. "That two-bit charlatan has done something again, hasn't he?"

Wow. No love lost here. "Yes ma'am, you can say that. He died."

She blinked at me. "Died? When did this happen?"

"Several days ago. There was a notice in the paper. You didn't see it?"

"I actively avoid the man," she admitted openly. "Any mention of his name, and I firmly direct my path and attention elsewhere. Please, come in. I'm not sure if I can be of any help, as I don't necessarily see his death as a detriment in this world."

In my experience, when people freely admitted their dislike for someone, they were not usually the culprit. Complaining to your friends and family was one thing, but saying that sort of crap in front of a policeman? A guilty person would never do it. They'd try to gloss over the relationship, make it seem trivial, and try to end the conversation quickly to move you along. She was inviting us in. It meant she was very, very clever or entirely innocent. Gut instinct said the latter.

So I went in to her beautifully appointed sitting parlor with its doilies and white furniture, sat on a settee that did not look strong enough to hold my weight, and gave her a charming smile. "I am sorry to bring this trouble to your door. I have to ask a few impertinent questions."

"Yes, of course," she assured me, sinking into a chair near mine. Every move graceful, not a hair or line of her expression out of place.

"Do you mind if I ask why you and Mr. Garner ended your marriage?"

"Two reasons, really," she answered in a forthright tone, a moue marring her mouth. "First, I learned that he was a charlatan of the first water. His magical license was a fake, he'd made it himself. I couldn't believe it. I thought I was marrying a man with a good education and occupation and here he was, a fraud. I demanded he turn himself in at once, that I wouldn't stay married to a man like him. He scoffed, like my opinion was worth nothing but a drop in the bucket. I tore his license right in half and walked out."

Interesting. So she'd known. "I see. You said two things?"

"There were a great many complaints about his charms." Aimee's eyes shifted to the window as if remembering something. "It's why I actually questioned the license to begin with. Multiple complaints came to our door, strangers I'd never seen before claiming they'd been swindled. That the charms weren't working. It got to be that the stores didn't want to take his stock anymore. He was stressed, constantly shouting at me and throwing things. His temper scared me, frankly. I thought his business failing, and while that alarmed me, I would have stood by him through it. I thought it was an error on his part. But when I learned he didn't actually have the skills to be a charm maker, and that Mr. Timms knew that, I was horrified. They could hurt people with their shoddy knowledge of charm making. And they didn't seem to care. That was the second nail in the coffin, as it were. There was no remorse, on either of their parts. I heard them talking about it one night over coffee, that they'd have to shut down the business and set up another one in a different section of the city and where to put it. I put my foot down that night. We had a terrible row. That's when I tore the license and walked out. I never saw either man again."

In her shoes, I'd have done the same, but more. "You didn't report either Mr. Garner or Mr. Timms to the police?"

"Well, I did, but it didn't seem to do much good." Vexed, she gripped her hands tightly enough the knuckles shown white. "I had no proof, just my word against theirs, and they'd already shut the business down by the time I'd arranged an attorney and made it down to the station. The police said there was nothing for them to investigate, and they wouldn't take the word of a soon to be ex-wife in any case. I felt defeated by the attitude and didn't press it."

I shared a glance with Penny. Even if it was from a woman on the cusp of a divorce, with that many other complaints against the man, they should have looked into it. I certainly would after this. "I see. Which precinct did you go to, Ms. Williamson?"

"Third Precinct."

"Do you happen to remember which officer you spoke with?"

"I'm sorry, I don't."

Darnit. No one ever remembered that. "Thank you, Ms. Williamson. By any chance, do you know of a specific individual who would like to see your husband dead?"

"Detective Edwards, I'm afraid in this case, I know too many."

We left shortly after that, having learned some things but not enough to put the picture into proper focus. I stared at the house thoughtfully as I started the car up. "Penny, I got the sense she told us the bare truth."

"So did I." Penny put the folder onto the bench seat between us, matching my look with one of her own. "She disliked him, but not enough to kill him. And there's no other motive that I can see. You think one of his new girlfriends did him in instead?"

I shook my head slowly. "No. I still believe it was charms-related. Still, let's go check out the three girlfriends, see what they have to say and if they have an alibi for the day in question. Maybe we're wrong."

"I doubt it," Penny opined.

"Yeah," I sighed, putting the car in gear. "Me too."

See, Henri? Penny trusts my driving.

I trust your driving too, Jamie.

Why thank you, Sherard.

You are all insane.

Report 08: The Kingsmen Arrive

The boys are back in town!
The boys are back in tow-ow-ow-ow-own~

...That's a song, isn't it?
don't worry, it's all I remember

Seeing a room full of Kingsmen interact with Jamie was an eye-opening experience in several ways. I'd heard the story, knew of her history. She had lived the first six months in Kingston with Seaton, and had many of the Kingsmen either teaching or training with her. She had many close friendships among the Kingsmen and met or spoke with all of them regularly. I knew all of this intellectually.

Still, seeing these veteran crown agents come in and greet her with wide smiles and hugs made it seem more like a family reunion than a meeting. I naturally was introduced to them as they came in, and was able to put faces to names. They shook hands all around with Gerring and McSparrin as well before taking seats at the narrow conference table.

Gibson was the last to arrive, a large bear of a man who dwarfed every other man in the room. He swept Jamie up in a bone-crushing hug, which got her to laughing, then set her back down again before regarding the rest of us. "Cheers, mates! I hope you've had better luck than I, as it's been piss poor going."

"Not really," Lewis answered dryly, stroking at the bushy mustache he sported. The auburn red mustache made an interesting contrast to his very dark brown hair. "But come in, take a seat, we're about to compare notes. You met either Officer McSparrin or Gerring yet?"

As Lewis handled the introductions, Seaton put the finishing touches on the Kingston map on the table, comprised of the two sections we were investigating and nothing else. As he did so, I made a timeline of events on the blackboard. When it was completed to my satisfaction, I turned, then started to find Gibson standing right behind me. My heart threatened to leap into my throat at the frank way he loomed over me. "Kingsman Gibson, I believe?"

My steady response amused him, or at least I took the twitch of his mouth as a sign of amusement. "I am. Dr. Henri Davenforth?"

"Yes, quite." I offered a hand, not surprised when his hand practically swallowed mine.

"We owe you," Gibson informed me in a low voice, expression sincere as he released his hold on me. "Jamie told us how you kept her breathing last time she went down. And the Felix, of course, that's been good for her. I'm a touch mad, don't mistake, as I'd nearly convinced her to let this whole nonsense of being a detective go. We've wanted her in our ranks from the beginning, despite her objections that she didn't know enough of the world yet. I figured one more bad partner would make her come back to us."

"It might have," I acknowledged, a touch sadly. It was no surprise to me that the Kingsmen wanted to keep her—more that they'd let her pursue her own course to begin with. "Although the general opinion in the precinct is improving, as you see."

"Yes, so I do. And I'm glad for her sake, but still mad, mind you. I'd rather have her with us." Sighing gustily, Gibson glanced at her over his shoulder, his expression softening. "But she clearly adores you, and it's good for her to have a dedicated partner who doesn't patronize her. You're a smart man, Henri Davenforth, for seeing her as she is."

He said that, and yet I felt a threat lingering in the words. I gathered the impression that if my attitude or opinion ever changed, Gibson would be the first man on my doorstep to straighten me out again. "Trust me, Kingsman Gibson. I have stupid colleagues who couldn't find their way out of a paper sack. Jamie is not one of them."

Chuckling in a low tone, he agreed frankly, "That she isn't. You, ah, do know of the importance of the anniversary coming up?"

"I'm well aware." Knowing well what he was really asking, I added in a lower tone, "And she's tired, no doubt having some bad dreams, but otherwise fine."

"There's more than—" he cut himself off and glanced over his shoulder. "I have a feeling we'll talk more after this. For now, however—Jamie! Shall we get started?"

She'd been leaning over the table, conferring with Evans, but at this hail lifted up enough to give Gibson a nod. "We should. And I vote we all go for dinner afterwards, as I'm half-starved."

As it was just past end of shift, I did see her point. "If we're quick enough, we might beat the dinner crowd at Yorkshire House."

"That's an excellent thought," my partner informed me happily. "Then let's quickly get down to business. Evans, why don't you start us off?"

"We visited every store listed on the invoices, took out all of Garner's charms," Evans answered with a grimace that drew his mobile expression upwards. "Bit not good, that. Some stores were happy to see bad charms gone, others were not happy having us do it openly. Said it was bad publicity. Anyway, after we hit them, Bennett said—"

"Might as well see what stores they used to use in the east end of town and if they have any charms still in stock," Bennett pitched in as if reciting from rote.

With a nod of agreement, Evans smoothly picked back up in his surprisingly low voice, "And we all thought that a good notion, so we went 'round them too. Pulled anything bad, of course, not just Garner's. Did find some of his, though. We're a bit foot sore, but we're sure we cleaned out the lot, at least. After that, hit every morgue on Rose, Watts, and Armstrong Road. I have a list of fifteen dead from suspicious illnesses, some of them surely a charm backfiring. I'll interview families tomorrow." For such a thin, short man, he had incredible lung power.

That was an excellent start. He'd covered a not insignificant amount of ground in six days. Seaton obligingly switched to a different hue of red and marked off the roads that he'd listed.

"Bennett?" Jamie prompted.

"West Street, Hudson Lane, and Newport Road," Bennett answered precisely. He seemed to be a man of few words. In fact, I'd barely heard him say more than ten altogether since his arrival. Leaning forward in the seat, his stocky frame made the wooden chair creak in protest. "I've got three suspicious deaths, but most were natural."

I marked them off, noting that they were on the outside of the eastern section of the city where we knew the first charm business had distributed their wares.

Seaton apparently observed the same, as he noted, "You're likely on the fringe territory. Might want to step in closer tomorrow."

"Planning to," Bennett answered succinctly.

"Marshall?" Seaton inquired.

"Thirty-six cases and I only went through Dunn Road," Marshall answered flatly.

I paused in marking the map, giving him a sharp look. "You're quite certain that all thirty-six are charm-related?"

"The reason I only managed the one road was that after inquiring at the morgues, I went to visit the families to double check. I found the same story with each family. In fact, three of them gave me a copy of the police coroner's report as well as a copy of the report they'd filed with the police against the charms business." Feral pleasure graced Marshall's narrow face. "I'm sure."

"I'd like to see those reports," Seaton informed him, staring at him with sharp interest. "In fact, I think Davenforth would as well."

"You're quite correct," I confirmed. "What else did you discover, Kingsman Marshall?"

"I did ask for occupations while I was interviewing the families, but no one was a powder monkey. A few mechanics, though." Marshall shrugged. "I asked if anyone knew that the two charm makers had pulled up stakes and simply relocated. They hadn't heard that and were blistering mad to learn of it. If anyone was guilty of killing those two men, they were too fine of an actor for me to spot them."

Jamie accepted this with a judicious nod. "We'll still want to look into the mechanics, though. Gerring?"

"I started with Third Precinct's morgue," he answered with a long, drawn out sigh. "It took me most of the day just to get the forms filled out to even look at their files. I did find reports on charm-related deaths, but I only made it through to the D's, and there were seventeen cases that fit the profile."

"You are quite likely at the right spot and asking the right questions, not to mention giving us the perfect list to compare to," Jamie assured him with an encouraging smile. "Keep at it. Penny, do you think you can go and help him with that tomorrow?"

"I certainly can," she answered forthrightly.

"Excellent. Gibson?" Jamie asked, turning in her

chair to face him. "I know you got a late start compared to everyone else, but did you hit any of the morgues?"

"Only the ones on Parsons Road," he answered, gesturing to the map. "But that was a bit of a hot spot, that. Twenty-nine confirmed cases, and the undertaker actually had two charms that he'd kept aside. Said he tried to turn them in as evidence to the precinct only to have them rebuff him—I'll be having words over that."

"They got tired of disposing of them," Gerring filled in with a grimace. "So many people figured out that the charms were bad, but were scared of doing anything to them, so they turned them into the precinct. The Magical Examiner got stuck with the job of disposal, got tired of it, and told people to just burn the things."

I flinched at the notion. Eerily in unison, Seaton and I both demanded, "What is his name?"

Wincing at our loud demand, Gerring held up his hands in a gesture of surrender, silently pleading we not shoot the messenger. "Carr."

"Interesting," Jamie observed in a tone that indicated her interest did not bode well for the man. "Garner's ex-wife reported to Third Precinct too. They apparently have very selective hearing."

"I'll have stern words with him tomorrow," Seaton promised us all in a voice filled with doom. "That is incredibly irresponsible and dangerous. I'll have the man strung up by his toes for this."

I dearly hoped that he did. Burning unstable charms was just as likely to cause severe illness to the person near the charm as it was destroyed. That tactic could account for half of the illnesses and deaths reported in this case. Really, I'd thought Sanderson bad. At least his behaviors were more often than not self-destructive.

Wishing to move the meeting along, I queried my partner, "Jamie? What did you and Officer McSparrin discover?"

"Quite a few things. Some of it might or might not be relevant," she answered forthrightly. "Burns-Cross Demolition did, in fact, have a missing stick of dynamite. They were quite alarmed by that, as they should be. They promised a thorough investigation and audit with the hope that a stick just got misplaced somewhere. We've heard back from most of the sixteen places that we visited, still waiting on a few others, but so far that's the only place for sure that is missing dynamite. We have a list of four powder monkeys who have lost a loved one in the past six months. Two of them lost a grandmother, which I'm fairly sure won't tie in with our case, but I'll interview the families tomorrow to double check this."

I noted this information as well, feeling alarmed myself at the idea of a stick of dynamite just missing. One would think that with such a highly volatile material, it would be better contained and kept track of. Although what that said of the two companies that couldn't even answer the question....

"There's a great many victims because of these two idiots," Jamie tacked on with a groan. "Which doesn't help our investigation any. I'm almost too sympathetic right now to care if we catch the murderers or not. Seems like they did the world a favor by stopping Garner and Timms."

"Unfortunately, can't disagree," Gibson sighed, slumping back in his chair. "RM, what did you and Dr. Davenforth discover?"

"Interesting things," Seaton answered, steepling his fingers together. "We made some inquiries of our own today after examining the charms. Allow me to paint the picture for you.

"Trevor Garner as a teenager went through charm school at Harper Institute of Magic. He attended for exactly four semesters before dropping out due to poor attendance and low grades. He was, in fact, failing before withdrawing from the school. We're not sure of his employment history, but a year later he opened a permit for a vendor shop at the docks, selling charms. That lasted eight months. Then three months later, Charms Against Harm opened on the east side. It was open for exactly a year before closing down. Our erstwhile charm makers dodged multiple lawsuits and fines by declaring bankruptcy—which is not supported by the ledgers we examined; the shop was actually making a hefty profit—and then opened their new shop two months later."

The entire table groaned in understanding except McSparrin and Gerring. They'd followed to an extent, but I could see the full details of the matter failed to connect in their heads. For their benefit, I further explained, "Garner's interrupted schooling is very obvious in the charms' craftsmanship. He used the wrong paper, the wrong ink, included random elements into the charms' design that we're not sure would actually function correctly, and used a printing press to do it all with. Those elements combined made the charms dangerously unstable. I couldn't lay hands on a charm that he'd produced with his previous business, but I believe he repeatedly did this very thing, not having learned from his mistakes. The results bear out with that, at least, and tell us that he truly didn't understand why the charms failed. From what he learned in his schooling, theoretically it should have. It's as much a crime of negligence as ignorance."

"And arrogance," Jamie grumbled in a rhetorical fashion. "What kind of moron fails school and then thinks he can still make a business out of it?"

"A dead one, now," Seaton responded scathingly. "Disturbingly, we also found traces of Destroying Angel in the ink."

Every magician in the room grimaced and Evans swore aloud.

Jamie raised a hand. "Explain for the non-magicians in the room, please."

"It's a powerful source, especially if extracted in sprouting form," I filled in, keeping my explanation concise. "The fungi itself, however, is deadly toxic and isn't something to be trifled with."

Pulling a face, Jamie muttered, "Lovely. How deadly is it in ink form?"

"Fortunately not," Seaton reassured her. "Higher in potency than we care for, but it would make someone sick, not deathly ill. We found an invoice with their records indicating that they had bought a batch of an ink from a reliable retailer. Still, the addition of the Destroying Angel element is oddly out of balance with the rest of the ink, which makes the charms further unstable. Please bear that in mind when handling the charms."

With the mood of the room, I understood their opinion very well: these two men had neatly dug their own graves. Still, that didn't excuse vigilantism and I, for one, didn't like the idea that someone had come up with a creative method of killing Garner, introducing yet another method of murder into the populace. Despite having no sympathy for our victims, I had no desire to let their murderers simply walk free, either. "Do we continue where we left off tomorrow?"

"Yes," Jamie sighed, pushing her chair back, clearly preparing to stand. "Knowing what and where Garner and Timms came from gives us a clearer picture, but at the moment it doesn't give us any answers. We still need to know who did the deed. I'm going to return to Burns-Cross Demolition tomorrow. I have to know if that missing stick of dynamite is really missing or not. We might have found the powder monkey's company if it is."

If the culprit had stolen from his workplace, then I felt sure he'd fudged the records as well. The manner in which Jamie delivered her intentions suggested to me that she hoped the man hadn't been able to completely cover all his sins. Detective work, however, more often included eliminating possibilities than discovering clues. This instance represented such an occasion.

Clearing my throat, I paused the table before they could get their feet under them. "There is one more facet of the case that bothers me. When I went back to retrieve the magical license in Garner's building, I took a second, closer look at the building. The second story of the building has been entirely blocked off from the first."

They all looked at each other askance, all but Jamie and McSparrin, who had been with me when we examined the building in the first place.

"You didn't find a way in?" Jamie inquired sharply.

"I did not. The staircase was removed, there was no exterior staircase or ladder, and every window along the second story has an iron grill placed over it. I'm quite baffled." Also very, very curious. It might not have anything to do with our case. Then again, perhaps it did. Either way, we needed to find a means of entering the second story and validating that one way or another.

"Henri," Jamie invited with that sparkly look she got when she contemplated mischief, "why don't you come with me tomorrow? We'll stop in and find a way upstairs."

Knowing very well what she contemplated, I asked dryly, "Are you by any chance contemplating punching your way up through the ceiling?"

She batted her big brown eyes at me. "Maaaybe."

My partner enjoyed inherent destruction far too much.

What are you trying to say, huh?

I believe it's self-evident.

You and walls meet frequently.

That's all we're saying.

Jamie's Additional Report 08...ish

I am now forced to enter more blank pages so that I can write my own observations. That is not a good sign.

Nonsense, I'm fleshing out the story.

"So that's Dr. Henri Davenforth." Gibson sat on the bench with both elbows on his knees, a towel in one hand, a glass of water in the other. He looked well warmed up and mussed, as he should, considering we'd already had three rounds of sparring this evening.

I so enjoyed cutting loose with the boys. I could never do this with Henri, he was not the athletic sort. He'd be appalled if I even suggested it. But that was fine. I'd let my easy-going partner curl up with his chocolates and books instead of beating him up in the ring. We all had our quirks. And Gibson was marvelously fun to spar with. He was one of the few men I knew who had strength almost on par with mine, and that made him less breakable.

We'd taken one of the training rooms at the police precinct, as the Kingsmen's training area was still under quarantine, and it was getting late. I'd definitely worked off the company dinner at this point. It had been the first time in a few days that I'd really felt like eating. PTSD was hard on the appetite. I'd learned a way to cope by cooking for Henri, because anyone would regain their appetite while watching that man eat. I swear, Henri spoke of food the way most men would a sexy woman.

I still breathed a touch too hard, considering, which meant I needed to spar with Gibson more often to keep in better shape. Eyeing him sideways, I gulped down some water before asking, "You sound approving of Henri?"

"Got a good impression of him," Gibson admitted frankly, returning my sideways look. "He's intelligent, he's got good manners, and he doesn't treat his female colleagues like they're inferior. Seaton says he's pulled off a few minor miracles in order to keep you safe and on your feet, which makes me like him even more. He's just a little..."

"Quirky?" I filled in dryly. "In the best sense, yes, he is. Very staid in some ways, thinks exercise is a dirty word, and has little patience with stupidity. But still, a staunch friend if you need someone at your back. Did you know that he's actually smarter than Sherard?"

Gibson blinked at me in frank astonishment. "He is not!"

"He totally is. It's a sore point with Sherard. That magical examination you take to get out of school? Henri's score is higher. In fact, no one's scored higher to date." I felt a little smug about that. Sue me, I could be proud of my partner.

An inarticulate noise of disbelief escaped Gibson's mouth. He was having some trouble getting his jaw to stay in place. "But if he's that smart, why isn't he a Royal Mage himself?"

"Doesn't have the magical power to back it up, sadly. But that's part of why he's such an amazing Magical Examiner. He doesn't need much power to do the job, just intelligence and a good knowledge base, which he has." I shrugged, splaying a hand. "And that's why Sherard consults with him. Those two, when they put their heads together, start talking in a completely different language. I understand one word in twelve."

"I can see that." He took another pull, emptying the rest of the glass before setting it aside. "Jams, I'll be honest. Before you partnered with him, I'd hoped that you'd come back to us. Be a Kingsman."

I wasn't completely surprised by this. Many of the men who had helped me find my footing in this world after escaping Belladonna had become like brothers to me. They hadn't taken my refusal to join the Kingsmen ranks well. Only a few had agreed that I had a good point—I needed seasoning in this world, in this culture, before I could really do the job right. Gibson was one of the more vocal ones about it not being necessary, that he'd show me the ropes. "And now that you've met him?"

"It'll make convincing you harder now that you have him as a partner," Gibson responded wryly. He lifted a shoulder up in a shrug. "He works well with you, he likes you, and he's got the magical know-how to keep you safe on cases."

Not all of the Kingsmen were magical themselves. Some of them had mediocre talents when it came to magic, but amazing detective or combat skills. Gibson did have magical talent, a mid-level magician at best, but was extraordinary in other ways that made up for it. I knew what he meant, but I didn't want him to feel inadequate. "Come on, Gibs, you know I'd partner with you any day."

"That I do. I'm just willing to admit he might be a better match for you."

I slung an arm around his shoulders and hugged him tightly, because that? That was big of him to admit. "Just keep being my sparring buddy and big brother, okay? 'Cause only you can do that."

He leaned in and kissed my temple. "Like you can get rid of me. But Jams, if you and he don't work out for whatever reason, you come back to us. We'll take you in a heartbeat."

It felt good, having another place to go. In this world where I had no relatives, I still had family. It made it less lonely, and I harbored the hope that the day would come when I wouldn't always have the fact that I wasn't from this world at all in the forefront of my mind. "Okay. I'll remember. Honestly, it…helps. Knowing that you guys will take me in a heartbeat. I feel randomly homesick sometimes and out of joint with this world. Being around you guys is like having a pack of brothers. It's hard to feel homesick around you."

"Glad to hear it." He got that cautious look on his face that people wore just when they were about to ask the question I was sick of hearing. "You're alright, otherwise? I mean with the anniversary coming up."

"People need to stop asking me that question," I responded before I could check the words. Then I thought, no, why not be frank about it? "I'm alright. It's not like the nightmares have disappeared, and some days I don't feel like eating, but I'm doing okay. But if one more person asks me that question, I swear to you, I will deck them."

Lifting both hands in surrender he gave me a grin. "Just asking. One more round?"

I now felt ready to beat him up and immediately stood. "One more round."

Report 09: Destroying Angels

Is this a Supernatural chapter?
A what?

Cass, are you there?
Dean?
Sam?
No, truly, what?

"No, you may not just punch your way through the ceiling," I informed my partner flatly.

Jamie gave me a pretty pout, fluttering her eyelashes at me like some innocent damsel at a picnic. "But Henri—"

"Sometimes," I cut her off ruthlessly, still standing on the step of Garner's charm business, "I do believe that you say outrageous things just to get my dander up. You know very well that doing such a silly thing would be dangerous. We have no idea what's on the second story, what area of the floor is clear, or anything else."

She reinforced the pout, which looked patently ridiculous. "But that's half the fun."

"You're deliberately tweaking my nose," I accused, shaking a finger at her. "Do stop. Go through a window like a normal person."

"You take all the fun out of things." Huffing, she stripped off the light jacket she wore, tossing it into the front seat of the car. Limbering up, she stretched both arms over her head, twisted her waist a little from side to side, then gave me a nod. "Ready."

I helped her pull the rope ladder from the boot, then magically lifted it in place with a carefully placed wand movement so that it rested just below the windowsill to the right of the door. There, that should be attached quite firmly. It would hold her weight, at least.

"You know," Jamie mused, and this time she didn't have a teasing note in her voice, "I bet I could actually parkour this."

A trifle alarmed, I snapped about to stare at her. "I beg your pardon?"

She flapped a hand at me, still staring at the building with that thoughtful expression. "Like, carve out handholds against the door trip, catch on to the iron grill over the window, stuff like that. I'm seeing enough handholds to make it doable."

I stared at her steadily, silently daring her to ignore my very nicely placed ladder.

Grinning, she soothed, "I'll use the ladder. Stop twitching."

"You're in quite the mood," I observed, not entirely pleased about it. She was more reckless than usual, and Jamie took more risks than my heart considered healthy to begin with. My eyes sharpened on her, studying her in a more careful way from head to toe, not sure if this was a symptom or not. I didn't think her sleep deprived, but she seemed antsier than usual.

"Had four cups of coffee this morning," she admitted cheerfully as she scaled the ladder as nimbly as any monkey. "I might be a little wired."

"Heaven preserve us," I grumbled. That explained her overenthusiasm quite adequately. I hoped the caffeine rush would die down soon—before I was forced to do something drastic like make her run laps around the city.

Jamie paused with her head just below the window sill. In a casual show of strength, she grabbed the iron grate and tore it off, the screws rending in an awful screech of tortured metal. I leaned up as she passed the grilling down to me and grunted at the weight of it, as it was by no means light. Setting it carefully aside, I turned my face and attention back up towards her. "What do you see?"

"That...is not good. Henri, do you have growth houses on this world?"

Slowly, I responded, "I am not familiar with that term."

"Places that look like ordinary houses on the outside, but a criminal grows something illegal on the inside, turning the entire thing into a greenhouse?" she explained, still peering through the window.

"Oh. Yes, we do, although fortunately they're not rampant. I'm almost afraid to inquire, what do you see growing up there?"

"Looks like fungus. Lots of white mushrooms."

Alarm tingled in the back of my mind, sounding bells in a growing klaxon of noise. I knew precisely what they were, because I had detected the use of them in the charm ink several days previous. Seaton and I had remarked upon the stupidity of it at the time, but why hadn't I questioned the source of the mushrooms? "Roughly three inches tall, perfectly white with no other stripes or blemishes?"

She twisted to look down at me, eyebrows drawn together in a frown. "I can tell from your face that isn't good. Do I need to get down?"

"Immediately," I rasped. "That's Destroying Angel."

Ignoring the rungs of the ladder, she stepped free of it and dropped all eight feet without issue. Her bent knees took the brunt of the impact, and she straightened, alarm growing over her face. "Wait, that poisonous mushroom thing used in the ink?"

"First, hold perfectly still," I instructed, then hit her with three different cleansing charms before examining her magic core carefully. No fissures. Still, I'd have Seaton take a look at her in the next few hours, just in case. "Yes, that poisonous mushroom. It's considered to be one of the most toxic mushrooms on this continent. Careless contact with it, such as inhaling its spores or coming into skin contact with it, can be lethal. Magically speaking, it's quite potent if harvested in its seedling state and distilled in alcohol. It makes a very strong base to ink."

"Craaap," Jamie groaned, looking back up at the window she'd just been spying through. "I thought you said they got their ink from a reliable source?"

"They did. And apparently boosted it with their own farmed Destroying Angel filaments," I agreed grimly. Mentally, I cursed myself for three kinds of a fool. Seaton and I had assumed that the result of Destroying Angel was from a licensed source, as the ink had been properly purchased from a supplier. We had an invoice stating as much from their files. It had never occurred to me that they would seek to double the potency of the ink by adding in their own crop of Destroying Angel.

Glancing at me, she said softly, "You couldn't have known. You thought you knew the source of the ink."

"I should have asked more questions," I denied, still mad at myself.

"Henri." Exasperated, she pointed at the second story and the horrors it contained. "What are we doing, right now, if not asking more questions?"

Well. Put like that, she might have a point. Still, I should have detected something strange about the charms when examining them. It irked me that I had not. But it wasn't the time to sit about and feel pitiful, either. That dangerous crop on the second story demanded my attention. "Jamie, let's message Seaton. I do not want to tackle this alone and we need to report it to a Royal Mage regardless. The potency of a crop this size demands such protocol."

"Okay. Say, you don't think that they've done this before, do you?" Her brown eyes went large with horror. "The previous shop they had, did they have a crop there too?"

I bit back the urge to swear like a stevedore. "That is entirely possible. We've not heard if someone else has taken over the building. Even if they removed the crop, traces of it could still linger."

"I'll message Evans, he's got the best magic ability of the group," Jamie informed me, already striding toward the car to fetch her texting pad. "You tell Sherard about this."

I pulled out my texting pad, scribbled in the name of the addressee in the delineated box at the top of the screen, and then wrote quickly, barely keeping my handwriting legible: Seaton. We have Destroying Angel growing on second floor.

It took him a few moments to respond: WHHHHHAAAAT

I'll lock the place down until you get here.

Coming now.

Looking up, I saw Jamie biting at her bottom lip, a sure sign that some word had failed her. "Need me to take over?"

"No, but how do you spell Destroying Angel?"

I told her, watched over her shoulder as she carefully spelled it out, checking the rest of the message as well. She had done well with everything else. Satisfied, I stepped back two feet and retrieved my wand from my interior coat pocket, putting in a temporary quarantine spell on the building. It might be tossing good effort after bad at this juncture, but policy was to lock down any large plot of Destroying Angels immediately upon discovery. I wasn't going to argue the point.

Putting the pad back into the car, she informed me over her shoulder, "Evans says he's going directly there to double check."

"Excellent."

"I suppose it's too much to hope that Garner and

Timms disposed of the Destroying Angels properly at their previous location?"

"I'm personally praying that they just hadn't planted them."

"Ah. Safer bet," Jamie agreed sourly. Looking at the building again, she crossed both arms over her chest, tapping a finger in an idle rhythm against her sleeve. "Henri. Just a thought, but…you said some of the charms actually caused sickness. Can that be because of the mushroom ink?"

"Quite possibly. If they didn't distill it properly, if they harvested mature shrooms instead of seedlings—you catch my drift. A dozen little things could have been done wrong to ill effect. It's why the distillation of the Destroying Angel mushrooms is government regulated and audited to begin with." I glared at the building. What an infernal mess.

"And they had no way of getting up there and clearing out the mature ones anyway," Jamie added in a grumble. "Or they had a trap door somewhere that we just didn't find."

"I assume the latter. They'd have no way of harvesting their crop otherwise. Or watering it, and it would require constant moisture."

"Ah. Good point." Looking about her, she prophesied in a voice full of doom, "We will be here all day."

"For once," I riposted, already feeling as if the day were a decade long already, despite it not being lunch yet, "I want you to be wrong."

She was not wrong.

It took the rest of the day to clean out the second

story, mostly because we had to craft a viable means of entering first. If there was a trap door leading up to it—and there must have been, I'd stake my reputation on it—then it was devilishly clever in design. We couldn't find it, even with locating spells. Once proper spells were built, it was a far easier task for the professionals to enter, clearing things carefully out and into containment bags before hauling it back down.

Jamie wasn't allowed anywhere near this process. She saw the danger as well as Seaton and I did, and chose instead to keep the onlookers well back, explaining the general dangers to them, not allowing the crowd near us.

I stayed planted near the wagons, keeping track of everything brought out. Seaton dashed in between the second level and the wagons, double checking that everything remained sealed tight, his expression far more grim than usual. He stopped next to me, sweat beading his brow from the constant activity, his eyes on the clipboard in my hand. "Sixteen bags so far?"

"As you see. How is it up there?"

"We're about halfway through." Grimacing, he acknowledged my unspoken look at the three wagons resting alongside the curb. "I've already called for more. Zounds, Davenforth, I don't mind telling you that if these two fools were still alive, I'd murder them with my bare hands for this. Stupidity should have a limit."

"I'm inclined to agree with you." I tucked the pencil into the clipboard to rub a hand along my forehead, feeling a headache brewing like a gathering storm. "Seaton, I know that we collected all of the inventory from the stores, but that doesn't account for the charms already sold. We put out an official notice, but…."

"I put in another one with the Kingston Gazette," he assured me, the kohl around his eyes smearing with perspiration. "And I've asked all of the theaters to announce a health warning for the charms and to notify the police immediately if anyone has one. I can only hope that between those two things, we'll catch most of them before they do any damage. The person that I truly want to strangle is the one who issued them a business license."

"We're still searching if they had one," I reminded him. "But we can hardly blame the clerks at City Hall; they're not able to tell a genuine magical license from a forgery, and we know Garner's was forged."

"That," Seaton growled, tone sour, "might be true, but I can still be upset about it. Alright, let's get the rest of this cleared out, then I vote we all go to dinner. Queen's treat tonight, as we've earned it."

"Hear, hear!" Jamie called over her shoulder.

"I swear she has hearing like a bat's," Seaton observed to me lightly.

"I heard that!"

Pointing to her smugly, he arched an eyebrow at me. "See?"

Considering the amount of times she'd overheard something she should not have, it didn't surprise me. Then again, Jamie's senses were superior to the normal human's. "So I do. There's one other issue, Seaton. Have we heard if there were any Destroying Angels in their previous location?"

"Evans reports there wasn't. Apparently they had this bright idea after moving into this building. I thank all listening deities for that small favor." Someone called Seaton and he acknowledged it by lifting a hand before adding, "Stay strong, old chap. We'll see the end of this in the next few hours."

I certainly prayed so. Standing was quickly becoming uncomfortable, the balls and arches of my feet not happy with the constant pressure of staying upright.

Cleaning was a laborious endeavor complicated by the mushrooms' deadly nature if someone mishandled them. The wrong exposure would lead to vomiting, delirium, convulsions, liver and kidney failure, soon to be followed by death. Few survived the experience. The magicians carrying out the task understood the risks very well and had suited up accordingly in suits of oiled linens, magically enhanced to repel any invasion of a magical substance, which covered them from the crown of their head to the soles of their boots. They looked rather like overexuberant beekeepers, in my humble opinion. It had to be sweltering hot in the garment, not to mention awkward to see around the small glass visor of the headgear, but not one man even hinted at taking it off.

"Henri," Jamie called out to me.

I half-turned, keeping my place, and found her regarding me with a mix of sympathy and amusement. "Yes?"

"Christopher's Steak House?" she suggested.

My mouth instantly filled with the flavors of a thick, perfectly grilled steak. "Thank you. That is exactly the motivation I needed to keep going."

Chuckling, she went back to the crowd, leaning in to answer a question from a child still in his knickers.

I checked off another three bags on the clipboard, mentally writing a formal report for this in my head, and imagining my captain's response. He would not be pleased about this. At all. While I understood and shared the sentiment, it did not mean I looked forward to reporting this either.

Please, please let there not be any further incidents like this one.

Oh, I see what happened. <u>You</u> called on Murphy.

Surely not. Such a simple wish wouldn't be enough to do so.

Yeah, apparently I didn't explain Murphy well enough.

Of all the things for you to bring from Earth, must Murphy be one of them?

What, you think I did that on purpose?

I'm not <u>that</u> crazy.

Report 10: Not the Sharpest Egg in the Drawer

I love malaphors

Captain Gregson was not happy.

Since I shared that sentiment, I gave him a commiserating nod and sigh. Jamie sat in the chair adjoining mine, perfectly peeved, and I had no doubt she would raid my chocolate stash in the lab at the first given opportunity. For that matter, I had every intention of joining her.

Listing to one side in his chair, Gregson leaned his head against a propped-up hand, weary and aged a decade older than his actual years. "Twenty-seven bags. You're telling me that you hauled twenty-seven bags of a deadly mushroom out of our crime scene."

"Yes, Captain, unfortunately." Giving a tepid smile, I winced before offering, "There's two silver linings to this particular cloud."

"Please do elaborate, Davenforth," he encouraged in a growl. "I could use them."

Ticking points off on my fingers, I intrepidly forged ahead. "First, it was entirely contained. Fools they might have been, but not without some survival instincts. Because they'd closed off all access to the second floor, no one tumbled into their little farm; otherwise we'd be looking at dozens of victims instead of just the two."

"Yes, by all means, let's avoid a bigger disaster than we have now," Gregson groaned. "What's the second?"

"Because this has basically become a government

case," Jamie pitched in smoothly, "we were able to immediately pull in experts to clear the area out. The bill for the cleanup and the aftercare of treating the building to prevent the spores from infecting anyone else who inhabits the area after this is also on Sherard's tab instead of ours."

Gregson lifted his head, expression lightening. "Truly? Music to my ears. You're correct, Davenforth, they're nice silver linings in the cloud. I'll take them. What about their previous location? You said they had a business on the east side of the city before moving."

"Clean," I assured him, not blind to his open relief. "Kingsman Evans checked it yesterday. They apparently hit upon this hare-brained scheme after moving. I'm inclined to be grateful for that, even as I curse them for thinking of it at all."

"I'm just cursing them," Jamie grumbled. "Idjuts. Those two were not the sharpest eggs in the drawer. As it stands, Cap, we've got something of a lead but a very large suspect pool. One of the demolition companies in town has some missing inventory they can't account for. I was supposed to follow up with them yesterday, but, well…."

"Things happened," Gregson waved her on with perfect understanding. "Pick up the trial tomorrow. How big of a suspect pool?"

"These two did a lot of damage," she continued sourly. "Half the city's out for their blood, or at least it feels that way. The guys report that whenever they bring up bad charms, and who our victims are, they get rants and sob stories. Poor Marshall got surrounded by a virtual mob yesterday from half the people working the docks after asking the question, all intent on getting their piece said."

"We'll have to narrow it down by expertise and opportunity," I stated, inclining my head to indicate my exasperated partner. She was going to eat my stash bare, I could see it now. "There's simply too much motive in this city."

"Truth," Jamie groaned. "Cap, I gotta be honest with you. We might not catch these guys. And after all the crap the victims pulled, I'm going to lose little sleep over it if we don't."

"I'm inclined to think this was justifiable homicide as well." I splayed both hands under the sour look he gave us. "I didn't say that I approved of their vigilante style, just that I'm tempted to murder them myself at the moment."

"It's not like they could call on Batman," Jamie muttered as an aside.

I let the nonsensical words pass. "We'll, of course, investigate this. If nothing else, I don't want them to get into the habit of thinking murder, no matter how justified, is a viable means to an end."

"At least you understand that," Gregson grunted. "And I don't want this car bomb method spreading any further either, although that's probably nothing more than words in the wind right now—"

A quick knock sounded on the closed door before it was abruptly swung open and a harried looking McSparrin stuck her head in. "Sorry, Cap. We just got bad news. Dr. Davenforth, Jamie, we got an emergency message from Dockside. There's an outbreak down there and it looks like it's magically caused. A doctor just sent us a message asking for help, he can't lock the area down. He's asking for anyone who has authority to come help him. Think it's our bad charms?"

Jamie leapt for the door, not even answering that question. I scrambled to stay on her heels, fearing that McSparrin's intuition was correct—this might very well be caused by our victims' shoddy work. Curse them to the ninth circle and may their souls be hung upon the devil's bedroom walls.

"Penny, you know the address?" Jamie demanded as she moved.

"I do," McSparrin confirmed. "Doctor, you need any equipment?"

"Quite a bit of it. We'll need the wagon for this, it has most of my gear already loaded. Let me swing by the lab and snag my bag." I hustled toward the lab but didn't just grab the bag. Instead I paused to grab a small box of chocolates I had purchased two days ago. Pocketing it, I went through the back door and found that both women had already started the process of hitching a team of horses to the wagon. Pitching in, we got the team harnessed in record time and quickly loaded up. McSparrin was quick to get the horses in motion, demanding enough speed that we took the first curve nearly on two wheels. I hung on with one hand, but the crawl of traffic forced her to slow to a more moderate speed.

"Penny," Jamie demanded over the din of horns, clattering hooves, and engine noises, "how did you hear about this?"

"The doctor sent a telegram to all police stations, hoping for a response," she answered. "I stopped by the front desk to help Mitch sort through the correspondence, as he looked overwhelmed, and saw it. It's probably our charms, isn't it?"

"Even if it isn't, we need that area locked down before it can become an epidemic," I assured her. "I can do that with my authority, and if nothing else, can get one of my fellow Magical Examiners to work the case. However, I'm inclined to believe in your instincts. A bad anti-sickness charm will cause harm to the people in immediate contact to it, but it never spreads further than a household. It doesn't have the power to do so. I would have said the same of Garner's charms, except he's added the element of the Destroying Angel mushrooms."

"That's a game changer, I take it," Jamie stated with a glance at me.

"Yes, quite. It would have the power, or at least the deadly influence necessary, to cause an outbreak." This was why half-finished degrees were so dangerous. The student left school believing they were sufficiently trained to go about the business. Nothing could be farther than the truth.

Leaning to the side, I gained the leverage necessary to retrieve the chocolates without elbowing Jamie in the ribs in the process. I handed it over to her and she cast me a thankful look before opening the top and popping one into her mouth. In a bout of charity, she tilted the box toward McSparrin, and the other woman juggled the reins long enough to fetch a morsel as well.

We'd need the sugar to see us through the rest of the day. Yesterday had been harrowing, emotionally speaking, and we'd stayed very late making sure that every particle of Destroying Angel was properly taken out. Today saw us drained of our normal energy and motivation. I'd need artificial stimulants to offset the mood. If there really was an outbreak here caused by the charms, we'd have our work cut out for us.

McSparrin drove directly to a doctor's office on Sea Lane, pulling up in front of a two-story building that looked old, but well-cared for. The white and black sign out front announced it the practice of Dr. James Cartwright. Stepping off the wagon, I offered a hand up to Jamie, then went around to hitch the horses to the post. I took in the measure of the place as I did so, and didn't care for what I saw. The building bulged so full of patients that some made do with the wide front porch. Grimly, I grabbed my bag before hustling down the gravel pathway and up the front steps.

The interior was as fully crammed as I'd anticipated. Patients lined the hallways—some of them too ill to remain standing, instead sitting apathetically upon the hardwood floors. I saw signs of influenza immediately upon entrance. Every person was coughing, sneezing, their noses running, faces unnaturally pale or flushed with fever, and sweating. An outbreak, yes, we definitely had that.

I stopped abruptly and pulled out an anti-sickness charm amulet, thrusting one at each woman following me. "Keep this on you at all times."

Jamie held up a staying hand. "I won't need it."

Perplexed, I cocked my head. "Of course you will."

"No, remember?" she replied in a patient, somewhat smug manner. "This is a magically started sickness. If it's magical, it can't do anything to me."

I kept my hand extended, the amulet still in my palm. "Jamie. The first generation of the sickness is magically caused, yes. But once released, a virus can adhere to other strains of sickness and become a different beast altogether. That you will have no immunity to."

Her smugness dropped abruptly. "Oh. Well that's no fun. Alright, amulet it is. Will it do the job in my pocket?"

"Yes, as long as it's on your person." With them sorted out, I put an amulet into my own pocket, searching visibly for a nurse or the doctor who had called for help. There was a staircase and hallway dead ahead of me, a receiving room crammed full to my right. Did that mean his patient rooms were to the left?

I attempted it and found to my relief a nurse behind her desk, frantically filling out prescriptions from the look of it. She looked entirely exhausted, hair escaping her bun in tendrils, the white uniform and apron far from clean or pressed. She looked up at us with a hopeless

Charms and Death and Explosions (oh my!)   139

resignation, then spied the uniform McSparrin wore and straightened abruptly, hope flaring to life. "May I help you?"

"I'm Doctor Henri Davenforth, Magical Examiner for Fourth Precinct," I introduced myself. "My colleagues, Detective Jamie Edwards and Officer Penny McSparrin. We received a telegram asking for aid and are here to give it. Can you direct us to Dr. Cartwright, Nurse…?"

"Fraser," she introduced with a relieved smile. "Yes, please wait one moment." Springing up from her chair, she rushed through the door and into the room behind, calling as she went, "Doctor!"

Jamie stepped in and murmured near my ear, "Henri, this looks bad. Can you tell if there's magic behind this or not?"

"It would take an actual analysis, I can't tell from sight alone," I responded in the same low tone. "As soon as the doctor gives us parameters to work from, can you have the streets cordoned off to quarantine the area? I'd rather it not develop into an epidemic."

"Sure, Penny and I won't be much use here anyway. The thing that bothers me, though…" she half-turned to indicate the view through the front window, "is that. Those are company apartments, aren't they? For Reggie's business?"

In my preoccupation of cause, I had overlooked the obvious. I swore roundly, pushing a hand roughly through my hair, my fingers catching on the curls. "Blood and magic, so they are. Jamie, do you know how to reach my brother-in-law?"

"I do. I'll send him a quick message alerting him to the problem."

Dr. Cartwright—I presumed him to be so, at least—bustled into the room at such speed that he nearly skidded the last three feet. His white coat hung askew, shirt untucked from his pants, tie missing altogether. His blue eyes latched onto mine with fervor as he asked, "Dr. Henri Davenforth?"

"The same, sir," I returned, extending a hand, which he latched onto with more eagerness than politeness. "We received your telegram and believe it might be connected to something we've investigated for the past several days. A charm maker released bad charms into the market, ones that we know for a fact sometimes cause sickness. I'll help you investigate this further and help as I can, but first, can you tell me which areas need to be cordoned off? Detective Edwards and Officer McSparrin can see to that."

"Yes, of course." He gave both women the widest smile, tinged with overly bright eyes. I felt that this was a man at the end of his rope, desperately glad to get any helping hand. "I've had patients from Sea Lane to Harvest Street, the furthest north being Market Corner, and right down to the docks."

I followed that direction, aligning it with a mental map in my head and winced. That was a nearly two square mile radius. "Good grief, man! You said outbreak, but it's more along the lines of an epidemic with that kind of area."

Jamie's mouth was tight, flat and unhappy. "I'll say. Doctor, you tell Henri everything you know. I'll handle the situation outside. Penny, chop chop."

Trusting that my partner could handle things sufficiently, I turned to Dr. Cartwright. "You said in your telegram that you believe this was magically inflicted. Why?"

"Every person has complained to me that they shouldn't have been sick because they have an anti-sickness charm in their house," he answered, anger rising in a hot tide across his cheeks. "I didn't pay much attention to it at first, as this is a poor area. These people are factory workers, for the most part; they wouldn't be able to afford good charms. Mostly bargain bin charms, and those are practically useless. But by the twentieth patient, I started to question it. By this morning, I was sure. It had to be the charms. I now have over two hundred patients. I literally can't see them all, and I've had to call in favors from other doctors in my acquaintance to manage the workload."

I took in what he said, turning my head to regard the multiple patients still waiting upon him. "Do you mean to tell me that their practices are equally as filled to the bilges as this one?"

"I'm afraid so."

There was one more question that I needed answered. "How long? When was your first patient?"

"Seven days ago to the day, I believe. Between my practice and the others, we have over seven hundred patients who have reported in."

Shaking my head, I informed him flatly, "That's not an outbreak, Doctor. According to the Disease Prevention standards, that's an epidemic. You have too many patients in a very short amount of time. I'm calling this in."

Far from being chastised, he nodded, exhausted in his relief. "Please do."

If he hadn't been so worn down, if he'd possessed more clarity of thought, I believe he would have already come to this conclusion and acted appropriately. But it is difficult to think clearly when the mind is fogged with fatigue. I 'cut him some slack,' as Jamie would put it. "I'll start examining patients myself after I've reported this in. I'll determine the cause and work on eradicating that."

"It'll make things simpler, cut out the middleman," Cartwright agreed. "I'm going back to my patient. Call me with any news or questions."

"I will, sir." As he left, I pulled the texting pad out of my bag and wrote quickly: Seaton. There's an epidemic near the docks, Sea Lane. Might be magically caused. I'm investigating, but send me help.

It took a moment for him to respond with his usual flare: Sod it, man, I want GOOD news! What kind of epidemic?

Influenza, I believe. Started seven days ago, reportedly by bad charms.

Zounds, that sounds like it might tie to our case. Alright, I'll notify the authorities, then join you.

Good, thank you. These texting pads were very handy in such emergency situations. I hoped I got to keep this one.

Shaking the thought off, I went back to the front receiving room, pulling out my wand as I did so. Stopping in the doorway—I'd little choice about that, as the floor was fully occupied—I cleared my throat and gained perhaps the attention of half the room. "Hello. I'm Dr. Henri Davenforth, Magical Examiner with the Fourth Precinct. I understand that you might be victims of a bad anti-sickness charm. Might I examine all of you?"

"Please do, Doctor," an elderly man croaked, his voice raspy, skin too bright with fever. He extended a shaking hand toward me, dark eyes beseeching. "Please."

Report 11: Where's Alcohol When I Need It?

I could've gotten you some, you only had to ask.
Gibs has a stash. Not that type of alcohol, darling.
But for future reference, where's the stash?

I had three different messages out to people, one via a message boy. Part of this territory fell in Third Precinct's area, and I had sent off a scorching note to the captain, not mincing any words about how they'd better back us up here because it was their own laziness that had allowed the situation to get out of hand. We were operating a little out of our jurisdiction as it was. I copied my own captain in on the message so he got one as well, fully explaining the situation. I knew Gregson, at least, took me seriously, as he sent in a dozen officers with several wagons of cordon rope to start locking the place down. I made sure to send a separate message out to Gerring, reinforcing that he was not to come help us. Right now, we needed him to continue his work through the morgues and going through Garner's files. If we had a better idea of just how many of Garner's charms had sold, we'd be better braced for how many patients we were likely looking at.

But at the moment the best that Penny and I could do was cordon off the roads, try to contain the influenza. It was regular police rope, nothing magical about it, but I had no doubt that when the cavalry arrived, the magicians would apply anti-sickness charms along the barriers to prevent anything from spreading. By itself, the influenza wasn't deadly, or so I was told. However, it apparently had a bad habit of blending with other viral strains and becoming some sort of super bug. People who were already ill, or had poor immune systems, would die from it. I'd like to prevent that as much as possible.

Penny was off on the north side with several other officers, cordoning off the area up there, and we had people on the east and west side, so I started with the streets down near the docks. I'd been reliably informed by the locals they had ten streets coming into the area, which meant a lot of rope. I was only taking three streets, but still. I'd grabbed more than a few rolls before leaving, thick golden rope with cloth 'keep out' signs woven into them. Hopefully I had enough to go the distance.

"Excuse me, young woman," a male voice hailed from behind me.

I turned, pausing in knotting the rope around one of the street lamps. He seemed a nice enough fellow, ordinary working class, brown hair tousled a bit by the sea breeze careening up the street. "Yes?"

"There's laws about tying something here or obstructing the street," he informed me, pointing to the rope.

"Yes, so there is," I agreed, a little amused. "I'm Detective Edwards, Fourth Precinct. There's an influenza epidemic here. We're cordoning off the area."

He looked alarmed by this, but not unduly so, as if I'd just said something that didn't jive with what he'd expected me to say. "But you can't do this without proper notice first."

Ah. One of those types. They did make my life difficult. "Proper notice is in the works. In the meantime, we want to prevent the disease from spreading. Now, do you live in this neighborhood?"

"Well, yes."

"Then you have a choice right now. Either go in and stay there for several weeks, or stay out." I stared him down, not impatiently.

Meekly, he backed up. "I think I'll stay out."

"Not a bad decision," I agreed. Picking up the rope, I carted it across the street.

I made it sound easy, didn't I? It wasn't. I had to stop traffic, explain to people over and over again that the area beyond was now quarantined. That they couldn't travel through. Some people were angry, some were scared, some asked me the same question three times in different ways, trying to find a loophole. It took me almost an hour to get it through their heads that quarantine meant just that—quarantine—and no one was coming in or out. Only when they were more or less cowed into

Charms and Death and Explosions (oh my!) 145

obeying did I dare head for the next street.

This whole situation just made me so mad. First, that so many bad charms could even be sold in stores to unsuspecting victims. That was just wrong, right there. People scrimped up the money to pay for a charm to keep sicknesses away, and instead it sabotaged them. And then, to add insult to injury, a doctor sees the problem and reports it, only to end up begging for help. Why would he have to do that? Why wasn't there a protocol in place for a more immediate response? The more I thought about it, the madder I got.

So, of course, the bane of my existence showed up.

I could hear her before she caught up with me, as the woman insisted on wearing heels on the job, and she had a very distinctive stride, like a mouse scurrying. Then again, she likely had rodent in her family line somewhere. It would explain much about her personality.

"Detective Edwards!"

Sighing, I let my head hang for a second, cursing the woman as vilely as I knew how. Then I turned around, shoulders thrown back, as you absolutely couldn't give any sign of weakness in front of reporters. It was like throwing blood in the water. "King. I'm a little busy at the moment."

She ignored me. She was good at that. Hand bag swinging from her elbow, ever-present pad of paper in her free hand, and a camera man jogging to keep up with her, she was the ever-unchanging picture of a reporter after a scoop. "Detective Edwards, what are your thoughts on this outbreak happening on the very anniversary of your killing Belladonna—"

"I think—" I bit my tongue, hard. I didn't dare say what I actually thought. Sensing she'd caught me at a verbose time, King's eyes went alight, limbs practically quivering in her lavender dress. I'd only ever seen her in that exact color. Didn't she own any other dresses? I deliberately rephrased. "I think the epidemic here isn't these people's fault. I think that when we do figure out who's responsible for this, heads will roll. I really think that my being here, and Belladonna, has absolutely nothing to do with it. And King, if you report me saying otherwise, your head will roll."

She paused in her scratching to give me a winsome smile.

"Of course, I wouldn't dream of doing so, Detective."

"Remember that I am not the most high-ranking person involved with this case," I tacked on in warning. "Don't think you can ignore me. They won't be as patient. Now, that's all I have to say. Get out of here before I slap you with an obstruction of justice charge."

She frowned, a pretty pout of frustration, got one picture of me frowning at her, then clacked off.

Growling a curse to myself, I went back to hauling rope.

My safety valve for frustration was singing. For that matter, my safety valve for basically everything was singing. People who knew me well no longer batted an eye. The ones who really knew me well joined in. As I tied ropes off to lamp posts, I sang to myself in a mocking tone, "This is the charm that never ends, yes it goes on and on my friends! Some people started using it not knowing what it was, and they'll get sick of using it forever just because—"

"I haven't heard that one yet," Sherard noted as he joined me.

I hadn't heard him pull up, but he must have just done so, as I saw his motorcar parked along the curb on the other side of my cordoned line. "Yeah, it's not the original lyrics. You got here fast."

"I've been messaging Davenforth back and forth the past hour," he answered with a long expression. Cats dealing with barking, stupid dogs wore that sort of expression. "He's reasonably sure at this point that at the very least, a bad batch of charms is responsible for all of this. He's half-convinced that it's our murdered duo's charms, although he said he won't be satisfied on that point until he has their charms in evidence. Fastidious man, isn't he?"

"He's that, alright. Then again, he wouldn't be a good Magical Examiner if he were anything else. Are you here to hunt down the charms?"

"Yes. That, and declare this area officially under quarantine so that we might have more ready assistance from the other government institutions. A division of labor, as it happens. Not that it'll be just the two of us, I've called on other colleagues to aid the cause. Davenforth intends to go about sticking true anti-sickness charms all over the area to keep it from spreading. I'll do the same while conducting the search." Sherard paused and looked around the area with a grimace. "What worries me is that we're in a very poor area. These people can't afford to take two weeks leave from work in order to properly recover. How are they to meet their obligations and afford medicine? They're living on very tight means as it is."

One look at the place told the story of just how tight. The place was clean, I'd give them that, but very worn. There wasn't a single sign of a car or horse stabled here, because those were luxuries people couldn't afford. Laundry, tattered and worn thin, hung from one window to another, with no sign of cold boxes hanging out the windows that most apartments sported these days. No toys littered the yards. I felt like I stood in a third-world country, in some ways, although these people at least had a proper roof standing over their heads.

"About six of these apartment buildings are actually company housing for Henri's brother-in-law's company," I informed Sherard with an illustrative gesture to the four-story brick building near us. "He owns three factories. I've sent a message to Reggie telling him the situation, asked him to meet me down here. I hope I can at least talk him into giving these guys full wages even though they can't make it to work. They're under quarantine, it's not like they have a choice whether they can go or not."

"That will certainly help a good portion of people here," Sherard observed with an approving nod. "You think he'll agree?"

"Reggie's a good guy. One of those quintessential 'good chaps' you people go on and on about. I think he'll help. The other problem I see is food. From what I can tell, people here don't really have a means of keeping anything perishable. They might not have much food in the house."

Sherard put a palm to his forehead, shoulders bowing in. "Bless you for thinking of that. I'm sure I would have, eventually. I'll send a message to our good queen, see if we can't get a disaster relief fund for this. I can have grocers deliver food to the lines every day."

One of the many reasons why Sherard and I had become

such close friends was that we had the same values. We looked at the world, saw the people who needed help, and moved to give them whatever aid we could pull together. We were both very service-minded people, and it showed in moments like this, as we were obviously on the same page. "Please, sooner rather than later. You'll need to put up anti-sickness charms to make that safe to do."

"Another colleague of mine is tasked with that and already working," he assured me.

That relieved me. "Good. But with the food, maybe ask that now, then go search for charms?"

"Yes, quite. The queen is quite enraptured with her texting pad and usually has it about her person. Perhaps I can reach her through that." Cheered by this thought, he whipped his out and started scribbling ferociously.

It never ceased to amuse me that people could now just 'text' their queen. At least, the few people who had the texting pad. It was about the size of a large smartphone now and thick as a cutting board, but it had to be to maintain the magical battery attached to the back. Ellie swore she'd find a way to make it more efficient and compact. I trusted she would. Ellie was a freaking genius.

Message sent, Sherard grumbled to me, "Maybe now she'll take me more seriously. I've been advocating for years that if we had a proper charms inspector, we wouldn't have near as much trouble in the city."

"From your lips to God's ears," I prayed, not at all joking. He wasn't kidding about the amount of trouble that a bad charm could cause. This was just a case in point.

"Ha, she has it on her!" Sherard did a little jig of happiness before reading off to me, words quick, "She's horrified at the news and grants me a budget to feed people with. She says to give her an estimate of how many people and how long they need to stay in quarantine."

"Estimate's about eight thousand people," I informed him.

Sherard winced, his emotive face making the expression almost comical. "Eight thousand?!"

"It's all apartment buildings in here," I pointed out to him, exasperated. "And we're quarantining about six blocks, with roughly twelve hundred people a block. You do the math."

He quickly did, using his fingers at one point, then groaned. "Great magic, you're right. I swear, if Garner and Timms weren't already dead, I'd murder them myself."

"Get in line. I already called dibs on that." Although I think Henri was actually the first to express that particular sentiment.

"She's not going to like this," Sherard muttered as he wrote a reply. He waited for her response with an anticipated wince on his face, his head half-turned away as if expecting the pad to suddenly develop into a Howler.

You have no idea how sad I was that I couldn't make Harry Potter jokes on this world.

The half-wince abruptly realized, a self-fulfilling prophecy, and he cringed. "I don't think a queen should swear like a sailor."

"Women have the right to swear when upset," I informed him drolly. Although it amused me that the queen was comfortable enough with him to swear. I'd spent a considerable amount of time with Regina when I'd first escaped the cave. She'd had many, many questions about Earth, and in the process of teaching her, and learning from her, she'd become quite a good friend. Regina was a remarkably down-to-earth woman—as far as anyone could be when born into royalty. "What did she say?"

"That she'd delegate someone to put the order in to grocers. Food will come in every morning and evening. She also says she wants a full report on just what caused this later." He jotted out a response before putting the pad away. "It's going to be a very, very long day."

"Understatement of the century," I sighed, shooing him on, then thought better of it. "Sherard. It's in the middle of the workday, which means most of the people who live here aren't actually here right now. What are we going to do about them?"

"We can't quarantine them at work," he answered slowly, head lifting to the sky as he thought the problem through. "Anyone who went to work sick, we drag back here to be quarantined at home. Anyone not showing signs, I suppose we find temporary lodging for them. Stonking deities, that isn't going to be easy."

"I'd let people choose, if they look healthy, as I'm sure most people would choose to be with their families," I advised.

"Yes, quite." Sighing, he dropped his head back down. "I'll arrange all of that. If someone wants in, let them in. If not, keep them out."

"Roger that."

"I'll put Kingsmen in charge of notifying the men at work and pulling them here," he muttered, scribbling once again on his pad. He grunted at whatever answer he received. "Very good. Alright, I need to verify that it was charms and what type is causing the problem. Where should I start?"

"That building. Start there. Most of our patients came from there."

"Right." Pulling his shoulders back, he marched for the building.

Belatedly, I realized the obvious and called after him, "You're wearing an anti-sickness charm of some sort, right?"

"Of course!" he responded over his shoulder, not breaking stride.

Figured. I could never get one up on Sherard. Many people misjudged him because of the guyliner, and the red double-breasted coats he favored, because really, he looked like a theatrical pirate in search of a stage. But he was one of the sharpest men I'd ever met, and that was saying something.

Another thought struck and I called after him, "Do something about the rats too!"

He paused, glanced sharply back at me over his shoulder and demanded, "Why are you concerned about the rats?"

"Proven thing, on Earth at least," I explained succinctly as possible. "Most plagues and epidemics are carried by rodents."

Swearing, he gave me a grim nod. "I'll post extermination charms too."

I love a man who's quick on the uptake. I went back to cordoning off the roads, explaining over and over again to anyone trying to enter or leave that quarantine was in effect. No one was happy about this—surprise!—and I got more than a few arguments. I was glad that I was now able to say that the queen herself was sending in groceries, that it was being organized right now for delivery. That put some people's fears to rest. Enough so that I felt people wouldn't be trying to sneak out, at least.

When I hit the docks, it became a little more complicated,

just because the area was more open. There wasn't much to tie a rope off to, or a clear line of delineation. I finally snagged one of the foremen, explained to him what was happening and what I needed, and he was quick to arrange some heavy crates to help hold the ropes. One of the smartest things I'd ever done was come up with my swimming lessons program for the sailors and dock workers. Even if they didn't know me personally, everyone on the docks knew *of* me, and that reputation saved me in situations like this. They might not understand fully what I asked of them, but they were willing to take whatever orders I gave them, and that was all I needed at the moment.

Halfway down the docks, Reggie finally caught up with me. His ruddy skin glowed an alarming shade of fire-engine red, fair hair sticking up in every direction, portly frame jostling a little as he ran toward me. He wore a suit, a nice one, so I assumed he'd been in his office today and not the factories. Thank heavens for small favors, as that meant my message boy had caught up to him quickly.

"Jamie," he greeted me with wide blue eyes. "What's this about, my factories are invaded with a sickness?"

He must have heard my messenger wrong. I'd not had anything to write with, so sent a verbal plea for help. "No, not quite. Your workers. A majority of them bought a batch of bad anti-sickness charms and put them up in the apartments, and now everyone in the area is down with a bad influenza. We're estimating about six city blocks have been infected."

Reggie blanched. "I'd heard reports that more and more of my workers weren't reporting to work, but—the foreman was just going to fire them."

"No," I groaned, but wasn't really surprised. Half the reason why I'd contacted Reggie to begin with was to prevent this sort of misunderstanding. "They're deathly sick, Reggie. Please don't fire them. In fact, right now they can't report for work even if they wanted to. They're under quarantine."

He looked at the rope still in my hands, followed the line of it with his eyes. "That bad?"

"Bad enough that the queen is sending in groceries to feed people, as she doesn't want this to spread to the rest of the city," I threw in, seeing if I needed to bait him more or not. I didn't think I would need to. Reggie was the type that liked to be helpful, after all.

"She has? Bless our good queen." He looked quite proud of the woman for a moment, although he'd likely never met her in person. "Alright, you summoned me down here for a reason. What do you need help with?"

I loved Reggie. "First, can you write a message for me to take in to the workers, assuring them they're not fired and they'll be given full pay until the quarantine is lifted? I estimate it will take about two to four weeks."

"Done," he agreed instantly. "What else?"

"If you can talk to your fellow businessmen, the ones who own these company apartments, and get them to agree to do the same? It will ease a lot of fears."

"I can certainly do all of that, but you know that when my Emily hears of this, not to mention my mother and mother-in-law, they'll want to help in some way too."

"Good point." I thought about it. I wasn't sure of what common symptoms the influenza on this planet might have with Earth's, but from the way Sherard and Henri described it, it was more dangerous and contagious. I'd had the flu often enough in my life to know what sort of cleanup it involved. "Reggie, I'll be frank. This stuff is contagious as all get out. They're going to need very strong soap in order to clean anything they touch in the next few weeks. I'll send a letter to your family later tonight, explain the situation in depth, but for now could you give them the message that people just need new things down here? Strong soaps, blankets, towels, things they can use to replace the ones already infected."

"I'll tell them first, then meet with the owners of Hartman & Hartman and Tender Textiles," he swore to me, already on fire with purpose. He was alive with energy, nearly vibrating in place, a man on a mission. "They're two of the biggest owners with company housing in this area. If I can get them to agree, the rest will fall in line. Those two own most of the area anyway."

"I owe you dinner," I responded in heartfelt relief. He'd just saved me a lot of time and arguments.

He gave me a boyish grin. "Looking forward to it. I'll touch base with you again in a few hours so you know of our prog-

Charms and Death and Explosions (oh my!) 153

ress."

I waved him off, watching him go for a moment. I now totally understood how he'd charmed Emily Davenforth into marrying him. What a good guy. If it wasn't frowned upon by this culture's rules, I would bear hug him and squeeze the stuffing right out. I might do it anyway if he really pulled all of that off.

My texting pad rang in my pocket and I pulled it out, pinning the cordon rope under my elbow so I could write a responce.

It was from Sherard: *Our bad charms.*

I took a moment to lift my face to the sky and swear. I hated being right. Dropping my head back down, I scribbled back, *Ok. Reggie promises pay to his people. Working on others.*

Glad to hear it. Will pass the word.

That should relieve many people's minds. I knew in their shoes, that would've been one of my main worries. Finances always were a worry, a weight dragging at the spirit. Remembering what I'd said to Sherard, I passed along: *Most diseases carried by rodents, FYI.*

I didn't need to see his face to know how Henri would react to that, but the only thing he said in response was: *I'll see to it.*

Good man. I almost put the pad back in my pocket before a thought struck. I scrawled out, *Ellie?*

It took a moment before she responded, *What, Jamie?*

How much of that rubbing alcohol do you have made up?

Report 12: I Despise Epidemics

    I found myself with cramping calves and feet by the time our reinforcements arrived. Granted, I was not accustomed to staying on my feet for long periods of time, which was likely the reason. I'd been darting about Dr. Cartwright's practice for several hours, examining the patients. As far as I could determine, the malady had been started by the charms, and reinforced every time they were exposed to the charm again. This particular strain seemed worse than the usual influenza—I blamed the addition of the Destroying Angel ink into the mix—as we'd already lost an infant and three elderly. High statistics indeed in just seven days.

    In an effort to cleanse the area and give these people a fighting chance to get well, I volunteered as one of the magicians responsible for cleaning out the bad charms. I'd need to witness their removal for the sake of the case anyway, so it was two birds with one stone. I took on several apartment buildings, applying true anti-sickness charms, trudging up multiple flights of steps, and removing any of the bad charms I could find. It meant, of course, that I had to stop at each apartment and explain the problem to the occupants before they'd allow me inside so that I could retrieve the charm. Usually each family had a collection of charms, not just one, but the one I hunted for often lurked in the collection. Not every apartment had one, only roughly seventy-five percent of them did, and half of those were Garner's charms. It was a deplorably high number and I could only believe proximity had stacked such odds in favor of this probability. The main shop for Garner's wares resided in the marketplace closest to this neighborhood. Of course most of the goods would wind up here.

Our Kingsmen, several other doctors, magicians, and roughly two dozen policemen arrived and started in on a different apartment as I worked. Captain Gregson coordinated several officers outside to help patrol the area outside of the quarantine line, to make sure people didn't try to either enter or leave. Of course, some people who lived here wanted back in, and that was quite a different kettle of fish to deal with. I wasn't sure what the protocol for that would be, as epidemics weren't something I had experience with.

The last apartment on the fourth floor was locked, with no one at home. I marked it on my reference sheet so that I remembered to return to it later. A few of the apartments had been unoccupied, and I assumed the families to be at the doctor's office. A return visit would be necessary. I turned away and wearily made for the stairs. Mercy, I needed something to eat. I'd skipped lunch altogether; not only was my stomach complaining at my negligence, but my energy was dropping sharply. Something of sustenance would be greatly appreciated. I didn't dare hope for the opportunity to rest. That would not come for hours yet.

Halfway down the stairs, I could hear my partner's voice carrying up the narrow brick stairwell.

"—yes, ma'am, don't you worry. We have a Royal Mage himself combing through, looking for those bad charms. And my partner, he's a Magical Examiner, one of the best in the city. He's looking through this building right now. In fact, I think Henri was applying good anti-sickness charms as well as removing the bad."

"Oh, bless him, bless them both," a raspy female voice responded. "But what are we to do for food if we can't leave? And my husband went to work this morning, can he come back in?"

"The queen is sending in groceries for everyone. It's being organized now and the first delivery should come in this evening. You'll get one every morning. As for your husband, there's quite a few people on the other side of the line. We're examining everyone first. If they're already sick, they come straight in. Is your husband sick?"

"No, he's the only one who wasn't."

"Then he'll be given the option. He can stay outside—there's temporary lodging being arranged for people—so he can still go to work if he wants to. Or he can choose to come in and help nurse all of you. Either way, he's got a guaranteed paycheck. I spoke to the owner myself and Mr. Robichard swore no one has to worry about being fired or getting anything less than a full paycheck."

A choked-off sob came from the woman. I could imagine her relief. So many worries to juggle, none of which she had the power to solve, and my partner was relieving each worry one by one. Although, it was news to me that Jamie had already spoken and arranged things with Reggie. When in the world had she managed that?

Turning the next corner, I came into view of the two women and discovered the error of my assumption. The reason why Jamie walked with the woman was that they carried three small children between the two of them. The mother looked dead on her feet, beyond exhausted and ill, as did her children. Two boys and a girl, the youngest appearing to be no more than a few months old, the eldest perhaps five. Jamie had a child on either hip, leaving the baby for her mother to carry. This, no doubt, was one of my missing tenants.

"Jamie," I called down to her, watched her head come up and locate me at the landing above her. "Do you need assistance?"

"I'm good," she denied, "but get the baby, please."

Charms and Death and Explosions (oh my!)

My calves sharply protested at the thought of climbing back up the steps. I mentally told them to hush and went down, shifting my bag onto my right shoulder to free up both arms. The mother gratefully handed the sleeping baby over to me, and I could feel her arms shaking during the transfer. Jamie's request for assistance made more sense now. I took the baby gingerly, not having the broadest experience with small children. Then again, perhaps I should view this as good practice for when my own nephew arrived in a few months.

The child felt hot in my arms, a heavy weight who was not sleeping peacefully, judging by the frown on that small face. I carried her carefully in the crook of my elbow, trying to disturb her as little as possible. She needed her sleep. Looking up at her mother, I inquired gently, "I'm Dr. Henri Davenforth, Detective Edward's partner. By any chance, are you a tenant of apartment 304 or 420?"

"420," she answered tiredly.

"In that case, madam, let us escort you up, and then if you'll allow me to examine your apartment, I'll remove any bad charms and replace them with a quality anti-sickness charm."

"She said you would," the mother responded with an inclination of the head toward Jamie. "Thank you, Doctor, of course you may."

"Excellent. Then do lead the way." I followed her up, Jamie right at my heels, not at all struggling under the combined weight of two children. I envied her strength some days.

Upon entry to apartment 420, it became readily apparent that the mother had not cleaned in days. Dirty dishes lay piled haphazardly in the small kitchen sink, the great room had nests of dirty towels, discarded blankets, and glasses of half-consumed water lying about. From somewhere in the house stank a collection of dirty diapers.

I could tell the matron was embarrassed by the state of the house, and I deliberately kept a bland expression on my face to save her any further embarrassment. Even if my nose did want to wrinkle at the stench.

As I went through the small two-bedroom apartment, searching for charms, I could hear Jamie in the main room.

"Mrs. Dodd, let me help you straighten things up here. At least until your husband can get back to you. It's important that all of you are in a clean environment to recover with. Tell you what, you get the kids settled, I'll tackle the dishes and the garbage."

"Oh no, I can't let you do that, you've got more important things to do," Mrs. Dodd protested.

"Not really, not for the next hour. I'm just extra hands while the magicians do the magical legwork. How many clean diapers do you have left?"

I smiled as I examined the walls of the couple's bedroom. Mrs. Dodd might as well give in. Jamie was nothing if not determined.

There were in fact four anti-sickness charms upon the walls of the master bedroom, children's bedroom, and one in the miniscule bathroom. All of them were of very poor craftsmanship and one of them, once again, Garner's. My anger with the man grew upon every apartment I entered. The deplorable conditions of these people because of his work was simply inexcusable. The demands of a man's greed came at too high of a price.

Depending upon the nature and strength of a charm, there were different spells used to dispel the charm's magical properties before rending the paper into ash. For a charm of this low-level caliber, I used only the most elementary of spells to first strip the magic from it, dissipating it harmlessly into the air, then disintegrating it into fine ash into my hand. I disposed of it promptly by flushing it down the sink.

I admit to using a few cleaning spells on the bathroom, the children's room, and the master bedroom. Since Jamie had taken it upon herself to help this particular family—and indeed, they sorely needed it—it behooved me to make myself useful as well. I cast several anti-rodent charms while I was about it, as I saw evidence that at least a few mice had taken up residence in the walls. As I exited the children's room, Jamie caught my eye and winked at me in approval. I flushed a little (of course she'd caught my muttered spell casting) and quickly focused on Mrs. Dodd. She was seated at the table, making out a list of groceries and necessities, it looked like. Judging by the slow, careful way she printed each letter, I judged her to be barely literate. I was more surprised she was literate at all, as most of the working class could barely write their own name.

"Mrs. Dodd?" I called her attention to me in a gentle voice.

Blinking tired blue eyes up at me, she responded, "Yes, Doctor?"

"I've found four charms in your house, is that correct? There are no others?"

"Just those four," she confirmed with a shallow nod.

"Three of them were entirely useless, they have no power in them whatsoever." I watched her lips tighten in an angry line. "The fourth charm, the one in the bathroom, was in fact the one that caused everyone to be ill."

Jamie paused in washing one of the dishes and gave me a sharp look. "Garner's?"

"Yes," I confirmed in a clipped tone. "Mrs. Dodd, I noticed that you don't remove a charm once it's expired. I found a small stack of them in the corner of your window. Is there a reason for that?"

"The refuse man won't take them," she explained

wearily. "And I was told not to burn them, that's dangerous. Didn't know what to do with them."

It was a common problem, and I'd heard this explanation more than once. "The refuse man will be given a stern talking to. He's supposed to take them. He doesn't because it's a cost for him to dispose of them, and he's cutting corners by avoiding the problem. But that's a cost the city compensates him for; he has no excuse. Even if he gives you such trouble, if you'll bring the charms to Fourth Precinct and report the problem, I will take care of it. Old charms piled up like that can eventually bleed into each other and cause a very dangerous magical back-blow."

Mrs. Dodd's pale face turned ghostly white. "How dangerous?"

"House fires are not uncommon," I answered frankly. "So please don't do that, and spread the word to your neighbors not to do that either. Even if the refuse man gives you trouble, bring them to me, I'll properly dispose of them for you."

She nodded vigorously. "I'll do that."

"Good. Now, the anti-sickness charm I've applied in your bathroom is a very strong one. It's good for five years. If you will remove it occasionally and let it soak in the sun, it will last a good seven years. It runs off of light and water. Just don't let it get wet directly and you'll have no issues with it. I highly recommend you purchase any other charms from Roberson & Sons, Inc. They're very reputable and their son is a hedge wizard; he's got quite a good eye for charms. No bad product is allowed through their doors. They're a little more expensive than a bargain bin charm, but affordable enough for your purposes, and guaranteed to work."

"I'll remember," she swore to me. "I'll pass that along as well."

"Very good, please do." To Jamie, I reported in a lower voice, "There's another apartment in this building I couldn't get into, 304. If you see anyone go in there, please report it to me so I can double back for them. Other than that, this building is clear. I'll start on the one next door."

"That's fine," she encouraged with a worried eye on me, "but stop by the cordoned line off Maple, would you? A nice vendor has pulled up there and he's feeding all of us for free. Fish and chips."

That sounded heavenly indeed and my mouth instantly watered. "Say that sort of thing sooner," I scolded.

Chuckling, she shooed me off. "Go, I've got this."

I dearly wanted to, but I had one further inquiry to make first. "You've clearly been in more recent contact with people than I have—are we allowed outside of quarantine?"

"Nope, we're stuck like everyone else. But Dr. Cartwright's brother-in-law has empty rooms at his house and he's invited us all to stay there. The two-story white house catawampus to the doctor's office? That house."

Trust her to think of the logistics while I ran about like a chicken with its head cut off.

"Oh, and your mother went to both our apartments and packed a bag for us," she tacked on, as if suddenly recalling the detail. "They're supposed to arrive tonight. She's also sending in some food for all of us. And she's heading some sort of ladies' drive in order to get new clothes, bedding, and towels in here. A lot of this will have to be tossed, it'll be too contaminated to salvage."

Yes, so it would, but... "And when did you organize all of that?"

"Henri," she responded with asperity, as if I'd failed to recognize the point, "I didn't do anything but tell Reggie what we needed in here. He's the one who passed the message along, and it's your mother spearheading all of this. I take no credit for it."

She'd thought to ask for aid, so in my opinion, she deserved at least part of the credit. But I sensed the argument would fall flat upon its face and didn't choose to pursue it. "I'll thank all of them properly later. I'll be in the next building if you need me."

"Roger." Jamie returned to doing the dishes.

I left, once again heading down the stairs. Even with six men actively hunting down the charms and replacing them, it would not be a day's work to clear everything out and replace it. More like three to four days. Three to four days of climbing stairs. Heaven deliver me.

I was perhaps halfway down the stairwell when my nose picked up the scent. Wood smoke had a distinctive smell to it, as did gas fireplaces, but this was neither of those—a far more pungent, acrid scent that scorched the interior nostrils. I'd only encountered that scent with particular instances—when magic burned.

I nearly tripped over my own feet, I moved so fast, desperately getting past the doors and walls blocking my view, to the first window I could find. It didn't take someone with magical sight to see that something had gone horrifically wrong. Something lay outside near the rubbish bins in a multihued blaze of smoke and sparks, alarming all who viewed it. Swearing roundly, I spun about and headed down the stairs, moving faster than safe.

Even as I took the stairs nearly two at a time, I realized what must have happened. Word had spread quickly since our arrival that the charms were bad, that they were what caused the sickness to begin with. Some fool had likely gotten it in their head to destroy the charms despite our warnings, and of course, people were quite accustomed to using fire to rid themselves of paper.

Although in this case, it was the worst possible method.

I slapped the door aside, spilling my way out onto the sidewalk, and raced for the burning pile. People shifted to let me through, fortunately, and I wished I had the breath to urge them back, but the mad sprint down had winded me completely. I barely had the breath to use any spells and contain the madness.

Even as I sprinted across the street and towards the scene, the small bundle there caught the neighboring stack of rubbish alight. It looked to be a communal burn pile, no doubt set aside for this purpose, as hexes were painted on all sides of the low stone wall to prevent sparks from spreading outwards. But its only configuration was for restraining conflagrations, not anything released by the blaze. Even as I watched, the fire released the magic of the charm and an eerie, unnatural green of virus spread out over the watchers' heads like an evil cloud.

Skidding to a halt three feet away, I threw out a containment spell first to prevent any other sickness from spreading, although it was a bit of damming the river after a flood. Still, I didn't want a face full of the stuff.

"Doctor!"

I glanced up, relieved to see Marshall running toward me. "Can you do an air dispel for this area and clear it? I'll take care of the charm."

"Of course, sir," Marshall assured me, already drawing out a wand.

As Marshall had more magical ability than I, I left him to it without worrying about his casting, focusing on the origin of the problem.

"What's the problem 'ere, gents?" a man demanded of me. He looked a little worse for wear, although I couldn't discern if drink or sickness made him wobble so. Perhaps a bit of both.

I ignored him, my entire attention on the sickly cast of the air about us. That grey-green hue made me nauseous just to behold. I could see from the saturation of the color that he had burned quite the stack of charms, although I could only guess at the exact number. Two dozen, perhaps? I drew a wand hastily, mentally revising which spell would be the most effective in dispelling the fire, and cast it with quick, clipped intonation. With the papers curling about the edges and smoldering, I cast two others in quick succession, dispelling the magic left on the paper and cleansing the area generally to wipe out any hint of sickness or aggravated magical properties. Only then did I focus on him. "Are you the one who burned it?"

Justified by his own actions, he jerked his chin to indicate the blaze. "Burn pile. No harm done."

"You imbecile," I grated between clenched teeth. "By burning a charm like this, you've released all of the magic contained in it. You're lucky it didn't explode like a bomb."

He was outraged until that last sentence, then the import of what I'd said hit him and he stared at the burn pile in silent horror, jaw hanging with words unspoken.

"And," Marshall stated brusquely, "you just released another wave of the sickness over everyone standing nearby. Well done."

"Now, hang on, I was cleansing it!" the man protested wildly. "Fire cleanses things!"

"Fire does not cleanse magical charms," Marshall argued back, at the end of his patience. He jabbed a finger toward the soot still smoldering. "And if not for Dr. Davenforth's quick reflexes, you and the two-dozen people watching this would have likely been dead in three days. Kindly do not burn charms!"

Abashed, the man hung his head and refused to

Charms and Death and Explosions (oh my!)

answer.

I hoped that message would spread but unfortunately most people were cooped up in their homes now, not chatting with their neighbors. I had no doubt that some other idiot would think to try this, to solve the problem, and that possibility would keep me up for several nights in paranoia. As if I didn't have enough to worry about.

I stood on the sidewalk and looked about me, nearly overwhelmed for a moment. All I saw about me was sickness, frustration, lethargy, and tears as the living struggled to survive. I stank of sweat after so much unaccustomed exercise, dirt crusted my hands and wedged under my fingernails, and the state of my clothes was not to be spoken of. The people around me were in no better state, having not the energy to launder their clothes or go through the struggle of bathing. They would need to haul water up from the wells, as there was no such thing as indoor plumbing in this area, and some of them didn't have the strength to haul up buckets of water to their apartments.

So many people passed me, trying to assist ailing family members, coughing, hacking, sneezing, their skin pale except high spots of color on their cheeks. They looked weary and done-in. I felt a margin of sympathy for them, but mostly anger fueled my emotions. This deplorable state, this suffering, could have been avoided if not for the arrogance of two men.

My anger ignited my motivation, and I would have immediately tackled the next apartment, but my stomach chose that moment to grumble in loud complaint of its neglect. Deciding I needed sustenance before tackling that other apartment, I followed my partner's directions and headed for the food cart. The street was crowded on either side by the apartment buildings sitting so close together, and I shortly found myself grateful for Jamie's general directions. I couldn't see the food cart until I'd walked halfway down, my view was so obstructed. As I walked, I hit myself with a general cleaning charm, as I had no desire to either carry the sickness to the food vendor or eat in this state. The vendor was one I recognized, as he frequently put up his stall near the police academy. I'd visited him often while attending the academy some decade ago. Seaton stood near the stall inhaling a basket of golden fried fish and chips, wearing the expression of a man who had found heaven.

"Davenforth!" the vendor hailed me, a wide grin on his face. He leaned through the narrow opening in the front of his cart, his hands braced upon the thin wooden bar that extended over the side. "Fancy seeing you here. It's been a number of years since you came to my cart."

"Indeed it has, Mr. Houghton," I greeted before inhaling deeply. "The smell alone tells me that this will be delightful, as always. Have you any of your chowder?"

"I do, I do." His ham-sized hands were already moving toward the small stove behind him. "Want some of that?"

"If you don't mind." No one made clam chowder as good as this man. I'd yet to wriggle the recipe out of him, but it would happen eventually. I was determined on this point. As I waited for a bowl to be served up, I greeted the Royal Mage eating nearby. "Seaton. How goes it?"

He had to swallow before he could answer. "I've cleared two buildings, but had to stop and help organize people. I'll show you the map of who's been allotted what so we don't repeat each other's efforts. You?"

"Some fool tried to burn a stack of charms." At his open wince, I added sourly, "We contained it. Marshall came and helped me dissipate the area before another wave of sickness could hit us."

"I'll try to discourage people from burning anything. Have you seen Jamie?"

Charms and Death and Explosions (oh my!) 167

"Just now, yes. She's helping a young mother. Mrs. Dodd's husband apparently wasn't ill and is outside of the quarantine line at this moment. I understand quite a few families are in a similar situation, but they can enter if they wish?"

"Yes, as long as they understand they can't leave again for three weeks. We estimate it will take two weeks for this to run its course, but it will be another week before no one is contagious."

I winced at the thought of being cooped up in this section of the city for three weeks. "Us too?"

"As long as we don't get ill ourselves, and we can pass a health inspection, they'll let us out sooner than that. But it will require staying in quarantine outside of the line for forty-eight hours to make sure we don't show any symptoms." Seaton leaned in to confide, "I've got another shift of workers getting ready to come in here, but it will take a few days to organize everyone and the supplies, so we have to tough it out until then."

That was all understandable. I nodded, resigned to my fate for the next several days, and accepted the warm bowl of chowder. The first spoonful was sheer ambrosia, and I sighed happily. At least good food was to be had during this turbulent time.

"Davenforth," Seaton murmured for my ears alone, "I do have one fear. It might be irrational, but…."

I eyed him sideways. "What?"

"We've already had several deaths from this. What if we have another person who wants revenge for that, and attempts their own version of a car bomb?"

As much as I wished I could dismiss the concern, I couldn't. "It's entirely feasible someone will react that way. But who could they blame? The makers of the charms are already deceased. The shop owners? They are victims as well."

"They might not see it that way," he cautioned. "They might blame the person who sold it to them. After all, they're supposed to be screening for quality. These charms are supposed to be viable."

"You and I both know that a non-magical person doesn't have a guaranteed method of ascertaining if a charm is good or bad," my shoulders slumped as I said this, "but that's unfortunately not common knowledge. Curse it, you're likely right. I'll request protection for the various shop owners for the next month and hope that deters anyone with vengeance in mind."

"Good. Hopefully it doesn't come to that, but I'd rather not have another case complicating this one."

Yes, I must agree on that. I went back to eating my chowder, my body quite pleased with the sustenance making its way into my belly. In fact, I requested another bowl, and was on my third when two frantic looking men approached the cart.

"Are you Royal Mage Seaton?" one of them demanded of Seaton.

"I am indeed," Seaton responded, wiping his hand of the fish oil before offering it. "Who might you gentlemen be?"

"Dodd, Mark Dodd," he responded, taking Seaton's hand in a quick shake. "This is Butcher. Sir, we've got family inside at home, wives and kids who are sick, but we're told we're not allowed in because we're healthy. Can't you override this, let us in? Our wives, they can't be taking it all on their own—"

Seaton held up both hands. "Wait, wait, I think there's a misunderstanding in play here. Gentlemen, the deal is this: You have a choice of whether you go in or not. If you choose to go in, you can't come back out for three weeks. Your bosses have guaranteed you'll have pay either way, but your freedom will be cut off for three weeks to leave the area. Is that what you choose to do?"

The men exchanged confused glances.

"Sir, that's not what the officers up on Sea Lane said," Butcher informed Seaton with a shake of the head. "They said if you're healthy, you're not going in."

"Oh, devil take it," Seaton grumbled. "That's not what I ordered at all."

Scraping up the last bite from my bowl, I inquired, "Mr. Butcher, by any chance, are you the tenant of room 304 in that building?"

Butcher blinked at me. "I am, sir."

"Dr. Henri Davenforth, Magical Examiner," I introduced myself belatedly. "I'm one of the men replacing the bad charms that caused all of this. I believe your family is still with Dr. Cartwright, being examined. Mr. Dodd, my partner is with your wife and children helping to clean things up a little so the children can rest comfortably. Gentlemen, why don't you ask Mr. Houghton if he will be kind enough to share a few bowls of chowder with your families; that way your children have something nutritious and easy to eat tonight for dinner?"

Houghton nodded encouragement to this, his hands already moving over the small counter to dish up the bowls.

"And I'll escort you both in myself," I finished, trying to keep my exhaustion out of my smile. "Mr. Butcher, if you'll let me into your apartment first, so that I can cleanse the place magically, you may, of course, go to your family afterwards."

"Bless you, Doctor," Butcher said with open relief. "I'll do that."

"Your partner is with my family?" Dodd seemed quite astonished at this. "Have they taken a turn? Worse than the others?"

"No, no," I hastened to assure him. "She's a detective,

non-magical. Detective Edwards is intent on helping anyone who needs an extra hand, and your wife was so exhausted trying to manage all three children, Edwards stepped in to offer assistance. I assure you, they have medications and are resting now. There's no cause for undue alarm."

"Oh. Thank you, Doctor." Dodd seemed on the verge of sinking to the ground and having a well-earned moment of hysterics. I sympathized entirely. In fact, if he chose to do so, I would be obliged to join him.

Handing Houghton my empty bowl, I accepted two full ones from him. Seaton waved himself off, heading towards Sea Lane and likely going to give the officers on duty there a blistering lecture on listening properly to instructions the first time. To the two harried husbands, I encouraged, "Come along. It'll be fine, I promise."

Report 13: An Anniversary

Sometime in the chaos of the afternoon, we received word that a panicked individual in Fourth District tried to set fire to several charms. It caused an explosion that took out half of his apartment building, prompting Seaton to teleport in order to take care of it. It violated the quarantine, which certain doctors were unhappy about, but I didn't think Seaton could contaminate anyone, considering the very powerful anti-sickness charm that he wore.

When he returned, Seaton brought back word that news of the epidemic had spread via an article in the morning news, one somehow featuring Jamie's picture. He'd also learned that ours was not the only outbreak. Another one on the far end of Fourth Precinct's jurisdiction had occurred. It was in the beginning stages, not as advanced as the problem here, but several of the specialists we needed had been diverted to stamp that out before it could grow any larger. The help that we expected would be delayed several days.

None of us were best pleased to hear it.

Near midnight, I finally stumbled to the house where we were supposed to lodge for the next few days. Despite the lateness of the hour, I found that most of the lights were on in the main floor, with people coming in and out, so I assumed we still functioned in round-the-clock emergency mode. I myself had worked eighteen hours and was due a hot meal and a bed.

The house was a nice one for the area—well-kept, the lawn precisely manicured in its cuts, the furniture that I could see through the windows well appointed. I had no idea what Dr. Cartwright's brother did for his living, but it was apparently well enough for him to afford this nice home. As I approached the door, I debated what to do. Should I knock? Just enter? It seemed rude to do the latter, but I had no desire to wake the sleeping occupants of the house, either. Fortunately, as I made the porch, the door opened and one of the Kingsmen stepped out. Bennett gave me a nod but passed without a word. I assumed him to be on some errand.

I slipped past him then paused in the carpeted foyer, unsure of my direction. The stairs were straight in front of me, which I assumed led to bedrooms, but the idea of just brazenly going up and searching for an empty room sat ill with me. As I paused, I heard a faint singing coming from my right. I recognized the voice instantly, as I'd heard Jamie sing often in the almost three months I'd known her. I swear, instead of the Shinigami Detective, she should be known as the Singing Detective.

Following my ears, I stepped through a front parlor and toward two wooden sliding doors, ones that I supposed led to a library. I was mistaken, as they were half-open to reveal a nursery. My indomitable partner sat in a rocking chair, an infant in her arms, singing a lullaby I'd never heard before.

Her tone was gentle, sweet, a promise of warmth and safety. "—soft the drowsy hours are sleeping, hill and dale in slumber sleeping, I my loving vigil keeping, all through the night."

I came to a natural stop at the doorway and watched her for a moment. I rarely saw Jamie in a tender state of mind, affectionate and peaceful. I knew her to be good with children, I'd seen several instances of that, but this was the first time that she looked more motherly to my eyes. I stood there silently, taking in the scene, my heart aching. Any chance she had of being a mother had been

Charms and Death and Explosions (oh my!) 173

robbed from her by Belladonna. Jamie's system was so unstable that the changes pregnancy required would undo her utterly. It would kill both her and the child, likely in the first trimester.

Jamie Edwards would be a wonderful mother. And she'd never get the chance.

My head fell back for a moment, strong emotion rippling through my facial muscles as I controlled the urge to violently swear. If Belladonna were still alive, I'd murder her myself with my bare hands for all of the harm she'd done my friend.

"Sir?"

I snapped about sharply, unaware that someone had come up behind me. I took him to be Mr. Cartwright from his appearance, as he bore a striking resemblance to the good doctor. Not wishing to disturb the child peacefully slumbering in Jamie's arms, I quietly shut the door, muting the lullaby to a mere whisper. "Yes. You must be Mr. Cartwright."

"James," he offered, extending a hand.

"Pleasure," I returned, shaking his hand. "Dr. Henri Davenforth."

"Ah, Detective Edwards' partner," he responded in an enlightened tone. "I'm glad you've finally come in, she was quite worried about you. Come, this way. There's still dinner to be had in the kitchen. We've kept it warm on the stove."

"Bless you, sir," I responded, as food sounded quite divine at that moment.

He led me through a formal dining room and into a kitchen with a large farmhouse table, white cabinets, and butcher block tops. The place was clean, but in a state of higgledy-piggledy, I assumed from the many people eating at all hours. He ushered me to a seat, which I gratefully took, and loaded up a plate on my behalf. It was a lovely concoction of glazed ham, mashed potatoes, green beans, and fluffy biscuits.

I tucked into it with hearty thanks, not minding the company when Mr. Cartwright sat nearby.

"Has the situation improved out there?"

"We still have patients who need medical attention, but everyone has food in their houses, and we've got a third of the houses cleared of the bad charms," I filled him in between bites. "We're making steady progress. I expect we won't see any overt signs of improvement for another week, sadly."

"I'm glad you came as you did," Mr. Cartwright responded with transparent sincerity. "Charles was worried, and rightly so, but couldn't get any of the authorities interested in responding. I guess because so many sicknesses sweep through this section of town, it's old news to them. He couldn't seem to get it through their heads that this was different. That it was dangerous because charms were likely involved."

"I'm equally glad that our young officer stopped by the desk and randomly saw his call for help. I might not have known about this situation for days otherwise." In fact, the idea that I might well have missed that telegram scared me witless. So many of the sick were either elderly or infants. They would not have survived the onslaught of the influenza, not with that sickness charm constantly reinforcing their illness, giving their bodies no respite.

"Yes, so Detective Edwards said." Mr. Cartwright paused, eyeing me with a trace of caution. "Forgive me for asking, but...her name is familiar to me. I read an article this morning in the paper detailing the destruction of Belladonna. That is the Shinigami Detective, is it not?"

I paused with a fork halfway to my mouth and mentally cursed. The anniversary. With all of the madness of the epidemic, I had quite overlooked that the anniversary was tomorrow. Or today, considering the time. Had anyone else read that article? Likely so, if he'd seen it. I looked him right in the eye. If he started some outcry because of her reputation, I would not be merciful. "She is."

He sat back, puffing out an astonished breath. "I thought she was, because of the name, and her likeness in the paper. It could only be her. But it's hard to reconcile her reputation with the woman I met this afternoon. She's so…"

"Charming? Personable? Kind?" I filled in dryly. He did not seem inclined to make a scene. Good. "Yes, many are surprised by her true nature. You realize, I hope, that her reputation came from a singular act. An act forced upon her in order to survive. It does not define the woman as a whole."

"No," he murmured in thoughtful agreement, staring steadfastly at the table. "I can see that it doesn't. She was so tender with my daughter earlier, giving both my wife and I a break, as we couldn't get Emma to settle. She sang her to sleep. I didn't recognize the lullaby, but she has a lovely voice."

"Yes, she does. She sings often." I chose not to comment on the song itself. Jamie didn't care if people knew she was from another world, but I remained more cautious about divulging that information. People were not tolerant of differences and Jamie was already very different from the women in this society. It would do her no favors to add upon them.

His eyes returned to me as I continued eating. "How did the two of you become partners, if you don't mind my asking?"

"There was a case some three months ago that required a person with magical training to investigate it. You heard of the case with the Night Foxes? Yes, that one. Jamie was automatically assigned to it, because of her reputation, and then I was thrown into the mix to assist her. It turns out we're a rather fine team, and our captain asked to make it permanent. We'd become rather good friends by the end of the case, and agreed." I shrugged, as it was a simple enough story. If you cut out all of the near-death experiences and drama that occurred during that time.

"Does that mean there are that many magical cases that it can keep you both occupied?"

"Not quite. Or at least, not at first. What cases Jamie took on that didn't involve magic, she normally worked herself, bringing on a junior member of the force to help train and mentor. I'd say half of the cases handed to us actually require my expertise." Which was just the right ratio, in my opinion. Any more than that and I wouldn't be able to keep up with the lab work that Sanderson refused to do.

"I see. I'm relieved to hear it. The thought of magical crimes becoming common place is not one that I relish." Shaking his head, he moved to a different topic. "I'm afraid space is limited here, as we're housing a dozen of you during the course of the next few days. RM Seaton assured me that you wouldn't mind sharing a room with him. Is that correct?"

"He and I are good friends," I reassured my host. "We'll be fine in the same room. Don't worry over that, we're all grateful to have a place to lay our heads."

"My wife and I are very happy to help. Relieved, really, at a chance for paying your help back. There are only two bathing chambers upstairs, I'm afraid, one at either end of the hall. But there are clean towels stocked inside each, and you may, of course, use any of the soaps available in the room."

"Thank you." I tucked away the last bit of ham and sighed in satisfaction. "My compliments to the cook, it was very fine."

He ducked his head at the compliment, pleased. "You're quite welcome. Please, let me show you up."

The next six days passed by with tedium and exhaustion. We divided up the workload amongst us, tackling each apartment in turn, stripping out the bad charms, replacing them with a good charm, then disposing of the ones not needed for evidence. It required repeating the same questions and answers over and over to the point of nausea. Jamie, McSparrin, and four of the other officers called on scene handled everything non-charm related, and I did not envy them their jobs. I believe Jamie was only able to manage because of her inhuman stamina. McSparrin kept up with her through sheer willpower.

The influenza was so much worse than the normal type. It had all of the symptoms of a normal influenza, but with the magical boost at its source, it attracted like viruses. People who should have been miserably ill instead tottered on the edge of dangerously ill, even people who had excellent health. I held many a person's hand, saw the fear and desperation in their eyes, and swore to them that we'd do everything in our power to save them. Only some believed me, I think. Hope takes energy to cultivate and these people had little to spare.

It took considerable cleansing spells to get the magical influence of the bad sickness charms out of the air, and only when we'd achieved moderate success at this did we make any headway. People's normal cleanly habits fell by the wayside during their sickness, and I'd waded into more than one apartment filled with leaking garbage, soiled linens, and pails of vomit. The assault on my nostrils was horrific, but not as much as the knowledge that these people suffered under such conditions with no energy to improve their own environment. I do believe I used as many cleaning charms as I did magical clarifying ones.

Warner, bless her soul, sent in a large batch of the rubbing alcohol, and Jamie immediately drafted Penny to help her spread it about and educate people on its use. With that solution's addition, we were able to cut down on the amount of cleaning charms, and the air smelled sharp and acidic instead of sickening after that.

Anyone who works in a hospital understands that caretaking can be particularly exhausting. While we had many specialists and doctors on scene, they still had to work nearly eighteen hours a day, and that took its toll very quickly. In an effort to keep them from dropping where they stood, we received orders to switch with a new set of professionals at the six-day mark. I must say we were all very glad to hear of it and only spent the bare amount of time necessary to catch our replacements up to date on the situation before thankfully handing the reins over.

We were given an official examination, which all of us passed, thanks to the anti-sickness charm amulets that Seaton and I had made sure everyone wore at all times. After the doctors cleared us, we loaded up in a wagon—the only vehicle both charmed and large enough to carry the entire group out—and went to a hostel across the street cleared for our use with orders to not step even a toe outside of the building for forty-eight hours.

At this moment, staring at the very inviting double bed in my room—away from Seaton's interesting sleeping habits—the concept of staying forty-eight hours inside of the building did not bother me in the slightest. They'd be lucky if I chose to leave this bed in the next forty-eight hours.

Shucking off my jacket, I tossed my bag to the carpet, toed off my shoes, and flopped gracelessly onto the mattress, face-first. Oh how lovely, the sheets were freshly laundered. I wallowed, snuggling further in, not caring that my nose pressed into the linens.

My body thrummed with exhaustion, an almost audible hum of tension and unhappiness. I could feel darkness encroach on my vision and the thought vaguely tantalized me that if I took off my suspenders, and properly got under the covers, I would rest better. I should do that.

Energy to move, I summon thee.

Hmm. That clearly failed.

A soft tap sounded at the door before it opened a creak. "Henri? Are you decent? Oh boy. You didn't fall asleep like that, did you?"

I turned my head just enough to stare at her from one eye. "How do you have the energy to check on people?"

Jamie snorted amusement. "Some of us possess more energy than others. Our hostess, Mrs. Kerr, is offering us a late lunch/early dinner. You interested?"

I thought of food, and while that did sound nice, my body was more interested in rest. More to the point, the idea of climbing down and back up the stairs to reach the room sounded utterly vile and I shuddered at the thought. "No, thank you."

Frowning, she crossed into the room and put a hand to my forehead. "Are you sick? I thought the only way that you'd turn down food was if you're dying."

"Just fatigued," I assured her, the words dragging. I could hear my own weariness in my voice. It was likely even more obvious to her. Although I liked the feeling of her hand against my skin. It was comforting, for some reason that I could not define.

She smoothed back a curl dangling over my forehead, nodding in understanding, but the frown continued to linger upon her features. "Alright. I'll let you sleep. But get under the covers, alright?"

I groaned in compliance, wallowing about like a seal until I got my arms under me. The door closed with a soft thump behind her, and I shed clothes down to my underthings before slipping back onto the bed, under the covers this time. I barely got my head situated on the pillow when the land of dreams rose up and snatched me away.

Jamie's Additional Report: FREEEEEDOM

I have never seen Henri that exhausted. I mean, he turned down FOOD. I thought he'd have to be at death's door for that to happen. Then again, I understood why, as he'd run about like a chicken with its head cut off for seven days straight. Sixteen to eighteen-hour days, a week straight—that would push anyone into exhaustion. It would have done me in too if I didn't have enhanced stamina and muscles.

Letting him sleep, I wandered back downstairs and into the kitchen. Mrs. Kerr stood at the stove fixing up hot sandwiches for anyone who wanted one, Sherard and Gibson being the only two not flat in a bed at the moment. It made the very large farmhouse table look empty, with only two men sitting at it, but I felt sure it wouldn't stay that way.

Gibson looked up as I entered the room, asking, "Not even Davenforth's coming down for food?"

"He said to let him sleep, he's too tired to eat." Sherard drew back, his expression poleaxed and I nodded in sour amusement. "I know. Believe me, I know. I figured Henri was the type to demand a plate at his own funeral, and here he is, turning down food. We really worked him into the ground on this one."

"It's magical depletion," Gibson informed me, passing a tired hand over his face. "He was doing just as much as the rest of us but didn't have the means to really pull that off. Magically speaking, he doesn't have as much power as the rest of us. Even I have about double his strength."

I paused in pulling out a chair, looking at him sharply. "Are you serious? I knew there was a difference in strength, but *that* much?"

"He's not powerful, barely above the level of a hedge wizard," Sherard clarified for me. "What makes him formidable is his intelligence and how craftily he uses his power. He does more with less, and does it with such finesse that he often shames magicians who have three times his power. It's truly elegant, his spellcraft."

Gibson nodded along in support of this. "I can see why he's such an excellent Magical Examiner and why he maintains that he won't be good at any other line of work. Although I think he'd make a decent Kingsman, myself."

I snorted a laugh at that, taking my seat. Oh heavens, that felt lovely, being off my feet. Chairs were invented by a wonderful person who never got as much recognition as they should. I vote for their nomination of sainthood. "You'd never get Henri in shape enough to be a Kingsman. He thinks exercise is evil and loves food too much."

"He's actually lost a good stone since partnering up with you," Sherard observed dryly, pointing an accusing finger at me. "Probably because he's constantly chasing after you."

"It's good for him," I retorted sweetly. "But getting back to the point, Henri's magically depleted. Check. What does he need to recover?"

"A lot of rest, food, and no demands for him to do anything magical for a good week," Sherard rattled off. His dark eyes flicked thoughtfully toward the ceiling and in the general direction of where Henri lay sleeping. "The last part might be more difficult to pull off. We got severely sidetracked by this outbreak, but we still have a case to solve."

"Yes," I sighed in agreement. "So we do."

Our hostess came over and tutted over us. "You poor dears, and you didn't even get to celebrate the anniversary of Belladonna's passing. Here, I've got a cake coming in, we'll make a small go of it, alright?"

I caught the looks my friends shot me, the worry and concern they felt when reminded that we'd let the anniversary slip right past us. To my mind, that was a better way to go about it. I was quite happy to let it slip by. Still, I appreciated this woman's efforts and gave her a smile. "A cake sounds lovely."

Sherard shifted uneasily and leaned in to murmur, "Jamie, if you'd rather—"

With a slash of the hand, I cut him off, keeping my smile firmly in place. "I don't mind missing the celebration, but doesn't a cake sound good? If nothing else, we can celebrate being able to leave quarantine."

Perhaps my eyes adequately conveyed the message that if he tried to wrap me up in wool and pat me like a child, I would stab him with my fork. Sherard instantly backed down. "Of course. A cake sounds wonderful."

You wouldn't have really stabbed me with a fork.

You keep telling yourself that.

Report 14: My Mother, the Burglar

Ooooh, Henri~!

I'm gonna tell her you said that.

She already knows.

At least now I know how she's getting in.

Forty-eight hours passed and we were released from our quarantine. All of us unanimously voted to take another day off to recover, as some of us were still magically depleted from seven days of straight magical strain. I believe that the offer was made more for my benefit than anyone's, but we all agreed to it. We'd tackle the case again come Gather Day.

Jamie and I shared a cab back to our apartments, and I let my eyes rest as I slumped into the seat, swaying with the rocking of the carriage. I was still too tired—not exhausted as before—but not my usual self yet. I hoped that by the start of the work week, I'd be back on my feet once again. If nothing else, I wished for the energy to at least be functional.

"Curry tonight?" Jamie offered casually.

I pried open an eye, a tired grin etched across my face. "As if I ever refuse that offer."

"I'll need to get the ingredients, so say in about three hours from now?"

"That's fine." I patted my stomach gently, promising it excellent food soon. If my anatomy was capable of purring, it would have promptly done so.

The cabby pulled to the curb, I paid the man, and we went about the business of getting our bags and ourselves up to our apartments. I dragged anchor more than a mite as we trudged our way up the stairs. Jamie did not bound ahead of me, as she normally did, but made short work of the stairs. Clearly, despite all that had happened, she still had energy to spare. She cast me a glance as she headed for the top floor, and I waved her ahead. If I could bottle that energy, I'd make a small fortune.

To my surprise, I found my door unlocked. Strange, I knew I'd locked it before leaving. A vague sense of unease filled me as I pushed the door open. I hadn't been robbed, had I?

"There you are," Ophelia scolded, immediately leaping from her chair and rushing towards me. She wore one of her plain linen dresses, hair done up in a casual bun, so clearly she hadn't dropped by while in the neighborhood, but instead waited on me.

"No, of course I haven't been robbed," I sighed to myself, setting my bag down off to the side. "My mother is a picklock. I'd failed to remember that for a moment."

"Tosh," she scolded, enfolding me in a quick, fierce embrace. "Mrs. Henderson kindly let us in."

"That now explains matters," I commented, more in a rhetorical fashion. "Father."

"Henri." Rupert came to thump a hand against my back, his eyes taking me in from head to foot, a frown gathering. He, too, was in a casual dark day suit, clearly waiting on his only son to arrive home. "You look done in, son. Was it very bad?"

"It was definitely not good," I sighed in answer. I caught the door with my toes and shut it before shuffling off to my favorite chair. Ah, sitting was truly blissful.

My parents quickly came to sit on the other chairs, focused entirely on me. I saw their worry, their relief, and knew that they needed to hear the details. I had the energy for that, but had a thought to explore first. Now that my parents knew Jamie was from a different world— she had taken it upon herself to explain matters to them some weeks ago—I had the freedom to ask questions like: "Jamie has offered to make curry this evening for me. If you wish to try it, I'll need to tell her immediately so she knows to prepare more than two portions."

"Oh!" Ophelia perked up immediately. "Yes, please. I've heard you rave about it and I'm quite curious. No, wait, that seems selfish of me. I'm sure she's tired."

I snorted inelegantly at the notion. "That woman can work a team of men into the ground. She's barely fatigued. Hold on one moment." I pulled out my texting pad from my pocket and scribbled a quick note: My parents are here. Dinner for four?

roger roger

Satisfied, I put it away again. "She'll make some for you as well. I'm sure you have many questions, but I'm not certain where to start."

"Start from the beginning. What caused this?" Rupert suggested, leaning slightly forward. "I understand from Reggie that it had something to do with bad charms? Charms causing people to be sick? How did that happen?"

From there, eh. I obligingly backed up to the very beginning, first explaining the murder case of Garner and Timms, then bringing the narrative forward to the present day. They exclaimed, asked questions, and interrupted multiple times, so it wasn't a straightforward presentation, but I didn't mind it. I wanted them to understand more than deliver the tale in some theatrical fashion.

"But those poor people are still stuck in there another two weeks?" my mother demanded in outrage. "All because of those two men making such horrendous charms? Devil take them, what an insane turn of events. I'm glad you caught on to the situation so quickly, that you were able to prevent it from spreading any further."

"We are all grateful for that," I answered, feeling the

chair gain a firmer grip on me. "But thanks are largely owed to Dr. Cartwright, for sending out a message for help and not giving up until someone responded; and Officer McSparrin, whose sharp intuition told her that it was part of our case. I might not have known about it for another fortnight without those two, and think of the damage that would have been done then."

"I'd prefer not to," Rupert denied with a shudder. "Bad enough as it is. Those charms, have you found them all, then?"

"There's no real way of knowing how many there are." And that aggravated me sorely. "At least, not at this moment. Officer Gerring was combing through the records to help us determine how many charms Garner made under his new business name. We hope to lay hands on every last charm, but, unfortunately, we've hit something of a roadblock there. We've pulled everything from the stores, and put out notices in the Gazette and through the local theaters asking for the charms to be turned in to us, but a large quantity of them are still unaccounted for. I'm afraid that we might be dealing with the repercussions of their stupidity for months yet."

Neither of them appeared happy to hear this, and my mother's mouth tightened into a telltale line of outrage before demanding, "What can we do?"

"We've already received a great deal of support from you," I hedged. Largely because I didn't know what else could really be done. "Reggie's financial support of his workers eased many fears. In fact, we wouldn't have been able to maintain quarantine without him and his fellow colleagues' support. I understand the queen is going to thank all of the men personally for that. And you, Mother, your aid in assembling all of those clothes, blankets, and towels—that was heaven-sent. We were able to throw away so much that was too stained or contaminated; it cleared the area of the other bacterial strains trying to complicate matters."

"But is it enough?" Ophelia pressed, agitated and gripping her hands firmly together. "Is there something else we can do?"

Rupert shook his head, expression thoughtful. "There might not be, not at this stage. Otherwise I imagine our son would have already said something. What about RM Seaton, is there anything he's mentioned?"

"Yes, but most of it's political in nature. He's advocated for years that there needs to be an inspection process of all charms before they're allowed to be sold on the market. This just proves it. I believe the queen is upset and focused enough on the problem to give in to his suggestions." Seaton had showed me some of the messages he and the queen had been exchanging. She swore as creatively as any stevedore and I'd gained the impression she would lynch the next bad charm maker without mercy.

"While I agree the situation definitely demands such actions, I can't help but feel like we're shutting the gate after the horses have escaped." Rupert tapped a thoughtful rhythm against his knee, a mannerism I knew well. It usually preceded something insightful and brilliant. "Henri. How many bad charms did you actually find in these people's homes?"

"Usually stacks of them," I answered with a wince. Just the reminder made my temples throb. "Several of the city rubbish men refuse to dispose of them, and people thankfully have been warned not to burn them, but that means they're not sure what to do to dispose of them. They find some place to stack them up instead, out of the way, which is dangerous in its own right. I'll have a stern word with the city waste management tomorrow, I assure you."

"That's dangerous, alright," Rupert muttered, vexed. "You explained the dangers of that quite clearly to us, years ago. But my thought was this: These people must spend a pretty turn to get the few charms they do possess. They'll not give them up lightly, even if there is a good possibility it's a bad or ineffectual charm. I think the only thing that you'll be able to do is offer them an exchange. Give them a better charm in return for every charm they possess in the house. You'll need to keep track of these people, of course; I'm sure some will try to cheat the system."

"Yes, certainly, there's always the con-artists," I agreed slowly, my mind spinning out the possibility. "But it's a thought with merit, I must admit. It would be far more effectual than simply warning about the charms. That's become very clear."

"There's more than a few good charm makers in this city, and stores that carry them," Rupert went on, gaining momentum and enthusiasm. "I imagine they're all as cross as you are about this whole bloody business. For that matter, I know a few of them. How about I go around, ask for donations, ask them to pitch in a hundred charms or so. I bet if we get enough of them together, they'll make the difference we need to see."

If it were anyone other than my father proposing this, I would not believe it to work. However, Rupert Davenforth had a very strong reputation in Kingston, one well regarded not just among his peers, but among every citizen. I often was given the benefit of the doubt because of my last name alone. If he were to ask for aid, to help the city as a whole, I had no doubt people would respond. Perhaps not all, but enough.

"That's a splendid idea, darling," my mother enthused, brightening. "I'll help you organize it. What do you think, Henri, will RM Seaton approve?"

"He'll likely do cartwheels," I responded, feeling a weight lift off of me. "Yes, Father, please do that. I'll ask the Kingsmen to coordinate the donations. Either Evans or Gibson would be the best to use, as they're quite clever with magic."

"Then let's do that." Rupert eyed my telephone sitting on its own table near the study door and beelined for it. "I'll make a few calls while we're waiting on dinner. You have a way of messaging that fellow, don't you?"

I took the hint and pulled out the texting pad again. Seaton, I wrote quickly, my father thinks that if we offer good charms in exchange for the bad ones, we'll get more people to hand theirs over. He's intent on asking people for donations of anti-sickness charms to exchange with.

My mother came around to see better, and I obligingly tilted the pad towards her so that she might more easily read the response. It came in Seaton's usual flowery script. Splendid! Tell him I owe him dinner, and reassure anyone who donates that I'll make sure they get tax credit for it. You'll need help to dispose of the bad charms and organize matters. Gibson?

And Evans too if we can spare him, I wrote. To my father, I said, "Seaton promises a tax credit for any donations."

Rupert paused in dialing and gave me a pleased nod. "Excellent. I'll pass that along, it'll help ease open the purse strings."

I rethought the decision to just pass the word along, as I knew at some point Seaton would need to step in and either answer questions or make suggestions. I bent to the pad once more. Jamie's making curry and my parents are at my apartment. Want to join us?

You fool, you should have said that earlier!

Chuckling, I wiped the screen on the pad to start a new message, writing in the addressee to return to my conversation with Jamie. Make that five. Seaton's coming.

Well, make it a party, she sniped.

It's a good party. You'll like the results.

Fine, fine.

"That's deucedly convenient," my mother marveled. "I know you and Jamie explained how it functioned, but it sounded so nonsensical. I couldn't see why you were both excited about it. But it's truly time-saving, isn't it? And you don't have to track down anyone's location, as it doesn't matter where they are."

"Yes, it's quite splendid," I acknowledged, laying it on the coffee table. I had a notion I'd need it again in a moment with the way things were working. "When I first heard about it, I thought it would be splendid. But I had no real concept of just how useful the thing would be. Guildmaster Warner is still making changes to the design, as it requires weekly charging, and she strongly feels she should be able to get around that somehow. She'll need to before she can put it on the open market. I fully trust she'll make a breakthrough soon."

"This was originally a notion of Jamie's, wasn't it?"

"Yes. Well, more a carryover of something she had on her world." I understood that our version only had a small fraction of the capabilities of her device, but she was limited by the technology of this world. She couldn't make everything progress all at once.

I could hear him well before I saw him. He always sang the same song when he was coming down to my apartment. In his high, child-like voice, Clint sang mournfully, "On my own, pretending she's beside me~ All alone~"

The sound of a song being sung directly outside my window made my mother start, but I knew very well who it was. I stood and opened the window to allow the purple feline in, and he sauntered through with casual grace, as if it were my privilege to open things for him.

"Clint, do cease and desist," I greeted the Felix with some exasperation. "You don't even know all the lyrics to the song."

Sitting on the outside window sill, he looked at me mournfully, neglected as only a child could be. "Come in?"

"Yes, yes," I agreed, amused despite myself. It was very difficult to stay upset with him for any length of time. His charm was lethal. "Bored upstairs, were you?"

"Bored," he agreed with a flick of the ear. He looked my parents over, who stared with some astonishment, then decided for whatever reason that my mother was more to his liking. He hopped lightly down from the sill and crawled into her lap, lifting one paw to lightly touch her breast. Head cocked, he purred at her enticingly, "Pets?"

"This is Clint," I introduced belatedly.

"Oh, Jamie's Felix," my mother responded, expression lighting up in understanding. "I've heard many things about you, Clint. Where do you like to be pet?"

"Ears, tummy, back," he instructed, then flopped down onto his back and presented his stomach.

Ophelia stroked him like one would a dog's stomach, and the cat squirmed and purred under the attention, quite at his leisure. Amused, she asked me, "Does he do this often?"

"If he knows I'm home while Jamie is out, he lets himself out of the window and comes down for the company," I explained, hand splayed in a shrug. I'd quite gotten accustomed to my feline visitor and I must admit, I didn't mind his company. "She leaves the window cracked so that he can go out if he wishes. He's quite intelligent and can navigate the streets without trouble. Mrs. Henderson adores him, as he spends most of his time dealing with the rat and mice population around the apartment. Sometimes the bugs as well."

"Fun," he informed me lazily.

"Yes, I'm sure that's your only motivation," I retorted drolly.

He ignored me entirely, focused on the adoring hand still stroking him.

"He's really quite effective," I continued the explanation. "Jamie informs me that pound for pound, the domestic cat on Earth is the fiercest predator known to man. That seems to be true of the Felix as well, as he's almost completely eradicated rodents in this apartment building. I understand the complexes to either side of us are now leaving their windows cracked on the main floor to allow him entry, give him a chance to hunt there as well. I wonder if his maker originally intended for him to be this way?"

"Perhaps so? He's meant to be a magician's familiar, you said. I imagine that part of his duties would be to keep rodents and pests away from the magical stores."

I hadn't thought of it in that manner before, but she was likely correct. I wish we'd been able to take him in with us into the outbreak area, as his skills would have been deucedly handy, but alas we couldn't. He wouldn't have been immune to the sickness and none us wanted to risk him.

Rupert gave his usual booming laugh, distracting us, and said cheerfully into the phone, "You're telling me. Right, I'll have a Kingsman swing by this week and pick them up. No, thank you." Hanging up with a clatter, he turned to us, cheeks ruddy with excitement. "Williams promised two hundred, and he said anyone who wants to dispose of charms can bring them to him—he'll make an announcement of it."

Two hundred charms. That was not a cheap donation,

and Williams could only be Hugh Williams, owner of the top charm store in Kingston. Just where had my father started? The very top of the food chain? I now regretted not listening in on that conversation. "Clearly I did not inherit powers of persuasion from you."

Tickled by this backhanded compliment, he picked up the receiver and dialed another number. I watched him work and felt, for the first time, that my efforts might not be in vain after all.

> *Your dad is so cool ♥*
> *He would be pleased if you told him that.*
> *After you explain what 'cool' means.*

Report 15: The Beatings Will Continue Until Morale Improves

Henri, I need more paper *Yes, I'll get right on that.* don't think I can't hear the sarcasm from here *And what do you mean "the beatings"?* read the report

I walked into work on Gather Day—I still call it Monday in my head—with a pep in my step and a smile on my face. It had been an incredibly good weekend. Restful in the right ways, surrounded by very amazing and supportive friends who had the political clout and connections to do what I could not, and a spoiled feline loving the attention. Henri's parents had pulled together and gotten us a donation of an insane fifteen hundred charms, and Rupert claimed there were a few people he hadn't managed to catch, but would chase them down today. I was beyond flabbergasted at this, but pleased as punch.

Sherard estimated most of the charms that people exchanged wouldn't be our charms, specifically, but Henri and Sherard were of the opinion that it didn't really matter. All bad charms could apparently cause this sort of damage. They were happy to get any and everything out of people's homes and off the streets. We just hoped that at least some of Garner's charms still in circulation made it back to us.

Walking to my desk, I put together a quick plan for the day. With specialists on the epidemic, I wanted to get back to the case that had started it all. Gerring had to be crying at this point, as we'd utterly abandoned him to all of the morgues and the paperwork. First thing, I'd track him down and catch up with everything he'd learned. I'd find a moment to formally write up Third Precinct as well, as their negligence in this case was absolutely inexcusable. I knew they were over the poorer section of the city, and they might feel overrun at times with cases, but when that many people complain? Someone had better properly look into it, not just write it off.

To my surprise, both Bennett and Gibson leaned against my desk, waiting. I hadn't expected either man, and from the worry lines entrenched in their expressions, I wouldn't like what they had to say. Bracing myself for it, I came in close and gave them a lopsided grimace, the closest approximation I could get to a smile. "You look like you just came from a funeral. Now what's happened?"

"We're just worried," Bennett said, keeping his voice low, ducking his head a little to keep his mouth near my ears. "The anniversary passed us, but you were so busy with the epidemic, I don't think you really had a chance to think about it."

"Or emotionally respond to it," Gibson tacked on, his words a low rumble. "Jamie, if you need to take a few days, we can cover for you—"

I held up a hand, stalling them. While they had the best of intentions, on this, they didn't need to worry. I'd handled the anniversary far better than I'd hoped, probably because I'd been embroiled in something that had taken all of my time and energy. I'd not had the opportunity to dwell on the past, and truthfully? I was relieved. No one chose to dwell in dark places if they could help it. "I'm fine. Really. I even ate breakfast this morning."

Gibson, at least, did not look sold. Bennett also looked as if he reserved judgment.

Exasperated, I planted both hands on my hips and stared them down. Bunch of overprotective mother hens. A mother cat with kittens could take lessons from these two. "Gibs. Benny. I am *alright* and I would say if I wasn't. Leave it be."

"Jamie." Gibson rolled those big brown eyes of his expressively, exactly the way my father had when exasperated with his daughters. "You told us you were 'alright' when you were literally flat on your back and barely breathing. Your 'I'm fine' doesn't ease our concerns any."

They mean well, they mean well, they mean well...nope. The mantra didn't help. I still felt my temper start to fray. "Gibson. I'm eating semi-regularly, I slept okay the past four days despite the madness, and I have a very cute cat that's being helpful. I don't know what else you want me to say."

"Just take two days off," Bennett suggested hopefully, gesturing toward the bullpen at large. "We've already had to take a few days off the case anyway, the dead aren't going anywhere—"

"And we're already short-staffed because multiple people are down with this influenza crap," I shot back, beyond irritated, "our leads are growing steadily colder, and people are now panicking enough to try burning charms. Sure, now's a great time to take a mini-vacation."

"We'll cover for you," Gibson soothed.

That tone was exactly the wrong thing to use in that moment. My temper frayed even further. I felt like hitting him. "News flash, gentlemen, I do *not* find it helpful to sit about and stew on my feelings. So even if I wasn't fine, taking two days off wouldn't be the right choice. No."

"If it isn't the right choice, why are you getting angry?" Bennett asked, also in that same tone, and if either one of them did it again, I would punch them. Right in the gut. *Hard.*

"Because you're making me angry," I hissed at them. "When a person says they're fine, *respect that.*"

Of course Evans chose that moment to slip through the desks, joining us, and he had that same stupid look of concern scribbled all over his face. "Jamie, are you alright?"

Snarling, I rounded on him. "The next person who asks me that will be *beaten*. Okay? I will beat them until I feel better. Your constant reminders do not help, they make it worse. I have a plan on how to deal with the stress, I have techniques to help me work through it, and just worrying about it causes more issues than it solves. So stop worrying, stop getting into my face and telling me that I shouldn't be fine, that is NOT. HELPFUL. Respect it when I say that I am fine. I was alright until you idiots started smothering me. Now I need chocolate. No, you know what, out! All of you, out! We have clues to chase."

Hands raised in surrender, and after a few apologetic looks thrown my direction, they scattered, leaving me standing there breathing hard. I might feel guilty about blowing up at them later, but not at the moment. Right now I was ready to administer smackdowns, Mortal Kombat style. They'd been watching me, waiting for the other shoe to fall for weeks, and I'd known it. I hadn't said anything, because I understood the concern, but I'd hoped that when I didn't show any signs of distress, they could leave it alone. More fool me.

Of course, my little rant had gotten the attention of the other detectives sitting near me. I'd kept my voice low enough to not carry, but there were no walls here, and eavesdropping wasn't exactly a challenge. I gave each man a stern look, just daring him to say something. Each of them quickly found something else to focus on.

I really needed to hunt down some chocolate, maybe find a punching bag to let off some steam. I doubted Gerring had any good news to relay, and I didn't want to take my frustrations out on him.

The front door to the station swept open with a bang loud enough to make everyone jump. I whirled around, instinct putting one hand on the gun strapped to my side, then realized that the person who had just stormed in was none other than Third Precinct's captain. A werefox, he stood barely waist-high on me, his orange fur bristled in every direction in visual outrage. He stormed right for our captain's office, snarling like a wounded animal as he did so.

"Gregson!" he bellowed in a surprisingly loud and deep voice for such a small creature. "Gregson, I won't stand for this!"

Gregson yanked his office door open and stepped out, first alarmed, then with the growing red of anger sweeping up his neck and over his face. "Captain Wood. I do not appreciate you barging in like this. Calm down and step into my office."

Wood either didn't want to calm down or didn't care that we all listened in. Probably both. He jabbed a sharpened dark claw at Gregson, tail lashing behind him. "The nerve, *the gall* of you, writing me up formally. For what! A single case went unnoticed, something that didn't even cause trouble in my district, and you—"

"I have thirty-six reports from the past month of complaints issued to your station of bad charms," Gregson cut through him, his icy tone brutal against Wood's hot anger. "You have one hundred deaths that can be linked with magical causes. The charm maker's own *wife* came and reported problems. The man was forced to close his business doors because of CIVIL suits rather than criminal, that's how negligent your detectives and officers were!"

I mentally cheered. Get 'im, Gregson!

When Wood tried to rally, Gregson ran roughshod over him, ruthlessly. "MY OWN OFFICERS had to respond to a call of distress from a physician that is in YOUR jurisdiction, and then were locked in there for days dealing with an epidemic. The cause of which was tied into those thirty-six complaints that you so easily ignored. So yes, Woods, I wrote you up formally. I have it on good authority that RM Sherard Seaton also wrote you up for this. Our good queen received a copy of both those formal complaints, and knowing her and her view on matters such as these, I have no doubt you'll be up in front of a review by the Police Commissioner before the week is out."

Because Woods wasn't the type to own a mistake, he snarled back, "I will not be held responsible for what my officers failed to do!"

"You will be held responsible for so poorly managing them that they literally overlooked murder," Gregson snapped back, and if he'd possessed a tail, he would have been lashing it as well. In fact, it was rather a pity he wasn't some type of were, as the fur would fly otherwise.

"The fault of my men—"

"Is entirely your fault as well! That is what leadership means. Don't come off on me like this, Woods. You're just blowing hot air about, being here. The complaints are in, I certainly won't rescind mine, and you're doing no good here. You're just validating what scum you are, trying to push the blame onto someone else."

I couldn't help myself. I started clapping.

Woods' head snapped about, his eyes landing on me. "That's insubordination, Detective!"

"Couldn't help myself," I responded with demonic cheerfulness. "My captain's being too cool. And really, Captain Woods, I'm well within my rights to clap. I'm one of the people who's had to clean up after your mess."

Woods' eyes narrowed and I could tell the minute he put together who I was. His dark eyes widened comically in his face, his body and tail stilling. "Shinigami Detective."

I met his eyes levelly, the smile on my face feeling unnaturally rigid. "The same."

He looked disturbed by this. I could only guess why. Wetting his lips with a quick swipe of the tongue, he turned his head just enough to hiss at Gregson, "You put the Shinigami Detective on this?"

"Edwards actually volunteered to take it," Gregson's smile was not nice, "as it overlaps with her area of expertise. Go away, Woods. You're only embarrassing yourself."

An inhuman whine exploded from his throat as Woods wheeled about, slamming his way back out of the station. I watched him go and nodded to myself. Yeah, he'd be the reason why Third Precinct was so terrible. A leader more interested in covering his backside had no time to actually do his job correctly.

Gregson caught my eye and asked, "What are you doing here?"

"Stealing Henri's chocolate before I go find Gerring to get an update," I answered truthfully.

"Then go."

I went.

My wonderful minion (you have no idea how sad I am that I can't make minion jokes either) had in fact been a busy little beaver while we had been quarantined. I found him in the back conference room, the one that no one liked to use because it was cramped, windowless, and a little musty smelling. He had the door propped open to offset some of that, the table buried under reports, and the blackboard covered in writing. With his ebony skin, the chalk dust all over him made it look as if he'd gotten into a fight with a flour mill. And lost.

Gerring looked up at my entrance with visible relief. "You're back?"

"I am," I answered, slinging myself into the nearest chair. "Sorry you had to muddle through on your own. We needed at least one person to continue working the case while we all got trapped inside. I'll treat you to dinner, okay?"

"Okay," he agreed happily. (I'm pleased everyone's picking up that word so quickly.) "You and Dr. Davenforth know the best places to eat anyway."

I snickered. "Yeah, well, I'm actually stealing his knowledge. Want a chocolate?"

Gerring happily accepted one, popped it into his mouth, and moaned appreciation. "Is this from his stash?"

"Of course. I only get the best. Hit me, kid. What have you found?"

"A lot, actually." Gerring gestured to the piles of reports and the blackboard. "I heard Captain Woods yelling earlier, and I know why he was, as he doesn't have a leg to stand on. I reported to Captain Gregson that there were thirty-six complaints, but actually there's more. Some of them were misfiled or maybe deliberately mislabeled so that they were 'lost' in circulation. Third Precinct has creative ways to get around actually working."

"Oh, lovely," I groaned. That called for another chocolate. "So how many do you think there actually are?"

"I've still got two piles to go, but there are at least seventy-two," he answered sourly, jerking his chin to indicate the two piles in question. When I started swearing, he grunted, mouth curling up in a snarl. "That's exactly how I feel about it. A lot of damage was done that could have been avoided, if they'd just responded to the first complaints. I mean, I know that I'm new, but if we had a complaint like this come in? I know for a fact that if I took it to Dr. Davenforth, and asked him to take a look for me, he'd do it."

"That's what makes him an exceptional Magical Examiner," I acknowledged. "As well as a good man. Alright, so we have lots of proof to get those idiots in trouble. Good. Glad to hear it. There has to be a silver lining, as this is too dark of a cloud. What else have you found?"

"All of the civil suits were dropped. The business filed a Chapter Twelve—they revoked their own business license and promised to close up shop in a week as the settlement. I think they begged for leniency, as they wouldn't have been able to pay the fine for damages and wrongful death against that many plaintiffs. Over a hundred families joined forces to put a case against them." Gerring tapped the binder in question, and while

I couldn't read it upside down easily, I made out the court's number and logo without a problem. So he'd gotten his hands on the court transcripts, had he? Clever boy. I owed him more than one dinner, it appeared.

"Alright, that's an amazing amount of legwork," I praised, heartily meaning every word. "Have you had the chance to run down any of these families, talk to them?"

"Not personally, no. I do have a list to work from." Gerring scooted his chair back in a scrape to stand, gesturing to the columns of names on the board. "This first list is every person who lost a child and has the right skills. They're either a powder monkey or a mechanic. Star next to their name is for the powder monkeys."

"Only six of those," I noted, counting quickly. Fourteen suspects. SO much better than a fifth of the city. "The other list?"

"People who lost a loved one due to the charms—that I could actually prove, at least. I think there's more. It would just take a Magical Examiner to verify my suspicions." He pointed to several underlined names. "These are the people who were part of the lawsuit."

I added them up quickly, estimating. "Gerring, that's a good hundred people to run down."

"Hundred and thirteen," he confirmed wryly. "I vote we split up the list."

"Motion carried," I agreed faintly. I was so not running down a hundred and thirteen people all by my lonesome. "Let's reach out to the Kingsmen, give them a portion of the list to work on. You and I will take the powder monkeys today, as I know where to go with them. And if we're very, very lucky, we'll catch people."

The day with Gerring had not turned up any obvious suspects, but it removed several people off our list, which I took as progress in the right direction. Many people had an alibi for the night and day in question, which made life easier on me.

Day two of being back on the job, I spent a few hours in the morning following up on the demolition companies that hadn't gotten back to me before the epidemic hit. I half-hoped they might have a suspect for me, but no one else had any dynamite missing. Only the one company, and they weren't entirely sure it wasn't just a misprint of sorts. I hardly wanted another cold lead handed to me.

Frustrated, I abandoned the search and trooped back into the station. I'd need to gather up Gerring again, see if we couldn't connect with the three men we'd failed to interview the day before. He'd come in late this morning, a doctor's appointment, but surely he was back to work by now.

My desk had a few reports on it, one scribbled message, and that made me smile. I was going on year two of being on this world and could finally read the simpler sentences. A lot of vocab was still missing, and slang went right over my head, but I was making steady progress. Give me another year, I might be able to pass muster.

Shifting my briefcase aside, I picked up the note first, as notes were rare. Most people just talked to me directly about anything case related. It didn't used to be that way pre-Henri, but post-Henri my relationship with my colleagues had improved by leaps and bounds. Henri openly teasing me had eased fears. I still unnerved some people—Berghetta, for instance—but I think that was less about me killing a rogue witch and more about my willingness to wear pants and shoot guns.

I couldn't just scan the note, the loopy style of the handwriting made it a little hard to decipher, and I had to puzzle through more than one word. Then the overall meaning of the note hit and a thrill raced through me. Holy crap, was this right?! Spinning about, I lurched around the desks and hightailed it for Henri's lab.

Not even knocking, I burst through the door but stayed behind Henri's line. I was not stupid enough to cross that, as he'd been in here hours already and had likely pulled out something dangerously magical.

He had a clear table, nothing more than a report and a sealed evidence case on it, so he must have just finished with something. He jerked around sharply at my entrance. Alarm spread over his face, eyes wide behind his glasses. "What?"

"I have a note that someone claiming to have killed Garner turned himself in this morning," I quickly relayed, words tumbling out and into each other. "He's waiting in the jail cell."

Henri looked as flabbergasted as I felt. "Criminals don't normally turn themselves in, do they?"

"More often than you'd think, but not as often as fiction inclines you to believe. Get us an interrogation room, grab Penny if you see her, but I'm hauling this man in to see if he's really the culprit." Sometimes people weren't. Sometimes the fame of the act drew the loonies in, and they wanted their fifteen minutes in the newspapers. Those were the dangerous ones. I'd have to be careful how much information I gave this man and test him to see if he was the genuine article.

I swear, being a cop some days was like playing cards with a gambler. Where was a truth serum when you needed one?

As Henri hustled one direction, I went the other, toward the back of the building where the internal jail cells were. We didn't have a lot of holding room back there, maybe enough to keep thirty people, and only two men on duty to manage the lot. At the moment, we had a largely empty house, with a drunk sleeping it off and another man who looked resigned, slouched on a wooden bed chained to the wall. I stopped at the desk just inside the door and leaned in. "Hey, Finch."

"Edwards," Finch returned with a nod. A portly man, Finch had a wife who was a good cook, three kids, and twenty solid years on the force. He was the steady sort that can be depended on to keep things from getting ugly. He inclined his head toward the resigned man on the bed. "That's yours."

I leaned in further, keeping my voice low. "Who took him in?"

"I did, actually. Poor Hurst didn't know what to do with him when he showed up. She called me, and I brought him back. He hasn't said a peep, except for he's the one who blew Garner to pieces."

Right. This might get strange. Although I hoped we actually had the right man, as that would further matters along nicely. "Alright, bring him out."

"You got a room?"

"Henri's arranging it."

Amiable, Finch got up in a clatter of keys and walked to the cell, slotted in a key, and waved the man out. "Detective Jamie Edwards is here to talk to you. Let's go."

He shuffled out and I got a better look at the man. Small, that was my general impression. Small and depressed. Short enough to hit my chin, thin in body and in frame, dark hair lank against his head, as if he hadn't washed it in days. This might be my murderer, but I'd wager he regretted his decision every second.

Stepping out of the cell, he looked up at me and his expression shifted from resigned to vaguely curious. I didn't see a lot of life in those eyes, and that was a bad sign. This wasn't a man anxious to live. Just what had he done to himself? Was the weight of another man's soul crushing his spirit? I understood that weight, all too well, but I had never acted out of vengeance, only self-preservation. Some might see it as a fine line but that distinction was soul-saving.

"I'm Detective Edwards," I introduced myself, my voice gentle, as I sensed this man needed gentleness right now instead of abrasion.

"Parkins," he rasped back, wetted his dry lips, and tried again. "Jake Parkins."

"Mr. Parkins, won't you come with me? My partner and I have many questions for you."

He nodded, a vague assent, and fell into step with me, his cuffed hands held loosely in front of him. I kept an eye on him, of course I did, as underestimating people got you quickly dead. Still, I sensed no danger from this man.

Henri stood waiting outside of the interrogation room, his dark eyes flitting over the man in a quick, intense study. He caught my eye, his own eyebrows arched in question, and I shrugged. I had no idea if this was really our man or not. At least, not yet.

We stepped inside the small interrogation room and I was relieved to see that Penny already stood in the corner of the room, her shoulders braced against the wall. I wanted her here for various reasons, but mostly for experience. She handled a lot of the low-key interrogations for domestic issues, or for witness statements, but this would be very different than anything else in her experience.

Parkins took a seat on one side, Henri and I on the other. Henri had his notebook out, a pencil lying on the blank pages, and I trusted him to take notes while I did the talking. We'd discovered that system worked best for us. I was trained in interrogation. Henri wasn't. We chose to play to our strengths, although I'd teach Henri the nuances of this eventually.

"Mr. Parkins, this is my partner, Dr. Henri Davenforth. He's a Magical Examiner." I casually folded my hands on top of the table, pitching my voice to be friendly, my body language inviting. "That's Officer Penny McSparrin. She's also working this case with us. Can you give us your full name, address, and occupation for the record?"

"Jacob Parkins, powder monkey with North Storey," then an address I vaguely recognized as being near the east side docks. He locked eyes with me, like a puppet upon its master, waiting for the next order. The guy seriously needed therapy.

I could tell the other two had picked up on it, too, but I ignored them for the moment and focused on Parkins. "I understand you confessed to killing Garner. Is that right?"

"Yes, that's right."

Nothing, huh. I tried again. "Can you tell us the story? Why did you do it? How?"

Curiosity flickered in those deep grey eyes. "You want my story?"

"I sure do. It's this thing with cops, we like to know motives."

A bitter laugh snorted through his nose. "They sure didn't."

"Who?" I prodded. Ha! Real emotion. Now we were getting somewhere.

"Cops at Third Precinct," he answered, rage tightening his fists until the knuckles shown white. "I reported the charms, we all reported the charms, but they said charms didn't do that. They didn't make people sick. They either worked, or didn't work. And that my—" he choked, faltered, eyes burning bright with unshed tears.

"They're quite wrong," Henri put in gently. "Bad charms can, in fact, cause the very thing they're supposed to prevent. And I promise you, after this, everyone will be very thoroughly educated on this point. RM Seaton is on the warpath about this very subject and our good queen is equally upset. Revisions will be made so that bad charms will have a hard time getting on the market after this. We've also written up Third Precinct's captain for this shameful conduct. An investigation into the station is now in the works."

That lifted Parkin's head again and he stared at Henri in wonder. "All of that, really?"

"The epidemic that broke out recently," Henri continued, tone lilting in question. "You've heard of it? Yes? That was mostly caused by Garner's bad charms. Because of it, I was able to report it to RM Seaton, and he in turn reported it to the queen. I assure you, no one is happy about the matter, and it's shoved the problem into the light. I believe we'll finally see regulation where charm making is concerned."

A shudder of relief went through Parkins, but it was a bitter sort of relief, leaving him brittle and angry. "So it takes more than once for that sort of change, does it? It wasn't enough we suffered under his hands?"

"Who did you lose, Mr. Parkins?" I asked, trying to not only get info out of him, but bring him back on point.

"My daughter," he whispered, face rippling with repressed emotion. "My little girl. Her lungs were weak, we bought a charm to keep the colds at bay. She was dead from pneumonia a month later. I knew it was the charm, she was fine before that, and for once no one else in the neighborhood was sick. There was no one to catch it from. And we got to talking, all of us, and it was always the same charm that set it off. We knew it was the charm. But we couldn't get anyone to listen, not at first. Then there were too many complaints, and Garner was gone. But he wasn't really gone. We didn't know that at first, we thought he was out of business entirely, and were glad for it. I might have left it alone if he'd learned his lesson. But I got a job over here on west side, to demo some of the old shacks and clear out land for a new neighborhood. And I saw him, coming out of that fancy building of his, climbing into that fancy car. And the sign on the window, that made it clear enough. He hadn't stopped. He'd just pulled up stakes, moved to another section of town, changed names, and was right back at it.

"I went home, told people what I'd seen, and they were livid. Like me. And we had to stop him, didn't we? Because we'd reported it once and got ignored, we couldn't just trust the police to do it." Here, he looked at Henri in apology. "I thought it at the time. But I heard what you did, Dr. Davenforth. I heard what you and your parents are doing, how you're pulling strings to get those charms destroyed. If I'd known you were here, that you'd help, I...well, things might be different, is all."

I felt my heart break for him. I'd seen grief and rage break good men, and when they felt like their backs were against a wall, they lashed out, because they didn't see any other option. Indeed, if he had known about Henri, he might not have made the same choice. But that bridge was well burned and cold ashes by now. There was no undoing it.

"It was the car that made me mad," he continued, eyes blind as he stared at the wall between us. "Silly, now that I think about it. But it was the car that really made me mad. My daughter's life helped pay for that car. And he drove it around, always with a different woman in it, playing at being a successful charm maker. I wanted to kill him for it. I said that for a week, and the more I said it, the truer it was. I wanted him dead for it, and I wanted that car to be what killed him."

He faltered there and I nudged him, just a little. I believed his grief was real, it was too raw and unapologetic, but was he really the culprit? Or was he covering for someone else? "Did you know how?"

Shaking his head, he denied, "Don't know nothing about cars. Had a buddy tell me how the engine worked. Once he explained the spark plug, I knew that was the ticket. That spark of electricity, to fire things up, that's all it would take to get a stick of dynamite going. I figured it wouldn't take more than one. I had a false start on it, day before, I didn't wire it right. I redid it, and the next morning, it blew everything apart first try."

I blinked at this. The timing of Timms' death now made more sense, the separation of the killings.

The odd hours of their business, where they generally worked in the afternoon, would have made later in the day prime time for the bombing. But it hadn't happened that way. Why? That question had bothered me, but here was the answer:

the bomb hadn't detonated as planned on the first try. Simple.

"At first I was relieved, because Garner was stopped. Timms was stopped. They couldn't do more harm." Parkins shook his head slowly, hands clenching and unclenching. "But I keep hearing and seeing the explosion. Even with my eyes shut. Even when I'm kissing my wife. I can't see anything but that. I thought it would bring my little girl some peace. Instead it torments me. I'm not sure if it's worth the price."

Murder generally wasn't. Not to good men like this one, who had too gentle of a nature to handle carrying another man's soul. "Mr. Parkins, I promise you that you will make peace with that eventually."

"If it's any consolation, his work has done a great deal of damage and caused multiple deaths," Henri added, words carefully tactful. "I wish you hadn't resorted to murder, of course, but the idiot was using Destroying Angel mushrooms to add power to his charms. That's why this round of sickness was so quick and horrendous. If we hadn't been called in to investigate, it would have taken over and potentially killed thousands."

Parkins looked at him as if Henri had handed him some measure of grace. "Thank you for telling me that, sir. I do feel better knowing it. I wish I hadn't killed him, either, but I suppose there's some good out of this mess after all."

All of the details lined up. He wasn't trying to bring fame into this in any way. I believed him to be our man. And relief washed through me, as I hadn't been sure we would have been able to find him on our own. There were just too many suspects to comb through. "Mr. Parkins, who else helped you?"

He shook his head immediately in denial. "I'm sorry, Detective, but I won't betray that confidence. I came in because I couldn't handle the guilt of it anymore. If they choose to do the same, I'll understand, but I can't drag them in with me. I don't think they regret it."

"I had a feeling you'd say that." Although I didn't think he realized that by coming in he would be the lynchpin that let me solve the case. I would catch at least most of his associates. I tried rephrasing, coming in with charm, reasoning, all of those interrogation techniques they teach you at the academy. He just kept shaking his head, over and over, mouth pressed together in a firm line.

Finally, I relented with a sigh. Just pushing wouldn't get me an answer at this point. I needed different leverage, and right now, I didn't have it. "Alright. We'll come back to this later. For now, I'd like a full list of every officer you talked to on this case. Every professional that failed to help you. I will personally ream them out for this."

That put a smile on his face, a brief, passing pleasure. "I will, Detective. I'll be happy to do that."

AL.
The man is now illuminated. Don't make the same mistake.
You too, Sherard.
    Yes, dear.

Report 16: One Step Forward, Two Steps Back

Jamie slumped forward in a dramatic groan, her forehead thumping against the top of the report. McSparrin and I shared a look over the top of her head, and I sympathized, as I knew how difficult it was for Jamie to skim reports. We had little recourse in this matter, however. Our one witness to the crime refused adamantly to name his co-conspirators. There was no other witness to the murders, and Jamie felt certain that at least two others were involved, a feeling I did not disagree with. Nothing about Parkins' narrative mentioned Timms at all, a very telling thing indeed. It meant he had been outside with the car, that he'd had nothing to do with the other murder, and it was hard to imagine Timms just docilely allowing himself to be tied up in that rather elaborate manner without trying to break free. There were no signs of struggle on his corpse, making this scenario unlikely. There must have been two people in that basement with him—one to hold the gun, the other to wield the rope.

Two murderers on the loose—even if I was sympathetic to their motivations—sat ill with me. I wanted them properly behind bars before something else untoward happened. We'd already had an additional thirty-six deaths to add to Gerring's earlier tally of seventy-two. But the only other lead we had to pursue were the complaints issued at the other police station, which meant a great deal of digging through reports, not all of them relevant to our case. Gerring's efforts notwithstanding, we'd learned that many of the complaints had been deliberately mislabeled.

He'd pulled everything that looked remotely relevant, but the complaints he'd brought with him didn't reveal our culprit. We'd interviewed all the mechanics and found them all with alibis. Gerring was disheartened by this and swore to go through every file in the Third Precinct if that's what it took.

He and Gibson took great delight in shuffling records back to us to check, and while it was helpful of them to do so, I think they did it to avoid the eyestrain currently threatening to make my eyeballs bleed out of their sockets. Of course, they had other excuses too. 'We have to check on Parkins' neighbors to see if any of them are mechanics,' and 'We'll verify how many of these complaints actually resulted in a death,' and so forth. But really? They wished to avoid the eyestrain. I was not oblivious to their tricks.

A full day into this, with only two hours left on the clock, my shoulders were locked in a hunched position, my buttocks numb from the hard wood seat, and a definite crick settled into my neck from the position. Tomorrow did not promise to bring any answers, nor relief, and I did not relish the prospect of doing this again.

"He has to know a mechanic somehow," Jamie repeated for the nth time, a near wail of disgust.

"We've interviewed all of his family members, all of his colleagues and friends, and none of them are of that profession," I reminded her patiently. "We spent three days doing that. I'm sure he does know the mechanic, but their acquaintance obviously isn't one that we can trace."

"What I wouldn't give for social media right now," Jamie muttered to herself caustically. "I'd be able to find the answer if we had Facebook. I guarantee it."

I labeled that statement under its usual title of, Earthling, Strange Sayings of and let it pass. I signaled for McSparrin to do the same when she gave Jamie a glance askance. An uneasy silence descended once more in the small conference room as we returned to the work. It was eerily silent in the room aside from the turning of the pages, even our breathing unnaturally loud. I wished the room had some sort of window, a way to open a breeze and stir the stale air, but it did not and I was unwilling to leave the door open to the bullpen. That would just invite distraction and unwelcome noise.

McSparrin straightened from her slouch abruptly and read aloud, voice climbing in excitement, "Mr. Harmum Lees, mechanic at Craig's Motor Garage, reported a bad charm at his residence on 11B Summers Lane. Mr. Lees attempted to turn over charm as evidence, quality reported as shoddy by Magical Examiner, who disposed of it. Mr. Lees demanded pursuit of charm maker, claims it killed his father. Case dismissed without evidence. This was dated four months ago."

Slamming a hand against the table, Jamie pointed at the report in McSparrin's hand with a victorious air. "Yes! If that isn't it, it's at least a reason to get out of this office and go hunt the man down. I'll take that at the moment. Let's go, Henri."

"Wait," I stilled her, asking McSparrin, "Did the report happen to mention where the charm was purchased from?"

"No," she denied thoughtfully, then dug through her pile of 'read' reports until she found one three down. "But this one did. Mellor Charms and Spells. It's in the same neighborhood."

"Let's combine trips," I suggested to my partner. "I've seen that same name several times now, and if nothing else, I want to prevent another outbreak and claim all of the bad stock from that store. If we're supremely unlucky, there might still be some of Garner's work amongst their inventory."

Jamie grimaced. "Lovely thought. Fine, let's do that. I'll message Gibson, have him meet us there. He's itching to do something aside from interviews anyway."

I agreed to her logical choice, as Gibson was already in the neighborhood. He'd chosen to go door to door, collecting names and faces in his own way of narrowing down who our mechanic might be. I had no idea which tactic might prove more efficient, and hadn't argued over methods, although I think my partner would have vastly preferred being out on the street with Gibson over locked up with reports she could barely read. For that matter, I was uncertain how the work had divvied out this way in the first place.

"I'll try and wrap it up here before heading home," McSparrin volunteered with a long sigh. "Maybe we can organize getting the read reports returned, help clear this out a little."

"Excellent suggestion," Jamie agreed, head already buried in her texting pad.

With hands on her shoulders, I steered Jamie out of the room. I'd learned it was safer that way, as she typically bumped into things like desks, her attention completely taken up by the device. We got a few funny looks and some snickers, which I ignored. Jamie either chose to do the same or didn't hear them. Upon reaching outside, she put it away and beelined for one of the motor cars. Resigned to my fate, I followed.

Jamie harbored a terrible tendency to speed when frustrated or jittery. Knowing this, I braced my foot and hand against the side of the car and still nearly slid out of my seat as she floored our way out of the back parking lot. "Jamie, do remember that I enjoy living."

Snorting a laugh, she eased back on the throttle. Just a touch. "If I ever get around to figuring out how to soup one of these babies up and get it going eighty, you're going to lose you're frakkin' mind."

"What a terrifying thought," I drawled, unconcerned. She'd already admitted her lack of engineering ability to me before. Then I remembered that Ellie Warner shared her love of speed and paled. Perhaps I shouldn't dismiss that thought so quickly.

Entering mid-afternoon traffic, Jamie wound our way down and around, heading to the docks before cutting over. It was the only sensible approach, as the docks had one of the broader roads, and thereby the clearest route of traffic at any time of the day. As she drove, I inquired, "How goes Warner's production of the rubbing alcohol? I meant to ask earlier."

"It's going rather well, or so she told me last night. Aside from the doctors field testing it right now in our quarantined areas, she's gotten seven doctors to field test it in their hospitals, and they're so pleased with how clean it gets things, they've all ordered batches of liters. Three doctors signed an endorsement of it on the spot when she asked, and she's in talks with a pharmaceutical to mass produce it and sell it in their stores. Leonard's Drugstore, I think she said."

I nodded approval. Leonard's Drugstore was very well-stablished, having been an icon for medicines even in my father's youth. The new head of the company, I understood, was the grandson of the founder, and he held no compunction about trying new products. Warner had indeed approached the right person with the right ware. "Excellent. I hope that spreads quickly. Has she found a way to keep production costs down?"

"She's still working on that, but she said it shouldn't be too difficult; she just has to get the right factory set up for it. After that, it'll basically pay for itself. More demand, more supply, and the basics of economics will take care of the rest." Jamie lifted a shoulder in a shrug, not worried, nor should she be. "It'll take a while for it to spread, but it will. Good things always do."

"Indeed they do." I eased the death grip I had upon the side, daring to think I could actually relax into my seat. "I'm often glad for your Earthly knowledge, as you bring excellent inventions to us, but this is by far one of the better ones you've introduced. It will cut down on rampant diseases and infections in a breathtaking manner. I can't wait to see it."

She shot me a small smile. Pleasure lurked in that expression but sorrow mixed in as well. "Silver lining."

My own expression turned bittersweet. For my sake, I was selfishly glad she was here with us. This amazing woman changed the world in better ways on a near constant basis. I shuddered to think how many lives we would have already lost if not for her interference. And yet…and yet. The price of that was substantially high. I could not pay it for her. I could only offset it so that the regret was not so bitter of a pill to swallow.

We rode the rest of the way in silence, until I had to provide directions to Craig's Motor Garage. Jamie didn't know this section of the city as well, nor should she, as she'd rarely needed to venture out this direction. Even I barely knew my way around it. At this time of the day, we knew Lees should be at work, making the garage the opportune place to stop. It seemed a successful enough place, as it had three cars up on the stilts in the bays, two others waiting, and a half dozen mechanics in blue overalls scurrying about working. Jamie parked in one of the few open spaces—the garage had little in the way of a parking area—before climbing out and striding toward the open door, myself on her heels.

The small reception area inside might have been nice at some point in time, but it was nothing more than

Charms and Death and Explosions (oh my!)

wood and grime now. The many greasy fingerprints left a residue behind, and while I was not particular about cleanliness, the idea of brushing casually up against something made me vaguely ill at ease. Did the employees here never clean the place?

A gruff looking man in his fifties sat behind the desk. He gave us a quick smile in greeting, barely discernable under his bushy mustache. "Welcome. What can I do for you?"

Jamie flashed her badge at him, professional smile pinned to her face. "Detective Edwards, this is Dr. Davenforth, from Fourth Precinct. We need to ask Mr. Harmum Lees a few questions about a complaint he filed a few months back."

Scratching at his thinning hairline, the man responded, "I'm Craig, the boss here. I haven't seen Lees in days. I actually fired him yesterday, sent a note to his house, as he'd skipped work without saying for nearly seven days straight."

That...did not bode well. Coming forward, I carefully kept my arms behind my back to avoid brushing up against the counter even as I inquired, "We read in the complaint that he lost his father due to a bad anti-illness charm. Or at least, that's what he claimed. Do you know anything about that?"

"Some," Craig allowed, "but his closest friend here is Wyatt, and he can tell you more than I can. Hold on." Ducking out a side door, he bellowed, "WYATT! C'mere!"

A thin man with hunched shoulders stepped in. I judged him to be tired, either from life itself or something else that prevented him from getting adequate rest. He looked us over with only mild curiosity.

Jamie once again introduced us before asking, "You're friends with Harmum Lees, right?"

"Yes, Detective," he responded politely, then stifled a

yawn. "Sorry, got an infant keeping me up at night."

Ah, that explained his exhaustion. "Quite alright. We're looking for Mr. Lees regarding a complaint he filed a few months ago. We believe there's validity to his claim."

"The one about his dad dying?" Wyatt's attention sharpened on us, his shoulders coming up. "About time. He was all bent out of shape over that. His dad's the only family Harm had left, sad to say. Man's a confirmed bachelor, he never did know what to do with women, and him losing his father…it was rough. Really rough. We couldn't get the coppers here to investigate, though. Despite his not being the only case."

"We're investigating that, too," Jamie assured him with a grim reaper smile. "I'm sorry to hear about his father. We really want to ask him questions, get to the bottom of it. Do you know where to find him?"

"Haven't seen Harm in a week," he admitted with a hangdog expression. "I meant to go looking for him at the house tomorrow, probably should have done it before now, but the baby's been sick and…well. I can tell you where he lives."

"That would be splendid," Jamie encouraged. "And a basic description, too, that'll help us make sure we have the right fellow."

"Sure, sure. 11B Seaboard Lane, just around the corner. He's got three inches on me, bit of a beer gut, black hair thinning on top, and he was growing a beard last time I saw him."

"Thank you, Mr. Wyatt," I acknowledged. Lees' disappearance from his place of employment without a word sat ill with me. It boded something dark and unpleasant. Was this our mechanic? It looked that way, although I struggled to keep from leaping to conclusions.

We left the shop, Jamie pausing before climbing into the vehicle. She turned to study the garage behind us with a thoughtful finger tapping her lips. "What do you make of this?"

"I find it suspicious," I admitted frankly, leaning my forearms against the car's door. "Why quit a perfectly good job without a word? Why fall out of touch with your friend? I know people don't always make sound decisions when mired in grief, so it could be just that."

"But his father died almost four months ago," Jamie returned, eyes narrowing speculatively. "People tend to make those decisions within the first couple months of losing a loved one. Not four months later, after the grief has had time to process. I'm not saying it doesn't happen, it's just rare for people to do it. Did he somehow hear that Parkins turned himself in?"

"I don't see how he could have. We've done very well in keeping that quiet. Unless one of Parkins' family said something to him. No, wait. Parkins came to us four days ago. This man's been missing for seven."

"The timing doesn't work out," Jamie acknowledged, still thinking. "Unless Parkins announced his intentions to come confess seven days ago, and Lees ran for it then. I don't know, I'm just throwing possibilities out there. It does look strange, this timing. It's making me jumpy. Gibs is supposed to meet us here, let's give him a minute to catch up before we try Lees' house."

Amiable to this, I chose to remain standing a little longer, as my cramping thighs did not relish the idea of sitting again soon. I'd been sitting far too much today. My muscles liked being upright for a change of pace. "Do you..." I trailed off when a funny expression crossed her face and her head turned, nose lifting like a dog catching a scent. "What is it?"

"I thought I caught a whiff of gasoline," she answered uncertainly. "But we're next to a garage, I suppose that makes sense."

"But you didn't pick up the scent on entering?" Something about it bothered her, I could tell. But the rational mind didn't always pick up on the logic of something, even while the instincts screamed warnings.

"No, I did, but this was stronger. Not contained." As soon as the words popped out of her mouth, she hopped up onto the boot of the car, using the height to look around us, head jerking about as she panned the area. "Lots of gasoline not contained. It's not something I like, usually leads to fires. Crap, where is it coming from?"

I had no answer for her. "Unfortunately, I can't do a seeking spell, it will lead us directly to this garage, as that's the nearest source for gasoline. You can't pick up the scent again?"

"It's completely gone," she groaned in frustration, hands clenching into fists at her side. "I now have complete sympathy for bloodhounds. This is frustrating. I just had it, when that random breeze came in, but now it's—"

A roar buffeted us, a wave of heat and noise. Glass shattering, people screaming in fright and stunned horror, like a tidal wave of disaster captured in sound. Thoroughly alarmed, I whirled about, as it had come from somewhere behind me, further up the street.

Jamie swore, as viciously as any sailor, hopping from the boot straight for the driver's seat. "Henri, get in, call for the fire department!"

I scrambled, demanding as I moved, "What happened? And by what means do you expect me to do so?"

She stared at me blankly for a moment, then swore. "Right. No cell phones. I HATE not having cell phones. Message Gibs, he's nearby and should be able to get the fire department out here."

That was reasonable and I hastily snatched the texting pad out of my pocket even as I demanded, "Did you see it?"

"Something just exploded," she answered grimly, then gunned it out of the parking lot. "And with that amount of smoke, I think it was a couple of buildings."

Report 17: A Broken Heart Bleeds Destruction
Amen

It was easy to see the epicenter of the blast. I stood up inside of the car, and even as I drew my wand, I couldn't help but hesitate a second to take in the scene. The building—it had likely been a shop of some sort—was nothing more than a shell of brick and fire now. A fanciful mind would think it akin to a burning jaw, gaping open from the mouth of the underworld. The neighboring buildings were the same: brick and fire and dark smoke, as if a demon lived and breathed in its depths, the inky clouds of smoke pillowing its way up into the sky. The air held so much smoke and heat that even across the street, I found it difficult to breathe. The intense heat scorched and tightened my exposed skin in a very uncomfortable fashion. I instinctively wanted to shed my coat but refrained, as I wanted the protection of the fabric against stray embers.

The heat, fortunately, kept the onlookers back. They watched in horror, exclaiming to each other, people hanging out of windows or crowded together in bundles. For their sake, I knew that I had to get this fire under control quickly, as it would spread to everyone's homes and businesses if I didn't. Gibs had called for the fire department, I was sure others had as well, but every minute counted in an inferno like this. It had taken us ten minutes to reach this area, and by a miracle Jamie had forced her way through the crowd until we were catawampus to the burning buildings, across the street from it. I didn't see how a fire wagon could get through.

I threw three suppressing spells directly forward, hitting the main building first, as it burned directly in front of me. The inferno sizzled against my magic, buffeting backwards, and I frowned in confusion. That should have worked...why hadn't that worked?

Jamie leaned down and shouted to someone over the roar of flame, "Is there anyone inside there?!"

"No one living!" a woman shouted back to her. "They all ran out as soon as the fire started! Oh, those poor people, it's just a charms shop, why would anyone set it on fire like this?"

Charms shop? My eyes went wide in realization, cold horror sinking into my gut. Mellor Charms and Spells? It had to be, it was in the right location for it. And that explained why my spells weren't having the proper effect—multiple magical charms were going up in flames right now, the fire would release the magic in unpredictable and very volatile ways. I'd seen some magic mixed in with the inferno, but I'd also expected to—there were charms and hexes on every business building for fire, theft, and other miscellaneous purposes. It would be stranger if I hadn't. But now that I was truly paying attention, I realized the majority of the flame was magical in nature. It wasn't because some chemical property had mixed in and threaded the blaze a strange green-blue hue.

"Jamie," I snapped out urgently, "get Seaton down here immediately. And Gibson. Every Kingsman you can. Magical fires can't be suppressed by water, the fire department won't stand a chance of getting this under control."

She lost no time in digging out her pad, and I left her to contacting the right people.

I didn't think I needed to say this, but I warned, "And do not, for the love of anything holy, go any closer than this. Just this proximity is likely straining your shields something fierce."

Jamie grimaced acknowledgement. "I'll stay planted 'til we need to move. Sherard's coming."

Meaning Seaton would likely teleport to us. I do bless people who could manage the higher magicks.

Somewhere not far from me, I saw a magical suppressant shoot out from the street level, attacking the side of the burning shop. I recognized the magical signature immediately and called to Jamie, "Gibson is on scene! Get someone else!"

"Got it!"

Now that I had a better idea of what I dealt with, and a friend with superior magic ability bearing down on the problem, I should have felt more confident we could at least keep the fire from spreading. Unfortunately, I had no such faith. The blaze was growing wildly out of control, spreading across the tightly packed buildings, every fire suppressant hex incapable of even buffering against this sort of blaze. People were forcefully evacuating from the buildings to either side, and still others past them, abandoning the buildings before they could be fully caught up in the conflagration. A different spell left my lips, one meant to suppress stray magic, and it buffered against the fire, barring its attempts to spread further down the block. Progress of a sort, but I didn't hold much faith we could put this out, not any time soon. Not with just two of us. It would require further magic and aid. Where was that theatrical mage when I needed him?

As if my thoughts had summoned him, Seaton arrived in a snap, took one look at the situation, and swore creatively enough to put a stevedore to shame. "What by all deities is this?!"

"Charms shop set on fire."

Seaton wasted no further time on questions, heading

directly to the right, further down the street, and throwing up a barrier between one of the buildings and another, squeezing it in the two-foot gap between the bricks, preventing the fire from spreading any further. I dared to take in a breath of relief. Surely with a Royal Mage we'd be alright. And with Seaton here, he could put an additional shield around Jamie, prevent her from collapsing under the magical strain. I felt buffered on all sides by errant magic, like I stood inside of a maelstrom. I couldn't imagine Jamie felt any better.

Jamie put a hand on my shoulder and leaned in, her mouth near my ear. "Henri. I think that's Lees."

I looked sharply to where she pointed, my wand not wavering from the spell, as I couldn't afford to drop that. Still, I saw who she meant, and the man did indeed fit the description that we'd been given—a little taller than average, thinning black hair, a scruffy beard not grown out, with a beer belly. The man looked horrified, mouth agape as he stared, and yet part of him seemed... vindicated? I couldn't put any other descriptor to his expression.

In that moment, he turned his eyes away from the fire and looked towards us. I've no logical explanation for what happened next. Jamie often claimed that a policeman developed instincts after a certain amount of time on the job, an ability to look at someone and know they were guilty, that they were the right person to pursue. I saw it happen in that moment, when Jamie realized Lees was somehow behind this explosion. She leapt off the car in a single bound and rushed for him.

Even as she did so, I screamed in warning, "JAMIE GET BACK HERE!"

She ignored me. Lees realized that he had been made and whirled about frantically, diving into the crowd. With so many people swarming about in the streets, edging around the buildings, it was impossible to make headway quickly. I couldn't begin to understand his aim—just where was he running to? Nothing lay ahead of him but fire and death, no clear path away from it.

Jamie dogged hot on his heels, calling for people to let her through, and people went hither and thither as they were shoved aside. I saw her try and dart through them but she couldn't gain any real speed, not with all of the obstacles in her path. Lees had the same problem, of course, but also a head start on her, and he used it to his advantage. He came out of the crowd faster than she did and an icy tendril of foreboding swept down my spine. Surely he wasn't—surely my paranoia was mistaken.

I'd seen multiple people commit suicide rather than be taken in by the police. I'd heard tales of criminals doing insane things in order to avoid capture. But this? My eyes took in the yawning mouth of flames, promising nothing more than a horrific death. Surely no one would choose that.

Even as I thought it, Lees wrested free of the last of the crowd, entering the dangerous no-man's land of intense heat and chaotic magic. I couldn't see his expression with his back to me, but his body language spoke of untamed desperation. His footsteps remained unfaltering as he aimed directly for what used to be the front door to the shop. A shout caught in my throat.

"LEES!" Jamie screamed in warning, even as she threw herself desperately after him. "Don't do it!"

She wouldn't catch him. I instinctively knew it. I couldn't aid her; I had no magic to spare, as all of my ability was focused on keeping the fire contained. People watching nearby tried to scream out warnings too, their words overlapping so badly that I couldn't pick out a single word from the rest. All anyone could discern was the tone of warning and horror as the scene unfolded in

Charms and Death and Explosions (oh my!) 227

front of their eyes.

I could see Jamie's core take a battering, already trying to unravel. Magic swirled around her, impacting like a sledgehammer. I couldn't stop her, but I knew she'd need Seaton any second, and without taking my eyes off of her, I threw a magical enhancement on my vocal chords and yelled, "SEATON, GET OVER HERE NOW!"

Jamie's body stretched out into a full-out sprint, her arms reaching desperately for the back of Lees' shirt, only to catch nothing but air.

A new horror tingled through me as I realized she wasn't watching her speed. Her legs shifted into that predator-stride that ate up distance but gave her no agility. "No," I breathed in panic, realizing that if she continued that speed for even another five steps, she wouldn't be able to stop herself before slamming into that wall of flame. "JAMIE, NO!"

Gibson apparently realized the same, as he yelled out a similar warning, barely audible over the din of noise. It did no good, as she ignored both of us, throwing herself forward once more.

Foolhardy idiot, what was she—I couldn't complete the thought, I didn't have the brainpower to spare for it. Lees succeeded in his course in that moment, throwing himself bodily in through the door, disappearing from our sight altogether. I expected screams of pain and anguish. I heard them from the crowd, but from inside the building, only the crackle of fire and magic could be heard.

Jamie had been so close to catching him, but as I'd feared, she'd gained too much speed. Her heels skittered on the soot-covered pavement as she tried to stop herself, only to fail utterly. Swearing mentally, I looked for Seaton who raced for us, or as best he could through the crowd of people.

He was too far from her. He wouldn't get here in time. I knew that by dropping the shield, it would put the other buildings around us at risk, but I didn't even hesitate. I dropped the spell I held abruptly, throwing every ounce of power I had into a different spell altogether, one meant to shield her from the flames and sparking magic. It came down hard about her, cracking visibly like a glass cage. I gritted my teeth and held, but this shield wasn't meant to withstand both magic and fire. I didn't have anything else in my repertoire safe to use with her, as anything else would tap into her unbalanced core, which would be disastrous.

She landed hard against the pavement on her side, still sliding a little, and her legs impacted strongly with the side of the building. Something heavy fell across her, I could see it blazing outwards, and my heart stopped. Was she burned? Trapped?

One man in the crowd tried to go to her, but a rush of sparks made him flinch back before he'd gone two feet.

I got off the car in a bound, ready to go and pull her out myself. It wasn't necessary. Jamie rolled, kicking off the thing that had trapped her before scrambling back up to her feet and back tracking. I couldn't see her expression from this distance, but I didn't need to. She'd be angry and upset about this for the rest of the day, at least. I anxiously scanned her for burns, and indeed her pants had seen better days, scorched and half-melted, but it disguised her skin so thoroughly that I couldn't ascertain her injuries.

I rushed to her as quickly as I could manage through the people, jostling everyone with a judicious application of elbows until they made way for me. I could hear the bells of the fire trucks as they approached, but spared them no attention. My partner took precedence.

Jamie met me halfway, her hair plastered to her skull,

soot covering one side of her like a dark rash. Pain and frustration marred her face, clenched her fists at her sides. She looked grey in the sepia-toned lighting of the fire, her magical core fluxing hard enough to leave her gasping for breath, wheezing for it like an asthmatic. I grabbed her strongly about the waist with an arm, clamping her to my side, as I felt she would collapse otherwise. The precaution was wise as her body weight slammed into me, her strength not sufficient to hold herself upright.

Seaton and Gibson converged on us from either side, Seaton already performing the various spells necessary to stabilize her core. Gibson was more focused on the outer skin, and he dropped to his knees, ripping the ruined pants aside and pushing the jagged hemline up to look. "You're burned?"

It took a moment for Seaton's spells to stabilize her enough that she could breathe, enough at least that she didn't stutter out a response. "Don't feel like I am," Jamie responded, tilting her torso to get a look herself. She did not even attempt to take her own weight, letting me completely support her. "I shouldn't be. Magical fire is one of the things I'm immune to. It's why I went in."

"It's why you shouldn't have gone in," Seaton cut in, smile more canine tooth than expression. "With this much magic in the air, what did you think it would do to your core?"

Wincing, Jamie sheepishly admitted, "I actually didn't question that until I was half-trapped under that beam."

This woman would be the death of me someday. She was too quick to leap into the fray and not consider the consequences, like inducing my heart to fail.

"She's trying to kill us," Gibson grunted, in complete empathy with my own feelings, then heaved himself back up to his feet. "She's fine, no burns, just a lost pair of pants. I'll get back to suppressing the fire on the left side."

I had no doubt that Gibson would have words with her later. Like I would. Seaton's look conveyed it all as he worked on stabilizing her core, to which Jamie gave him a helpless shrug. "I couldn't ignore him."

Her instincts terrified me some days. Resigned, I went back to casting a suppressing spell as well, trying to cover the area until Seaton could lend his aid once more. I looked for any sign that Lees might still be alive as well, but I had no hope for it. "Lees?"

"That moron," Jamie growled in response, finally shifting upwards and carrying her own weight again. "That utter moron. Is dying like this really preferable to spending time in a jail cell?"

Despite her words, I knew she would blame herself for this on some level. What-if's and maybe's would play through her mind tonight, leaving her to wonder if she could have saved him if only she'd been three seconds quicker on the draw. None of this was her fault, and telling her that wouldn't help, as logically she knew it as well as I. The heart, however, did not always heed the mind. I shifted my arm to go around her shoulders and drew her into a loose hug, giving her comfort for a moment. "The grief-stricken are in too much pain to make good decisions, my friend. Sometimes their pain unhinges their minds. His decision is not yours to carry, nor is his ghost. Don't put that burden on yourself."

Leaning into my shoulder, she hid her face from view for a moment, and I could feel her gusty sigh against the side of my neck. She needed that moment, we both did, then she pulled herself upright again, meeting my eyes levelly. "Thanks, Henri. Am I okay now, Sherard?"

"You are, but steer clear of the fire, otherwise you'll undo my hard work." Seaton paused and added, "I'll likely have to renew it again tomorrow. Your core took a battering."

I didn't think she'd come out of this completely unscathed.

Wincing, Jamie nodded. "Thanks. I'll handle crowd control."

Nodding, I let her go, returning my own attention to the fire. I knew that brief moment was not sufficient, but we couldn't manage more. Not in this situation, with a city block about to go up in flames. Seaton did as well, returning to his position off to the right.

I watched several men hop out of the fire wagon, heading for the hoses and tank attached to the wagon, and then I beelined for them. Catching one of their eyes, I gestured him toward me.

"Sir," he greeted civilly enough, his weight shifting as he fought the urge to ignore me and leap into the fray. "If you could step back—"

Overriding him, I introduced myself, "Dr. Davenforth, Magical Examiner with Fourth Precinct. That is a magical charms shop in flames behind me."

The man likely had ten years of seasoning in his career, as he looked nearly thirty to me, and his eyes widened as he took on my meaning. Firemen especially understood the problems of magical fires, and this man knew his trade well, as he instantly turned and bellowed, "GOT A MAGICAL FIRE HERE! SUPPRESSIVE WATER ON ALL BUILDINGS AND GET THESE PEOPLE CLEAR!"

As he turned back to me, I further clarified, "RM Seaton and Kingsman Gibson are also on hand, he's handling the other side of the building. RM Seaton is the man in the red coat over there on our right. I'll handle this front side until further aid comes."

"Yes sir, thank you, sir," he rattled out smartly before pivoting sharply about and lending a hand with the hoses.

I do adore the professionally competent. With a grim smile, I recast my magical suppressing spell, forcing the fire and magic back into a quarantined space. It would take a miracle to not lose this block altogether.

Somewhere around midnight, the last of the fires finally died out to smoldering wisps of smoke. I sat on the floor of the car, my arm hooked over the edge of the seat, looking wearily at the building. They'd pulled the remains of Harmum Lees from the building not five minutes ago, and that was a gruesome sight that wouldn't leave my dreams for many nights to come.

I felt weary to my core. Not just physically, although my muscles ached under the exertion of today's events, but emotionally as well. If a heart could bleed, mine did so, aching with all of the loss scattered about me. So much of this could have been prevented if two men had been stopped from making and selling bad charms. If only the police had taken the complaints seriously. If only we'd had proper inspections of the charms to begin with. If only, if only…I stopped myself before I could go any further down that road. I'd warned Jamie against doing this very thing, hadn't I? It would do no good and only serve to depress the spirits.

Seaton approached and turned to slouch against the side of the engine, appearing as fully soot-covered and weary as the rest of us. In fact, the soot seemed to find every line in his face, aging him a good decade. I fancied I fared no better.

"Jamie's still fine," he informed me with no segue. "I looked her over again. She doesn't have a mark on her, although her core is still fluctuating. I'll pop in tomorrow, reset the spells once more. I think that will hold her for another month."

"She's angry with herself," I responded softly. "She thinks she should have been able to catch him with her reflexes."

"On flat, open ground with no obstacles, she likely would have," he sighed. "I understand her frustration, but this wasn't of her making. I'm just glad she was able to pull herself back out again, although I do wish her self-preservation instincts were stronger."

"Have we an answer on what caused the conflagration?"

"Yes, the fire inspector just reported to me. Dynamite, he said." Seaton grimaced as he gestured to the charred remains of the building. "Some of this is supposition, and Jamie's trying to track down witnesses, but I think Lees decided to take matters into his own hands. He used approximately three sticks of dynamite to blow up the shop with. I assume this is where he bought the bad charm that caused his father's death. But he didn't take into consideration how much magical power was in the store or the effect that would have on the explosion. When the store blew, he was as horrified as everyone else how fast the fire spread to the surrounding buildings. It was guilt as much as anything that motivated his suicide. That's my take on it, at least."

"I cannot fault it," I agreed, passing a weary hand over my eyes. Dynamite again? Perhaps he'd had some leftover from Parkins? And since he'd collaborated with the powder monkey, thought he understood enough to use it here. It all made a neat sort of sense. Even if it wasn't entirely accurate, I believed part of our guesswork would prove correct.

My partner chose to join us, re-doing her hair into a messy ponytail as she moved. "Well, boys, we've been politely asked to go home. The fire department claims they have it from here. They did ask we write up a report tomorrow of events for their records, but we're done for the night."

"Sounds blissful," I admitted, gaining my feet with a groan. A hot bath would do wonders to relax me and get the soot off, and I was determined to do that before attaining my bed, no matter how lethargic I felt. "And tomorrow? I must admit, I intensely dislike the idea that Parkins might have left other people access to dynamite."

Grimacing, Jamie agreed, "You ain't the only one. I'll lean on Parkins tomorrow to give up anyone else involved in this scheme. I've got the leverage and I'm going to use it. I'm not going to repeat tonight."

Report 18: Gotta Catch 'em All!

Once again I sat in the interrogation room with Parkins, Henri sitting beside me, Penny standing in the corner and observing. I'd played nice last time, as sometimes it took several interviews with a person before they played ball. This time, I didn't have the patience for it. I'd gone to bed at one in the morning, woken up five hours later by nightmares I didn't care to remember, and spent the next hour cuddling Clint before heading to work.

Parkins seemed to sense I was not to be trifled with this morning. He had a hard time meeting my eyes. I deliberately kept my hands under the table so that I wouldn't reach over and smack sense into him. I chose my words carefully, pitched my tone into something approaching flat neutrality. "Harmum Lees is dead."

Startled, Parkin's eyes flew up to mine, his skin going white in horror. "Wh-what?" he croaked out, barely audible.

"He took three sticks of dynamite last night to the charms store in his neighborhood. Blew it sky high, set six other buildings on fire, and released more of the influenza virus in the air," I related in that same flat pitch. "It killed four other people, injured sixteen others. Then he dove into the burning building, committing suicide. We're still cleansing the area and the air about it to prevent another epidemic from occurring."

Parkins' expression crumbled and he slumped in on himself. I felt almost bad relating his friend's death in such a brutal fashion, but I had to shake this man out of his commitment to keep their secrets. I knew of no other way than this.

"Mr. Parkins," Henri inserted in the taut silence of the room, his manner soothing and quiet, "I don't know if the others have access to any other dynamite. I don't know if they're as sane as you are regarding this matter, if they're content to only kill the two men responsible. Or if they're like Mr. Lees, who was clearly not in his right mind, and caused horrific collateral damage as he pursued his path of revenge. I do know that I don't want to take the chance of last night being repeated, in any fashion."

Henri made a very good cop. I let my inner bad cop out. "Parkins, I want to know who else was with you. I can't trust these people to leave matters alone. Names. Now."

Parkins visibly hesitated, the names hovering on the edge of his tongue. He did not, however, speak.

"Spill, Parkins," I growled, slamming a hand on the table and leaning toward him. He flinched from me, ducking down into his chair. "So help me, if you make me live through another scene like that, I'll take it out on your hide. We had to haul the burned body of Lees out of that building. Do you really want other people to die like that? In agony?"

Whatever color remained in his cheeks fled, leaving him grey as a corpse. Swallowing hard, he shook his head no. It took a moment for him to find his voice, and my tension ramped up with every second he hesitated. If he didn't give me something in three seconds, I'd choke the answers out of his cryptic throat, I really would.

Head lowered to nearly his chest, he rasped out, "Rice. Mrs. Eliza Rice. She was the third person."

An exultant shout of victory nearly burst out of my throat. I had to throttle it back. "No fourth person?"

"No." Parkins hesitated, his attention drawn up to Henri. If it was easier to face my partner than me, I didn't care, as long as he kept talking. "Mrs. Rice is my neighbor. She lost her youngest grandchild. She's a gunsmith's daughter, knows more about weapons than we did. She's the one who shot Timms."

I sat back in the chair, scrutinizing him. I didn't think he lied. In fact, I felt pretty sure he didn't. "Thank you, Mr. Parkins."

"Just be careful with her," he pleaded to me, eyes imploring. "Her health is...not good."

Henri promised for both of us, "We will."

It took no time at all to get a warrant for the arrest of one Mrs. Eliza Rice. Parkins even gave us the address. I didn't really expect trouble, but the woman knew how to use a firearm and had one, so I didn't expect it to be easy, either. I just hoped she didn't open fire, as she lived in a crowded apartment off a very busy street, and lots of innocents could be hurt if she didn't come easy.

We approached the apartment up creaking wood steps, and I felt the claustrophobic space of the hallway keenly. How did people even get furniture up here? Seriously, the hallway was probably three feet wide, if that. Of course her place was at the end of the hall, and I knocked on the door firmly before stepping back, one hand on my gun just in case. I kept the grip discreet, camouflaged under my jacket. Henri had his wand in hand, also tense and at the ready.

Slow moving footsteps came near, then the door opened gradually, revealing a stooped old woman who couldn't be younger than seventy. She regarded us behind half-moon spectacles perched on the edge of her nose.

"I'm Detective Edwards, Fourth Precinct," I introduced myself, still not sure which way this would go. I didn't detect a gun on her person, though, that was a plus. "This is Dr. Henri Davenforth. Are you Eliza Rice?"

"Yes, dear," she answered in a sweet, grandmotherly way. "I've been expecting you. Let me get my purse and lock up, then we can go."

I blinked at her. Say what?

"Mrs. Rice," Henri pitched in, as confused as I felt, "we have a warrant for your arrest. Would you like to see it?"

She waved this off, stepping back enough to snag a purse resting on a small side table near the door. "As I said, young man, I've been expecting you. Poor Mr. Parkins couldn't take the guilt. I knew that he'd fold eventually. Ever since he went to turn himself in, I thought you'd come for me. It took longer than I thought."

For some reason, that last line felt like an accusation. I defended myself before I could question why. "He didn't want to name anyone until he learned about Harmum Lees."

She paused halfway out of the door, regarding me sadly. "Yes. I heard about that this morning. Such a sad thing. I thought killing Garner and Timms would help him, move him past his grief. It apparently didn't."

"Did you really think that it would?" I couldn't help but ask. Motivation wasn't necessary in order to close a case, not really, but it sure made it easier on me. Knowing why these people made the decisions they had helped me put the case to bed.

"Hoped," she corrected with a sad smile. "We started this because we had no hope that the police would do anything to stop them. And someone had to stop them. My poor Lizzie is gone because of those two fools. Many others lost a loved one because of them. You saw yourself how much damage they did."

I did. I'd experienced the aftermath first hand and had to clean it up. It was why I sympathized with her so strongly. It didn't make her actions right, she wasn't Batman, but...I felt that, in her shoes, I might have made a similar choice. "Yes. Yes, I did."

"You're the ones who reported it to the queen," she said in a simple statement of fact. How she knew that, I didn't know, except perhaps if our story had made it into a newspaper. I never paid attention to the things and Henri hadn't touched one in days, as we'd not had the time.

"Not quite," Henri corrected with a genial smile at her. "We reported it to RM Seaton and he reported it to the queen."

Mrs. Rice waved this distinction away as unimportant. "Regardless, it's been reported to the queen, and she's taking steps to prevent this nonsense from happening again. That's what we really wanted, you know. For someone to see the problem, to understand why we were forced to kill them. To prevent history from repeating itself. That's all we really wanted."

"I think we can safely promise you that; if nothing else, we'll all actively try to prevent a repeat of such sad circumstances," Henri promised her.

That sad smile lingered on her face. "Thank you, young man. It's worlds too late for my Lizzie, of course, but still. It's a leading light. I won't look at it askance." Shaking her head, she moved into the hallway, and while she was a tiny wisp of a thing, I had to give ground a good two feet to make room for her.

I didn't know what 'leading light' meant—assumed it to be something like a silver lining—but didn't ask. I had a more burning question in mind. "Ma'am? What's in your purse?"

"Nothing dangerous, I assure you." She latched the door properly, put the key into her purse, then handed it over to me.

I promptly took it. It didn't have the right weight to hold a handgun, but I wasn't above her packing dynamite. Dangerous little old lady, this one. Henri decorously offered her an arm, which she took with a smile of thanks, and as soon as her back was turned I opened the bag and took a look inside. Handkerchief, key, some sort of medicine bottle, a different pair of glasses, and four spare hair pins. Okay, safe enough. Relieved, I followed after them.

A few heads popped out of different apartments as we made our way down the stairs. I got a few evil looks, because of course this woman wasn't a known murderer, and they assumed we were here for some stupid reason. If they only knew…. I shrugged it off, helped Henri settle her into the front seat of the car, and carefully pulled out. I didn't think her balance was up to the task of me 'going at a rate of knots,' as Henri would put it, so I kept it down to a demure fifteen miles per hour.

I really missed going eighty some days. Okay, most days.

We reached the station and I parked out back. I normally wouldn't have, I'd have stopped in the front and taken the criminal in immediately, but she was just so amiable…I felt like I was taking Betty Crocker in for questioning.

Henri gave her another hand to help her down from the car, then escorted her in, for all the world like going to the Mad Hatter's Tea Party. We got many a bemused look from our fellow colleagues, Gerring actually stopping dead and watching for a moment before shooting me a confused look. Poor kid was a little out of touch, as he'd been running around gathering all the complaints and investigating the deaths touched by charms. I mouthed a promise to catch him up later but stayed on my partner's heels until I heard Captain Gregson call out to me.

"Edwards!"

Henri caught my eye, motioned for me to go ahead with a jerk of the chin, and I split off from him. I didn't think she'd cause him any trouble, and even if she did, she was surrounded by cops, for heaven's sakes. They'd be fine.

Our captain hovered in the doorway of his office, watching

Henri and Mrs. Rice head for the holding cells with a growing frown. "Edwards, who's the grandmother?"

"Mrs. Rice, the shooter in our case," I answered, starting to see the humor in this macabre situation. When he blinked at me, perturbed, I lifted both shoulders in a helpless shrug. "Parkins named her. She confessed. In fact, she informed us when we arrived at her door that she had been waiting for us. Don't be fooled, sir. That sweet little old lady popped a man in the back of the head, execution style."

He rubbed a hand over his eyes in a tired manner. "Can this case get any stranger?"

"Yes, yes as a matter of fact it can, and I'd appreciate it if you didn't call on Fate like that. She's a very fickle mistress."

Groaning, he conceded the point. "Alright. Give me a full report after you've got her booked. And please tell me that's the last person? There's no other suspects running about, correct?"

A true smile on my face, I answered in relief, "Yes. We've finally caught them all."

It's like Pokemon! We've caught them all!

Poke—what?

Oh dear. How do I even begin to explain this.........

Report 19: Loose Ends

Ellie Warner was in her element, running around teaching people about her new product, including its variety of uses and the proper means of storing it. Jamie was right there alongside her, repeating the same information over and over, somehow managing to keep a smile on her face. I'd never understood how she managed that. I found repetition tedious in the extreme.

We were overseeing the last of the cordon rope's removal, as the epidemic was over, the area safe once more. Due to the many professionals who had donated their time and efforts, we hadn't lost a single person more, and I considered that a miracle of epic proportions. I'd like to think my charms had some small part to play in that, but I could hardly claim more.

The area was cleaner than the city had seen it since the day the apartments were first built, I believe. The recent rainfall we'd had last night had something to do with it, the seasonal downfall washing the area clean, leaving patches of the road still damp and shining. It smelled fresh, the air not humid due to the recent storm, and I drew in a breath just for the pleasure of doing so.

The queen was due in at any moment to survey the area and see for herself that things had been taken care of. No one doubted she'd come, as Queen Regina had a very personal touch, and she always chose to see for herself how matters stood. Her common sense and accessibility as a ruler were part of the reason why her subjects adored her. More than one eager face looked anxiously toward the road, hovering on the sidewalks in anticipation.

I think they half-expected a multitude of cars, Kingsmen, guards...some sort of grand entourage. Instead, Queen Regina pulled onto the main street with a Kingsman driving, Seaton next to her in the back seat, and what looked to be a secretary of some sort in the front. Hardly the fanfare people associated with royalty, but from what I knew of her, very in taste with Queen Regina's usual antics.

Someone recognized her in the crowd and the word spread like wildfire. No one dared to crowd the car, but they inched closer, beaming as she waved at them. The Kingsman pulled to the side and parked, then hopped around to open the door as Queen Regina stepped regally out. As she did so, she looked all around, asking a question I could not discern from my position. I stayed on the porch of Dr. Cartwright's practice, as I had no desire to be crowded in on all sides.

Perhaps because of my position, Seaton spotted me. He lifted a hand and beckoned me closer. What the devil was he about, wanting me to talk to the queen? I couldn't think of a single thing to say to her, no information I could impart, that she hadn't already heard a dozen times. Sighing in resignation, I made my way toward them, forced to slip sideways through different pockets of people to manage it.

Queen Regina Kingsley, Fifteenth Queen of Kingston, did not possess the extraordinary beauty that bad novels always insisted queens should have. She rather reminded me of my sister, really, just one ten years older. She'd dressed quite sensibly in a plain blue skirt suit, well cut to her figure, dark hair done up in a loose bun that complimented her heart-shaped face. As I approached, Seaton said something to her in a low tone, and she smiled winsomely.

That smile transformed her into someone I

instinctively felt I could confide in. Strange, how that glimpse of personality affected me so. Drawing to a halt in front of her, I gave an appropriately deep bow before straightening.

"Your Majesty, this is Dr. Henri Davenforth, our Magical Examiner," Seaton introduced with a wave at me. "Davenforth, I trust this lady needs no introduction on my part."

"Perish the thought," I returned with a brief smile. "Your Majesty, a pleasure to meet you."

"And you, Dr. Davenforth," she returned, making no secret of her study as her eyes swept me from head to foot and back again. "I've heard much about you, most of it kind, some of it rather alarming. You didn't really turn down the offer to become my Kingsman, did you?"

She found that alarming? "Your Majesty, I have not the physical stamina for it, nor the magical power necessary. I'm best suited to the occupation I hold now."

Her blue eyes narrowed thoughtfully. "You are not one to be overly ambitious. I find that quite charming. So little in my acquaintance are of that nature. Well, I'm pleased to know the man behind the stories. Jamie is always telling me something you said or did, and Seaton's inclined to steal you away to work on his magical puzzles, so I knew you had to be a good sort. Walk with me, sir, and tell me what all has been done. I'm very anxious to know that preventative measures have been taken, as I do not want my citizens to fall prey to something like this again."

I found this sideways praise to be somewhat disarming, and I had no way to respond to it, so I felt grateful she directed me on what she wanted to hear. I fell into step with her, walking her through the many charms we'd painted on the sides of the buildings, hung along the walls, and the ones scheduled for renewal.

Queen Regina listened attentively, her eyes following where I pointed, then stopped me with an uplifted hand as we reached one of the refuse bins. "I'm told that the refuse man in this area refused to collect the decaying charms. You've confirmed this?"

"Yes, Your Majesty. I've reported the matter to his superiors as well."

"I find this quite distasteful, that the man would cause so many problems for other people in order to line his own pocket. Is this a common problem in my city?"

"More common than I care for," I admitted sourly. "I've encouraged the word to spread that if anyone has such a problem in the future, they are to immediately report it to me, and bring their expired charms with them. I'll handle it."

Her head canted as she regarded me. "That's kind of you, Dr. Davenforth."

"Not at all," I denied, and meant every word of it. "I've no patience with this sort of stupidity. I don't want my city plagued with illnesses or ablaze, either."

"On those two points, we are in perfect accordance," she assured me, smile razor sharp. "And I can promise you, the oversight for charms disposal will be more regulated from now on. I understand that you are also an advocate of an inspection system for charms before being released for retail?"

"Very much so, Your Majesty. Just that would have prevented this disaster altogether."

She nodded, not surprised. "I'm in talks with my councilors at this time, discussing the best way to go about it, and the budget for it. I trust that within six months, we'll have a rudimentary system in place."

A thrill of relief raced through me. For a government system, that was a very quick timeline indeed. She must be pushing hard to make it go through that quickly.

Charms and Death and Explosions (oh my!)

"I'm relieved, Your Majesty. If I can be of any assistance, please do inform me."

"Oh, I will," she promised dryly. "Seaton's already volunteered you."

I shot my friend a look. "Of course he has."

Seaton snickered and looked innocently elsewhere. The fiend.

"Your Majesty!" Warner greeted happily, practically skipping up to her. "How is my texting pad?"

"Thankfully durable," the queen responded with an airy laugh. "I dropped it three times this morning alone. You're close to working out the kinks soon, I trust? This needs to be in the hands of my policemen sooner rather than later."

"Almost there," Warner promised faithfully. "It's just the battery power that's giving me issues, but I think I'm close to a good breakthrough. You're here for a tour, I take it? Here, let me show you, we came up with a process to clean and sanitize everything—"

I stayed back as the women moved forward, Seaton hovering with me. "She's really not pulling your leg about bringing you in for consultation on this," Seaton advised me, dead serious. "I think it's because we kept mentioning your name in connection with some solution."

Rolling my eyes to the heavens, I prayed for patience. "Seaton, absolutely nothing that I've done has been a permanent solution."

"Davenforth," he returned, matching my tone, "you're still the one who thought up the temporary solution and put it into practice, which buys us time to think up and implement permanent solutions."

"The reward for a job well done," Jamie noted as she came to stand at my other side, "is more work. That's well-known, no matter what world you're in."

I wrinkled my nose slightly, as she smelled strongly

of alcohol. "Apparently so. How many things have you cleaned?"

"All the things, Henri," she answered lightly. "All. It's been a very productive day. I take it Ellie's turned tour guide on us?"

"They're over there," Seaton indicated with a general wave of the hand.

Jamie nodded, unsurprised. "How upset is our good queen?"

"Livid," Seaton answered cheerfully. "I'm quite happy about that. Angry women often change the world."

"Never meddle with a woman on a mission," Jamie agreed in the same manner, rubbing her hands together. "Well, gentlemen, don't just stand around and look pretty. We're not quite done yet. I found a whole stack of dead charms sitting in a closet under a stairwell."

I winced. "Great good magic, did you really? After I told everyone not to?"

"I think they'd actually forgotten about this pile," she admitted, already leading the way towards the apartment building in question. "It wasn't until we went hunting for a good place to put the gallon bucket of alcohol for storage that we found it. Come along, Sherard, there's a good chap. You can't make Henri deal with it by himself, he'd be here the rest of the day."

Seaton sighed gustily, trudging along in resignation. "I'm supposed to be escorting the queen."

Jamie didn't even turn her head. "And you'll do a splendid job of it when she wants to leave. Until then, Ellie and Marshall have her."

Sotto voice, I advised him, "Don't argue. She, too, is a woman on a mission."

"I sensed that, yes," he agreed wryly. "At least we're nearly done with the cleanout here. I don't think we'll have any issues for some time to come."

Yes, that thought cheered me considerably. I didn't want to ever come back here, in fact—although I was not naïve enough to think that people's habits would change because of the disaster visited upon this area. Still, I had hope for the future, that we would not repeat this particular mistake. That bad charms would not accidentally kill people, or be sold again on the market, or that the magic meant to protect would instead cause great harm. I had great faith that all of that would change, and for the better.

If nothing else, this case had been a simple lesson to me that I did not need to struggle alone under the weight of the problems I saw. I had a wealth of connections to draw strength from, including the remarkable woman who chose me as her friend and partner. And really, with her, could any problem be insurmountable?

As if sensing my regard, she turned her head, pausing just outside of the doorway to the apartment complex. "Something wrong, Henri?"

"Not at all," I smiled at her as I said the words, meaning every syllable. "Not at all."

Jamie's Notes to Herself:

• Green Tea exists on this world! It's brown, not green, but whatever. I'll take it.

• Parsley, cinnamon, and nutmeg acquired! My Kingstonpedia came through. Still hunting for a soy sauce substitute.

• Do NOT GIVE CLINT LIQUOR OR SUGAR WATER, OMG. THAT WAS A TERRIBLE IDEA, NEVER AGAIN.

• Also, "The song that never ends" is hereby BANNED from this house. Clint SANG IT FOR THREE HOURS STRAIGHT

Days of the Week
Earth – Draiocht
Sunday – Gods Day
Monday – Gather Day
Tuesday – Brew Day
Wednesday – Bind Day
Thursday – Hex Day
Friday – Scribe Day
Saturday – Rest Day

Months
Earth – Draiocht
January – Old Moon
February – Snow Moon
March – Crow Moon
April – Seed Moon

May – Hare Moon
June – Rose Moon

July – Hay Moon
August – Corn Moon
September – Harvest Moon

October – Hunter's Moon
November – Frost Moon
December – Blue Moon

Werespecies: werehorses, wereowls, weremules, werefoxes
Carmine berries: NOT A STRAWBERRY, JUST NO. CAN WE SAY GAG.

Report X1: Author's Note

The storyline for book two is interesting in its own right. It is, in fact, based upon real life cases. Specifically, I merged two different cases that happened in the early 1900's. One of them was the first televised court case to ever air, and it happened in Waco, Texas. The ex-son-in-law of a Texas socialite used a car bomb to kill her. The other was an interesting case where only half of the murders were actually solved, and the other half was left a mystery. A doctor famous in town for having multiple girlfriends was murdered by his wife, who lived separated from him. The doctor's office had the second story completely blocked off, and the clerk was found dead in the basement, although no one ever figured out if the wife had the clerk killed as well, or even why the man was murdered in the first place. The car bomb case came from Jason Lucky Morrow's collections such as "Famous Crimes the World Forgot." I quite adore this man's work, as he really does his research, and he has a good writing style that makes it easy to read and captivates my inner imagination. I just wish he'd write another one, as I believe I've read everything of his at this point.

Yes, I'm aware I'm rather the pot calling the kettle black right now. But in my defense, I DO write faster than he does!

I'll continue to do research on real-life cases, as I felt like doing so leant an air of realism to the book. The fact that I have fun researching cases has nothing at all to do with it.

Other books by Honor Raconteur
Published by Raconteur House

♪ Available in Audiobook! ♪
THE ADVENT MAGE CYCLE
Jaunten ♪

Magus ♪

Advent ♪

Balancer ♪

ADVENT MAGE NOVELS
Advent Mage Compendium

The Dragon's Mage ♪

The Lost Mage

WARLORDS (ADVENT MAGE)
Warlords Rising

Warlords Ascending

Warlords Reigning

THE ARTIFACTOR SERIES
The Child Prince ♪

The Dreamer's Curse ♪

The Scofflaw Magician

The Canard Case

THE CASE FILES OF HENRI DAVENFORTH
Magic and the Shinigami Detective

Charms and Death and Explosions (oh my)

DEEPWOODS SAGA
Deepwoods ♪
Blackstone
Fallen Ward
Origins

FAMILIAR AND THE MAGE
The Human Familiar
The Void Mage
Remnants
Echoes

GÆLDORCRÆFT FORCES
Call to Quarters

KINGMAKERS
Arrows of Change ♪
Arrows of Promise

Arrows of Revolution

KINGSLAYER
Kingslayer ♪
Sovran at War ♪

SINGLE TITLES
Special Forces 01
Midnight Quest

*upcoming

Dear Reader,

Your Amazon reviews are very important. Reviews directly impact sales and book visibility, and the more reviews we have, the more sales we see. The more sales there are, the longer I get to keep writing the books you love full time. The best possible support you can provide is to give an honest review, even if it's just clicking those stars to rate the book!

Thank you for all your support! See you in the next world.

~Honor

Honor Raconteur is a sucker for a good fantasy. Despite reading it for decades now, she's never grown tired of the magical world. She likely never will. In between writing books, she trains and plays with her dogs, eats far too much chocolate, and attempts insane things like aerial dance.

If you'd like to join her newsletter to be notified when books are released, and get behind the scenes about upcoming books, you can click below:

NEWSLETTER

or email directly to honorraconteur.news@raconteurhouse.com and you'll be added to the mailing list. If you'd like to interact with Honor more directly, you can socialize with her on various sites. Each platform offers something different and fun!

Printed in Great Britain
by Amazon